PROOFS
OF
AFFECTION

PROOFS
OF
AFFECTION

by
Rosemary Friedman

WILLIAM MORROW AND COMPANY, INC.
New York 1982

Grateful acknowledgment is made to Russell & Kegan Paul Ltd. for
permission to quote from *Service of the Synagogue* (New Year) and *Service of the
Synagogue* (Day of Atonement), translated by Arthur Davis and H.M. Adler,
and for permission to quote the final verse of *Had Gad-Yo* from *The Children's
Haggadah*, edited by Dr. A. M. Silberman and translated by Isidore Wartski,
B.A. and the Rev. Arthur Saul Super, M.A.

Library of Congress Cataloging in Publication Data

Friedman, Rosemary.
   Proofs of affection.

   I. Title.
PR6056.R49P7   823′.914   81–22450
ISBN 0–688–01106–3   AACR2

Printed in the United States of America

First Edition

1 2 3 4 5 6 7 8 9 10

BOOK DESIGN BY MICHAEL MAUCERI

For Emma

"... *The impression that one gained from her was of a family with few friends, or at least there were few known to her; there were a great many brothers and sisters dominated by Leonard's mother, a woman capable of heroism but usually perceived as timorous and sentimental, continually demanding proofs of affection from her children and, I think, receiving them* ..."

—VIRGINIA WOOLF.
Diaries. Vol. 1 xxv

PROOFS
OF
AFFECTION

1

YOU COULD TELL THE CHANGING OF THE SEASONS by the hats. The Day of Atonement, even if it fell, as it frequently did, in the middle of St. Luke's little summer, was the signal for velvet berets for the young and fur cachepots for the older women. Passover, although it was often freezing, brought out the straws, beige, white or navy blue trimmed with flowers or bits of ribbon, designed to go with everything and generally ending up by going with nothing. This was New Year, however, on the first day of which it was inscribed how many shall pass away and how many shall be born; who shall live and who shall die. Peach-bloom felts in mannish styles picked up the colour of a blouse or the shade of a suit—for the married women, that is. The single girls went hatless, long drifts of hair falling over their faces and their new clothes.

The synagogue was full, as it invariably was three times a year, when the backsliders, attracted by the perennial magnet of the Days of Awe, arrived like lemmings in the hope of acquiring "their eternity in a single hour."

From her front-row seat, Kitty Shelton, in a burgundy tweed suit with the new padded shoulders and a burgundy felt hat, from which hung self-coloured rouleaux, looked down through her bifocals onto the black and white mass of the male congregation below.

She looked down upon the mass, but her eyes focussed like homing birds upon the black trilby and navy-blue pin-

11

striped shoulders of her husband. Beneath the hat you could just see the curling of the freshly barbered grey hair. The congregation was standing and he was praying avidly, swaying back and forth, from the book in front of him. In response to her wordless signal, his shoulders rotated and he raised his head, looking over the tops of his half-glasses, to meet the gaze of his wife.

She opened her mouth and spoke clearly, silently. Only a lip-reader and Sydney Shelton, her mate for so many years, could know that she said: "Where's Josh?"

By way of reply he glanced at the empty seat next to him, turned up his palms and shrugged.

The message was received: "How should I know?"

Sydney returned to his prayers and the spiritual tempo of the day, and Kitty, joining in the refrain the choir was now singing, held her book with its red-edged pages in front of her and wondered what had happened to her son. He was very thoughtless. He knew his father got upset, although Sydney put on a brave front of pretending not to mind. It wasn't too much to expect a son to put in an appearance three times a year to keep his father company, even if he didn't believe. True, he was a busy man; but looking round she could see Louis Craig, M.P., and Morris Goldapple, who was gynecologist to Royalty, and Cyril Simmons, who had the financial ear of the Prime Minister— all busy men, busy and successful. If they could manage to get to synagogue on New Year, why not Josh? Ever since he'd broken off his engagement to Paula he'd been acting strangely. Sydney would have to talk to him over lunch. He'd be there for lunch all right; Rachel, too. The fact that she had not come to the service was less important. She was the apple of her father's eye, and that she came home for the holidays was in itself sufficient. She was not expected to pray. Carol, her elder daughter, who took after her father in her religious inclinations, stood beside her singing lustily. She was four months pregnant. Kitty hoped that it would be a boy; Carol had two girls already. And although Sydney said nothing, she knew that he was longing for a grandson to take to synagogue and to instruct in the ways of his forefathers. Morris Goldapple was delivering Carol as he'd done when she'd had Debbie and Lisa. They'd probably give him a knighthood one of these days, although her mind boggled when she thought of Cissie Goldapple, who was always having rows with the fishmonger, as Lady Goldapple. No knighthood in the world could make a lady out of Cissie. Morris himself wasn't much to write home about either, clever undoubtedly and at the top of the obstetric tree, but nothing to look at, not like Sydney with his grey hair and distinguished bearing. Sydney, who had always been good-looking, had become even more handsome as he grew older, but they didn't seem to give knighthoods to people in wholesale Fancy Goods.

Carol had lost the fatigued look of the first three months of pregnancy and was, Kitty thought, beginning to wear the quiet unmistakable bloom of maternity. She always had been a pretty girl with her dark hair, olive skin and enormous brown eyes. Even when she was a baby in the pram, people had stopped in the street and said, what fantastic eyes, she'll break a few hearts when she's older, *kain ein hara*.

By next New Year, if God was willing, Kitty would have three grandchildren and, with a bit of luck, Josh would have found another girl and settled down, although what was wrong with Paula, goodness only knew. Rachel, with her wild ways, was another matter; but she was barely twenty, there was time. She really was very lucky with her children, with her entire family in fact. In her row alone there was Rose Ingram whose husband had glaucoma and was virtually blind; Ettie Green who had lost her only and adored son in a car accident when a load of steel girders, from an

13

articulated lorry, had come adrift and crashed in upon him through the windscreen; Myra Graham, a widow for many years, who always looked so utterly bereft.

"What time does the Children's Service finish?" Kitty whispered to Carol.

Carol looked at the watch with the black face and the gold hands Sydney had given her for her last birthday. "Another half an hour. They keep them until after the sermon."

"There's no room anyway." Kitty glanced along the filled seats, knowing that when the girls arrived, standing politely at the end of the row, she would somehow squash them in, one on each side of her, expecting Rika Snowman and Barbara Brill to shift up a bit, as she would to accommodate their grandchildren, although Rika's daughter and son-in-law were living in Monte Carlo and Barbara's were more likely to go to Mass, since Nathan had married not only a *shiksa* but an Irish one at that. What was it Rabbi Magnus had once said? If everyone put his problems down on a table in front of him, there wasn't a person who wouldn't pick up his own again.

"Ve-zos ha-Torah . . ." the choir sang, waking Kitty from her reverie. She joined in the refrain as the first lopsided Scroll of the Law was held aloft by David Weinrib. Finding the appropriate place in her book, she tried to occupy her heart with contemplation of the New Year and its special promise of fulfillment.

Rabbi Magnus stood in the pulpit, tugging at the sides of his prayer shawl and waiting for silence. It was a case of diminuendo. First the shifty stampede of those who wanted to leave the synagogue before the sermon; then the shuffle, to find a comfortable position, of those who remained; the finishing of conversations, the single nose blow, the odd cough. Into the resulting quiet—old Mr. Gottlieb had already dropped off—Rabbi Magnus lifted up his beard and said:

14

"Hope is the keynote of every New Year."

As he sent the words ringing through the synagogue, through the serried ranks of men, the colourful rows of women behind the wrought-iron gallery, through the hanging pendants of the crystal chandeliers, presented by the family of the late Minnie Roth, he looked, Sydney Shelton was convinced, at the empty seat that should have been occupied by Josh. I'm certain he'll be along later, he silently reassured Rabbi Magnus with more conviction than he felt. It was already eleven-thirty. Perhaps there had been a dental emergency. What else could account for the fact that Josh was not in his seat; what other reason could there possibly be? Josh didn't particularly like going to synagogue, had let the religious observances go by the board, but he knew that Sydney liked him to put in a token appearance on New Year and the Day of Atonement and he had no reason to aggravate his father. Last night he had said to Sydney, "See you tomorrow" and Sydney had said, "Don't be late. It doesn't look nice to walk in late." Maybe he wasn't well, although he'd seemed all right when he'd left them after the Festival meal. It was the time of year for colds. Last New Year young Joseph Barnett, who sat behind him, had started to cough, and three months later they were saying prayers for him; something or other of the bronchus. Amazing the number of young people these days. It seemed to be the old who were the strong. Of course they weren't brought up the same. He couldn't imagine himself not being in the seat beside his father, God rest his soul, on New Year and the Day of Atonement, not to mention the Sabbaths and every Festival there was. Times had changed. Josh was a good boy, though, and certainly would have come had he been able.

"The *Torah* reading today," Rabbi Magnus said, turning from one side to the other, "deals with the birth of Isaac, and the exile of Hagar and Ishmael; the *Haftara*, of a similar

15

story of a child being born to a previously childless woman, the birth of Samuel to Hannah. Hannah's prayer, at the end of the *Haftara,* is one of the most beautiful pieces of Hebrew poetry . . ."

Sydney Shelton looked the Rabbi in the eye. "He's probably in bed with a cold," he told him silently.

He was partly right. Josh Shelton was in bed. But not with a cold. With Sarah MacNaughton, whom he had met the night before after dinner at his mother's, where he had eaten the symbolic apple dipped in honey, a token of the sweet year to come.

He dreamed that he was sleeping in a shallow rock pool. Fighting his way through the seaweed, which undulated over his face and which was Sarah's yellow hair, he fumbled for his watch.

"Christ!" he said, sitting up. "It's ten to twelve!"

"Lie down," Sarah said, snuggling further into the bed, which was hers, and pulling him down with her. "It's Saturday."

"I'm supposed to be in synagogue."

"Why?"

"Because I'm Jewish."

"Every Saturday?"

"No. But this is New Year."

"Lie down, darling," Sarah said soothingly. "We haven't even had Christmas."

Josh lay down, unresponsive to the welcoming frissons of her body. He was thinking of his father, of his disappointment. He had intended, really intended, to go to synagogue —and not too late either in order not to embarrass him. He couldn't think how it had got to be almost noon. Well, he could; there had been very little of the night left by the time Sarah MacNaughton had finished with him or rather the other way round—she could have gone on. He'd never met such an amazing girl, all give. He looked at her. What there was to see above the quilt: the hair long and blond, streaked with other blonds, the high cheekbones, the tan on her shoulder that wasn't only a colour sample but went all over after her summer on Skiathos.

"You didn't tell me you were Jewish." She didn't open her eyes.

"You didn't ask me."

"You didn't even tell me your name."

"Josh." She had said it in a million different ways during the night.

"The other bit."

"Shelton. It used to be Solomons."

"Solomons is nicer. Sort of judgmental. I adore Jewish men."

"How many have you known?"

She sat up. Her face looked as if it had been chiselled from fine marble.

"You're the first." She brought her face nearer. "If they're all like you . . ."

She drew away. "You don't like me anymore . . ."

"I adore you."

"What then?"

"I promised my father . . ."

She ran her fingers from his neck to his navel.

"All that hair on your chest and afraid of your father?"

"I said I'd go. I promised. It means a lot to him. Oh what the hell. It's too late anyway. I'll go tomorrow."

"Let me guess," she said. "If today is New Year tomorrow must be Easter."

"No," he said. "New Year again."

He lay back, pulling her down on top of him, and tried unsuccessfully to resurrect some of the passions of the night. He could not erase from his mind the image of his father sitting in the front row of the synagogue, opposite

17

the warden's box, and of the empty seat next to him.

He got out of bed. "I'd better take a shower."

Sarah rolled out the other side and stood facing him. "Me too."

She held out her hands.

He stared at her, wondering whether she was serious. Paula had never even allowed him in the bathroom.

2

THEY CAME OUT OF THE SYNAGOGUE, the men first, spilling into the sunlight of the courtyard. They kept their hats on their heads and carried gold-embroidered bags of blue or scarlet velvet in which were prayer shawls. The regulars had left theirs, together with the books, locked beneath their seats. The ladies, stepping carefully down the stairs from the gallery, infiltrated the navy blueness and greyness of the suits with their colourful hats and dresses. Husbands kissed wives and children and shook hands with the Rabbi, who stood on the steps. The passengers on passing buses stared curiously at the assembly. Gradually, in twos and threes, the men drifted out into the street, dodging the traffic as they crossed the road, their hands behind their backs, discussing the sermon, the decorum. Sometimes they stopped beneath the trees, pointing a finger or grabbing a lapel to emphasize a point. They fanned out across the pavement, the women, lagging behind in their heels, speaking of children and grandchildren and summer holidays now over.

At the parting of the ways, the late sun in their eyes, they used the ancient phrases:

"May you be inscribed for a good year!"

"A Happy New Year!"

Watching them from the window of the flat as they appeared in slow-moving groups from round the corner, Rachel Shelton wondered what it was that made them instantly recognizable as Jews. It wasn't only the hats; or the suits that were well-cut, too well-cut, in fine materials; or the New Year outfits of the women, some of which were neither right for the time of the day nor the time of the year. It was, she thought, more the last vestiges of attitudes derived directly from the ghetto.

Her father said she was anti-Semitic. She was not. Anti only this holier-than-thou exhibitionism, this public display. "For thou has chosen us from among all peoples," they had sung that morning in unison. Heaven help us, Rachel thought.

She had set the table for lunch, using the "meat" cutlery. She was acquainted with the theories, the rationalizations. She had been brought up strictly in the ways of her faith, but she had never discovered a satisfactory answer to the vexing question of how the injunction against seething a kid in its mother's milk had resulted in two separate drawers of silver in inviolate and distinguishable designs.

In the kitchen, remembering that she had had no breakfast, she took a fork, which she knew very well was "milk," and in an act of bad faith plunged it into the chopped liver her mother had prepared. With the same fork she rearranged the contents of the dish so that no one would know she had been at it.

It was quarter to two when Kitty and Sydney came in,

19

bringing with them, Rachel thought, an aura of synagogue and of prayer.

Kitty took off the hat with the rouleaux and ran her fingers through her hair.

"Quarter to two! I don't know why he has to drag it out so long."

"Likes the sound of his own voice." Sydney kissed Rachel and put his trilby down on the hall table.

"Is Josh here?" There was anxiety in his voice.

"No."

"What can have happened to him?"

"Perhaps there's been an earthquake in Bayswater," Rachel said.

Sydney went into the living room.

Rachel followed her mother into the kitchen.

"I don't know why you needle him," Kitty said.

Rachel opened her eyes wide. She was pretty and blond. "What have I said?"

"Just try not to needle him."

"I don't know why you make me come home."

"Your father likes you to."

"Why, if I upset him?"

"You talk too much." Kitty was cutting up a cold chicken on a board and expertly arranging the pieces on an oval dish.

"I'm not coming home for *Yom Kippur.*"

Kitty stared at her. "Don't talk nonsense."

"I mean it."

"Why not?" She held the drumstick in midair.

"I've got lectures."

"So have a lot of other Jewish students. Even that Israeli conductor has cancelled his concert at the Festival Hall the day before because it's *Kol Nidre* night. Everybody else manages."

"I don't want to come."

20

"That's different. Nobody asks you to want to. Who wants to fast? Of course you'll come."

"I've made up my mind."

"We'll discuss it later."

"There's nothing to discuss." Rachel picked up the parson's nose.

"Take your fingers out of the chicken," Kitty said.

"Any chance of lunch?" Sydney called.

"Go and talk to your father and don't go upsetting him about *Yom Kippur*. You'll change your mind."

There was little point in pursuing the argument. Rachel got down from the table where she had been perched.

The front-door bell rang.

It was Carol and Alec and the children.

"Hi," Rachel said.

Carol, still in her hat, a velvet beret, kissed her younger sister. "Happy New Year. Say 'Happy New Year,' girls."

"Skip it," Rachel said.

"They have to learn."

"Why?"

"Happy New Year." Debbie had no front teeth, and Lisa had freckles from the summer holidays. They wore long white socks and black patent-leather shoes, which Rachel doubted would be extant without the Jewish holidays, and had their hair in identical ponytails tied neatly with red ribbons.

She hugged them, loving them both. Debbie was dark, a little Carol, and Lisa, redheaded like her father. Alec had brought his medical bag in with him.

Kitty came out of the kitchen, wiping her hands on the piece of towelling that hung from the side of one of the aprons made yearly by a member of her Committee for the *Chanukkah* Bazaar.

"We met Alec downstairs." Carol took off her beret.

21

Kitty kissed her son-in-law. "Happy New Year. Have you had a busy morning?"

"Hasn't he been to *shul?*" Rachel asked.

"He had visits to make." Carol defended him. "Go and wash your hands for lunch, girls."

"Must have been private patients!" Rachel said.

There was no reply when they called Josh's flat. They had started lunch and were onto the soup when he arrived.

"What happened?" Sydney said. "We were worried about you." He looked at the dark circles under Josh's eyes. "You've got a cold. I knew you had a cold. I said to your mother you must have a cold."

"Shagged to bits, more likely," Rachel said into her *matzo* ball.

Kitty took the plate of chopped liver she had kept for Josh from the sideboard and put it in front of him.

"Thanks, Ma!"

"Well," Rachel said, "why *weren't* you in *shul?*"

"He told you," Kitty said. "He's got a cold."

"Don't come near the children," Carol said.

"He didn't say he had a cold. Dad said he had a cold. Josh didn't say anything," Rachel said.

"Stop making trouble," Kitty said.

"It's all right for him but it's not all right for me."

"I said stop."

"At least I'm in touch with my feelings."

"What's that supposed to mean?" Sydney asked.

"All this religion. It's a defense against facing the problems of your own mortality. Blame everything on God. O.K.?"

Sydney put a hand over hers. "It's New Year, Rachel! Be a good girl."

After lunch Rachel took the children to the park with

Josh. They made straight for the playground and the merry-go-round.

"Where were you anyway?" she asked Josh.

"They're going too fast on that thing," Josh said.

"Fancy upsetting your father like that," Rachel said mockingly.

"You can talk! Did you go to *shul?*"

"He doesn't expect so much from me."

Josh watched the merry-go-round, operated by a small boy, increase in speed until the images of Debbie and Lisa became blurred. Rachel was right. Their father stretched his tolerance, which wasn't very elastic at the best of times, to its limits for Rachel. She was the youngest, the baby, a girl. There was much that she was excused. Not Josh. What a ridiculous name to start with. Josh, Joshua. His grandmother, his father's mother, used to sing "Josh-u-ar, Josh-u-ar, how like a lemon squash-u-ar!" every time she saw him. She had been dead for years, but the ditty still rang in his ears. He couldn't get away with half the things Rachel did. He was the firstborn, the eldest, a son. From the moment of birth there were expectations to be fulfilled, rituals to be performed. Circumcision, Redemption of the Firstborn, Hebrew classes from the age of four, prayers on Friday nights and Saturdays and synagogue attendances on holidays until the first whisperings of the approaching *Bar Mitzvah.* At thirteen you became a man, or so they said. It seemed at the time to have more to do with gifts of books and cameras and hand-painted chess sets than with reaching his religious majority and becoming qualified for inclusion in the ten men necessary to make a quorum before many of the prayers could be said at all. In Josh's case, puberty came late and because he was so small, he read his portion standing on a box at the reading desk. His voice was high and reed-thin, his face smooth as a cherub's. In the eyes of the religion he had been a man for a year when

23

his voice broke; he took a razor to the down on his upper lip and at night, in the privacy of his bed, came to realize what it was all about.

Josh wasn't sure when he realized that to his parents mediocrity was unacceptable. They expected A's for everything and believed, when his finest efforts were rewarded with a B or sometimes a B minus, that either he wasn't trying or the teacher was anti-Semitic. He became neither prefect nor head boy, was not included in the rugger team, nor was he selected as outstanding in anything at all. "Pleasant but idle" was the comment on his report.

He had wanted to be a doctor, or rather Sydney had wanted him to, and he had had no strong objections. His failure to get a place in a medical school had compounded the disappointment they felt in him. He took a year off and went to Israel, then came back and applied for dentistry. The shame was manifest. He had no hope of redeeming himself, not even when he had passed the Fellowship and found in himself a talent for his work. He never seemed to come up to expectations.

"Be fruitful and multiply," the *Torah* said. After becoming a dentist, he did what was expected of him and became engaged to Paula, whom both Kitty and Sydney hugged to their bosoms. He found out in time that in marrying Paula he was expected to take on her formidable and demanding family. Six weeks before the wedding he decided he could not go through with it. It was the bravest decision he had made in his life, and it took Kitty and Sydney many months to get over it. Their disappointment was complete. He often wondered whether if he'd been born a girl, things would have been different.

He decided to tell Rachel about Sarah. Despite her ironic chidings he could rely on her to keep his secrets. They were quite close, forming a kind of mutual support society that helped them to cope with the demands made upon them by their parents. Carol was different. Like her mother in many ways, indistinguishable from the photographs of Kitty as a young girl, she never felt the tentacles of manipulation; her life-style differed very little from that of their parents.

They forgot about Debbie and Lisa. Rachel was telling him how she had put the cat among the pigeons over *Yom Kippur* when there was a cry from the merry-go-round.

Josh was up in a flash. "I told you!"

"She hasn't hurt herself," Rachel said.

Lisa was lying on the gravel with Debbie standing uncertainly over her.

"It's only a graze," Rachel said, dabbing at her knee. "Come on, Lisa, there's nothing to cry about."

"It hurts," Lisa said.

"It's bound to. Come on, we'll go back to Grandma's for tea."

3

Lisa, DECLARING HERSELF WOUNDED, limped convincingly.

"We'd better get on the bus," Rachel suggested.

Debbie looked at her with a horrified expression on her face. "It's *Rosh Hashanah!*"

Josh lifted Lisa onto his shoulders. Like his father, he was heavily built. Leaving the park they passed knots of people still in their New Year clothes and walking off their Festival lunches. The faces were familiar, but Josh and Rachel knew no one.

Carol opened the door of the flat to them. When she saw Lisa, her eyes widened with horror.

"Not to panic," Rachel said. "She fell off the merry-go-round."

"Just look at your socks." Carol's voice was angry. "And the new coat Grandma bought."

"Never mind the socks," Josh said. "Let's get the dirt out of her knee."

Kitty came to see what the noise was about. She took in the graze.

"There's peroxide in the bathroom. Show her knee to Alec straightaway. Never mind, darling," she said to Lisa, who was crying again but only because Carol had shouted at her. "Daddy will make it all better and Grandma will give you a chocolate button." Kitty picked her up and took her into the living room, to Alec.

Rachel lifted her eyes to the ceiling and went into the dining room to inspect the tea.

Auntie Mirrie was putting the finishing touches to the table.

"Hallo, darling!" She put her arms round Rachel.

They had always had a soft spot for each other. She was Sydney's youngest sister. The youngest of two brothers and four sisters—Sydney, Juda (Jules), Freda, Beatty, Dolly and Mirrie. She had never married and worked part-time in a knitwear shop. In return for being subsidized by Sydney, she was at everybody's beck and call. It was hinted at, but never verbalized, that she was a bit simple. Although there were rumours of her having been dropped on her head as a baby, Rachel had always found her particularly wise and perspicacious, and didn't give much credence to the story. When her grandfather died, it was Auntie Mirrie who had lived with her grandmother for twenty years, nursing her and loving her until her death, at the expense of her own life. It was a martyrdom Rachel had never understood.

26

Sometimes she incited Auntie Mirrie to revolt, but was only met with the half-smile, the gentle eyes.

"You're not eating," Auntie Mirrie said, holding her at arm's length. "You're like a rake! You need some of your mother's *Yom Tov* tea inside you."

"Who's coming?"

"Everybody. No. Austin has flu. Uncle Leon and Auntie Beatty are bringing the grandchildren. Dolly and Norman, if Dolly's back isn't acting up . . ."

"Auntie Dolly wouldn't miss a nosh up."

"Jules and Leonora. Do you think I've cut enough bread?"

"For a regiment."

"Freda and Harry. I think a few more slices wouldn't hurt. That grandchild of Beatty's can put away a plateful by himself."

Rachel looked round the dining room with the furniture which had been too big even in Hendon. The bow-fronted, glass-topped sideboard with the silver tea service, the candlesticks and *menorah,* the *Kiddush* cup on its silver tray, the photograph of Kitty's late parents, Momma and Poppa Greenberg, and a sepia one of her grandparents dressed in their sepia clothes. On the table you could hardly see the handmade Chinese lace cloth for the bread and scones and cakes and biscuits and cream and jam and salad and cheeses. Auntie Freda would say, she always did, "The table looks a picture, Kitty!"

Rachel regarded the teas with ambivalence, sometimes losing herself in the warm familiarity of them all and sometimes regarding them, hearing their sounds, as if the room had been invaded by unknown revellers wearing false noses. Of all her aunts and uncles, she liked Auntie Mirrie and Uncle Juda, Jules—she never could remember to call him Jules—the best. He had an art gallery in Belgravia, the Jules Stanley Gallery. It was Leonora who had changed his name. He had already changed Solomons to Stanley. They lived in Hyde Park and had a weekend home in Norfolk. Vanessa, their seventeen-year-old daughter, was being groomed for nobility at the very least. Of all her father's family Jules had prospered most, and marrying Leonora had been one of his best investments. Rich as he was, however, he was declared mean, not like her father. He spent his money on paintings and antiques, on taking Leonora and Vanessa to Bermuda and St. Moritz for holidays and on acquisitions for the three of them. It was not unknown for him to fly to Paris for the day to have a suit fitted, but he did not give Auntie Mirrie anything. When it came to weddings and *Bar Mitzvahs,* the Stanleys would send the smallest present of all, often something they'd had lying round at home. Strangely enough, they always liked to come to her mother's teas, as if they were something they missed in the vast flat, where the paintings were priceless but the atmosphere chilly. Since it looked as if tea was going to be late, she went into the bedroom to phone Patrick.

She flung herself onto her mother's bed, which was not allowed, and leaned against the quilted headboard with its carved cherubs embracing the twin divans.

At the sound of Patrick's voice her own became gentle. She had met him in the summer term. Listening to the account of his day, she glanced idly at the semicircular wall lights, the standard lamp, the "dancing lady and harlequin" on the bird's-eye maple tallboy, the dressing table with its triple mirror edged in peach glass, all of which had gone out of fashion and come in again.

She turned onto her stomach, twisting the telephone cord in her fingers.

"I have to wait until after tea," she said, "or there'll be murder. We have this huge tea . . ."

"There you are!" Kitty said, coming in. "Get off the bedspread. The tea's made."

28

"I've got to go," Rachel said.

Kitty opened the tallboy.

"I love you too," Rachel said.

Kitty counted out linen napkins, straightening an edge here, a fold there.

Rachel blew a kiss into the phone. "I'll come as soon as I can."

"The laundry ruins them," Kitty said, shutting the cupboard, "but I can't stand paper ones. Who was that?"

"A friend."

"What's his name?"

"Patrick."

Rachel waited. Patrick who?

Kitty had other things on her mind.

"I think I left the honey cake in the oven too long . . ."

Rachel got off the bed, leaving a pink satin hollow.

". . . I hope it's not dry."

Kitty crossed the room and banged at the hollow, smoothing it until it was at one with the other divan.

"Wait till you have a home of your own," she said.

It was as if locusts had called. Of the honey cake, made especially for New Year to add sweetness to it, only a triangle remained. Robert, who was six and was Austin's eldest son and Leon and Beatty's grandson, had five cake papers on his plate because his grandmother, busy with the new baby, hadn't been watching him. The jam and the cream and the scones were finished, the chocolate ring, which Kitty had decorated with cherries, was now a half-circle, and the teapot had been refilled twice. Kitty held out the silver bread basket to Josh, who was trying to lose weight.

"The *challah's* lovely," she said, as if it were different from any other week. "The brown bread's lovely too."

Josh patted his stomach. "You know I'm trying to diet."

"Yom tov you don't diet," Beatty said, reaching for a Danish pastry. She took two and put one on her husband's plate.

Leon looked at it doubtfully.

"It's only a mouthful!" Beatty said.

He must have a big mouth, Rachel thought. He and Beatty had a fur shop, which wasn't doing very well these days, mainly remaking and altering, because people weren't spending money for new coats. Of their two sons, they saw Austin more frequently. Charles was married to Angela and had two daughters, Melanie and Clare, but they lived in Reading. Beatty was holding her grandson on her lap. He was three months old and nuzzling at her bosom, over which a wool print dress was stretched tightly.

"Look what he's doing, Leon, he wants his Mummy. We'll have to go soon."

"Why can't you feed him, Grandma?" Robert said, unwrapping a wafer biscuit and watching his baby brother. There was laughter all round. Robert couldn't understand what it was about and no one enlightened him. In later years they would tease him about the remark, which would be added to the family archives.

"Have a fairy cake," Kitty said, handing him the plate. "Grandma made them specially."

"He's had enough by the look of things," Dolly said. "You're not paying attention to him, Beatty. I wouldn't mind more tea."

Mirrie held out her hand for the cup and saucer.

Dolly withdrew the cup a little. "Norman will do it. He knows how I like it."

Norman, large, amiable and unmarried at forty, lived with his mother and looked after her. Dolly was the next youngest to Mirrie. She had been married to Bertie Glicksman, referred to as "poor Bertie" since his untimely death in a train crash. She lived in Golders Green and kept her only child, Norman, who was an estate agent's negotiator, firmly anchored to her by means of a continuing and inventive stream of ailments, the latest of which was her "back." The family all felt sorry for Norman, although, on the surface at any rate, he seemed not dissatisfied with his role. In the early days he had brought home girl friends, but one by one, by fair means or foul, usually foul, Dolly had managed to get rid of them. As far as she was concerned, there was room for only one woman in Norman's life.

Norman poured the tea with care. Dolly's eyes, travelling round the table, said, see how he looks after me.

"I may have to have traction." Dolly was sipping the sweet tea, savouring it as if it were nectar.

"It's dangerous," Leon said. "You should stop in bed."

"Who can stop in bed?" Dolly, who had nothing else to do, gave her brother-in-law a withering look.

"You should try swimming," Leonora said. There were crumbs of a single cooky on her plate. It was how she kept her figure. "There's a divine pool at Grosvenor House."

There was silence as they all tried to cope with the image of Dolly diving into the pool at Grosvenor House. The only sound was Dolly herself, inhaling her tea and finding the suggestion too bizarre to be taken seriously.

"The *'refuah's* worse than the *makkah,' "* Leon said.

Leonora looked puzzled. She came from an old Anglo-Jewish family and was not acquainted with Yiddish.

" 'The cure's worse than the disease,' " Leon translated for her. "Even in Eilat, Christmas, I only put my big toe in."

Juda took Leonora's hand and wondered why she always seemed to do the wrong thing wherever his family was concerned.

"What about acupuncture?" Harry suggested. "There's this chap at the golf club who was crippled with his back, wasn't he, Freda? He had pills, traction, manipulation, you name it, he had it. Then he went to this man in Harley

31

Street. He put needles in, not deep, just under the skin, like a little pinprick, that's all, it's where they put them that's important. He's my partner in the Bogey Stableford next month."

"Does it really do any good?" Sydney said.

"Ask the doctor if you don't believe me!" Harry looked at Alec. "Not much use having a doctor in the family if you don't ask him."

Alec, who was in general practice and had been with the British Medical Association to China to see acupuncture demonstrated, opened his mouth . . .

"You believe what you want to believe!" Beatty said firmly.

"I don't fancy it," Dolly said. "I can't stand needles. I can't even have an injection, I pass out."

"If you don't try, you don't know," Harry said. "I can get his name if you like."

"Look, it's *my* back," Dolly said, "and I'm having traction. And if you don't stop that child eating, Beatty, he's going to be sick."

Sydney decided to say the evening prayers at home. He enjoyed his Festivals: New Year, Day of Atonement, Tabernacles, Passover, Pentecost. These were the semicolons, the regular cases of peace and tranquillity, which punctuated the year. There were the commas, too: the Sabbath, bringing a dimension of rest to every harassed week; minor fasts, lesser landmarks in the history of his people, each to be remembered in its singular prescribed way. Sydney enjoyed the whole cycle and participated in it with enthusiasm. He was not unaware of the burdens imposed by some of the precepts to which he adhered, but he felt that no matter how much he gave to the religion, how much he sacrificed by way of small pleasures and selfish inclinations, the gain was invariably greater. After each immersion into synagogue, Festival and prayer, he felt physically and spiritually refreshed, taking up his secular tasks with a spring in his step and a lightness in his heart he was unaware of at any other time.

He had tried to instil similar attitudes into his family. "Train up a child in the way he should go," the Proverb said, "and when he is old, he will not depart from it."

He didn't seem to have done all that well. Josh, on whom he had pinned his hopes, paid only lip service to the religion, in order, as Sydney was well aware, to please his father. Rachel wanted nothing whatever to do with it, talking through her hat about it being an opiate and a neurosis, as if you could dismiss almost five thousand years with trendy psychological phrases said loud enough. Only Carol carried on the traditions in which she had been raised. He was pleased, of course, pleased, too, that she had married Alec who, although less observant, came from a similar background; but paradoxically this did not gratify him as it should. It was Josh and Rachel he would have liked to see following in his footsteps, the footsteps of Abraham and of Isaac and of Moses. They'll come round, Kitty said. She was always ready with a panacea, a couple of mental aspirins, but there was no sign she was right. Sometimes he wondered where he had gone astray. He was aware that times had changed—since the days of the Bible there had been a few changes, too, but somehow the religion had endured. It had survived the mocking laughter at the birth of Isaac to his aged parents; the destruction of both the First and Second Temples; the expulsion from Spain; and the attempt of Adolf Hitler to exterminate an entire people. Today, with the less overt threats of apathy and intermarriage, the danger of extinction seemed equally great, but Sydney believed that as always, with God's help, Israel would stand fast. It would if he had anything to do with it. He had made that clear to all of them. He was not interested in any rubbish about the world shrinking and the advance of humanism. There was to be no intermarriage. No child of Sydney Shelton's was to be responsible for breaking a link in the chain. For any one who did, as far as Sydney was concerned, it would be as if he had died. This threat was not said lightly. He loved his children, but he identified with Abraham who, as they would read tomorrow in synagogue, did not falter when the commandment came from God to sacrifice his son.

Kitty was tidying the room after the invasion of the family which was Sydney's but which, an only child herself, she had come to regard as her own.

"Rachel isn't coming for *Yom Kippur*." She took the bull by the horns.

"What are you talking about?" Sydney picked up his prayerbook.

"She says she can't take time off this year. She doesn't want to upset you."

He put his skullcap on his head. "There's nothing to be upset about. She's coming. There's no question about it. She knows that as well as I do."

Kitty shrugged. She had prepared the ground. There was nothing more she could do at present. She looked at Sydney, surprised.

"Aren't you going to *shul?*"

"I've got a headache."

"It's too much," Kitty said. "The family."

"You wouldn't like it if they didn't come."

She retrieved a snakes and ladders board from beneath the sofa.

"It's nice to see them come and it's nice to see them go again. What do you think about Dolly's traction?"

"I don't suppose it can do any harm."

34

"What she needs is a man. It's been one thing after another since poor Bertie died."

"Well, she's hardly likely to get one now. She wasn't exactly an oil painting in her young days."

"I feel sorry for Norman."

"Be glad he's there. If it weren't for Norman, we'd have Dolly on our hands."

Sydney opened his book and turned to the Evening Service, regretting now that he had not gone to synagogue. It was his second home, the red brick building, less than ten minutes' walk away along well-trod paths, and he was deeply involved in its life. Every Sabbath and on every Festival he was in his seat. When his mother died, he had also attended the weekday services early in the mornings and in the evenings to recite the Memorial Prayer, never missing, not even when he'd had flu, for the statutory eleven months. He wondered whether, when he passed on, Josh would say *Kaddish* for him.

Kitty looked with satisfaction round the room, which reverberated with the low tones of his prayers. Order had been restored after the chaos of the afternoon. Ornaments, moved for safety from the children's reach, were back in place, cushions fatly plumped, sweet dishes refilled with chocolates and bonbons ready for new visitors.

"Have you seen the *Chronicle* ?" she said. "I haven't had a chance."

The praying did not stop. Without taking his eyes from his book, Sydney reached out a hand to the magazine rack at the side of his chair and handed the newspaper to Kitty.

Slipping off her shoes and curling her feet beneath her, she sank down into the blue velvet cushions of the sofa. It was the first moment she'd had to read the paper.

The Jewish Chronicle. It was more than "The Organ of British Jewry." It was the courier, the Telex, the tom-tom of Jews throughout the United Kingdom, the *sine qua non* of

35

Friday nights, the nepenthe of the weekend, the precursor of the Sabbath. It brought news of births, deaths and marriages from all over the nation, as well as of Jewish communities round the world. It provided a weekly challenge, played throughout the length and breadth of Britain, to see how many people, living or dead, one could claim kinship or acquaintance with. Over the years, the columns of the deceased acquired a morbid fascination relegating the "hatched" and "matched" to second place. There was something for everybody: a review section which could hold its own with that of any national newspaper; pages for women, for students, for the very young; profiles, short stories, learned sermons and commentaries on the *Torah*. Through its columns you could engage a nurse, sell your dining suite, arrange your holidays, buy insurance or a car. In the same issue you could read "Memories of the *Shtetl*," which took you back in time to Eastern Europe, an analysis of current trends in the stock market and recipes for *holishkes*. There were ads for scotch whisky, certified accountants and summer schools; letters about butchers and the Bible; articles on music and on *mikvas*. It was a barley soup of ingredients, a multifaceted amalgam of life itself.

This week, because of the New Year greetings, the paper was unusually large. Some people sent cards. Kitty's mantelpiece was already overflowing; others, through announcements in the personal columns, made public declarations, which some maintained were not in the best of taste.

"Margolis. Frank and Eunice of Thistlethwaite Road . . . wish their dear children, Kevin, Dean and Joanne and darling grandsons, Craig and Bradley, relatives and friends a happy, healthy and prosperous New Year and well over the Fast."

"Sugarman, Minnie and Joe . . . wish their children, grandchildren, *mechutanim,* relatives and friends . . ."

36

Why they didn't just ring them up, Kitty couldn't imagine.

"Sam Plotsker died . . ." she said.

"Retzay adonay elohaynoo . . . accept O Lord our God, thy people . . ." Sydney intoned from his book. ". . . He's been ill a long time."

"He couldn't have been very old."

". . . and let our eyes behold thy return in mercy to Zion . . . sixty-five . . ."

"I must write to Sonia."

"Yisgadal ve-yiskadash . . ." Sydney said, standing up to face the mantelpiece with its Magicoal fire glowing with false embers.

"Listen to this. They found a pig's foot outside Stamford Hill *shul,* wrapped in a *yarmulka* . . ."

There was no cessation in the prayers.

"That pretty Stern girl's got engaged," Kitty went on, "to a boy from Leeds. Beckman. I wonder if it's any relation of the Beckmans who had that big corner house in Hendon, with the monkey puzzle tree. I think his family came from Leeds. In the leather business. Sue Needleman's had another baby, that's Joy Kaye's niece, she had trouble with the first . . ."

Sydney, accustomed to her chatter, listened good-naturedly but did not hear. It was the beginning of the ten days of penitence, when every good Jew was expected to submit himself to severe self-scrutiny in order to improve the quality of his life. For ten days he would try to live at the highest spiritual level of which he was capable, in an attempt to set a standard for all the other weeks of the year.

4

"OPEN WIDE," JOSH SAID, "and turn your head towards me."

He gazed into Lady South's mouth and, having made a decision to take the nerve out of her painful tooth and to replace the small filling next to it, he allowed himself to think about Sarah. Not that he had ever really stopped for more than a few moments. He was so preoccupied with her that he had almost addressed his last patient as "darling," and had to prevent himself, between appointments, from lifting up the telephone just to hear her voice. If he managed to get through the day, it would be a miracle. He was already overbooked. He adjusted the chair with his foot and, swinging his instrument tray towards him, relived Friday night for what was not the first time.

He had gone to a farewell party given by Tim Davis, to whom he sent his orthodontic cases. Disillusioned with English dentistry and lured by the fleshpots of Beverly Hills, Tim was abandoning his practice and emigrating to the States. He lived in a basement flat in Eaton Square with his girl friend, Martha, who was famous for her wooden sculptures and her protruding upper incisors, which his friends imagined had attracted Tim to her in the first place. He had invited everyone he knew who had had any part in his life, including the milkman, the plumber who unblocked his drains and the woman from the dry cleaners.

When Josh arrived, after the New Year dinner at his

mother's, the flat was overflowing and the party, beneath
a pall of smoke, was in full throttle. Elbowing his way to the
grand piano, which was the bar, he greeted the friends and
colleagues he recognized among the media faces from
Tim's fashionable practice. There were plenty of opened
bottles but no clean glasses. He picked up an abandoned
one and fought his way into the kitchen. At the sink an
unsteady, sun-tanned arm, encircled by a dozen shiny ban-
gles, held out a glass. He looked into a pair of sapphire eyes
and turned on the tap. The water gushed onto a burned-
bottomed quiche dish and ricochetted onto a grey silk camisole, pooling it dark.

Apologizing, Josh looked round for a cloth, but there was
only a pair of Martha's tights hanging from a string across
the ceiling. He took the handkerchief from his top pocket
and mopped at the stain.

"I've spoiled your dress."

"It'll dry." Her eyes, which were not sober, delved into
his. She was not concerned about her camisole.

Tim, his hands full of glasses, stepped sideways into the
kitchen.

"That one's no good to you, Sarah darling," he said,
looking at them. "Josh isn't interested in *shiksas.*"

"What's a *shiksa?*"

Tim held the glasses under the tap and shook the drips
off over the floor.

"You are. Watch it!" he said to Josh. "She's on the re-
bound!"

She had long hair and long, dangly earrings, a straight
nose, and a full mouth with lips that curved upwards and
looked painted but were not. He noticed that she had
milky-white teeth, and that they were even, except for a
misplaced canine which lapped over the lateral, giving a
certain humour to her face.

He could not describe the evening. The camisole had

39

dried, and they had sat on the stairs oblivious to the people stepping over them. They had danced, and fought their way to the French bread and the Brie, and had held out their glasses to Tim as he circulated with the bottle. Sarah had come with an actor from the Royal Shakespeare Company. At three in the morning, she told him she wasn't feeling well and went back to her flat with Josh.

It was a studio with old comfortable furniture and a bed covered with a patchwork quilt made by her great-grandmother. There was a photograph in an oval silver frame by the bed. An elegant man in jodhpurs had scrawled loving words in an elegant hand across the corner.

"We were going to get married," Sarah said, looking at it and taking off her camisole. "Six years of my life!"

"What happened?"

She stumbled against the bed and sat on it.

"His wife wouldn't let him."

He turned the photograph to the wall. He was in love for the first time since Paula. He wondered if he had ever really loved Paula.

There were sounds of protestation from the chair. He switched off the drill.

"The water's going down my neck!" Lady South complained.

"So sorry." He flexed his back while Jacky, his dental nurse, dabbed at the wrinkled neck and fixed the bib more securely.

"O.K. now?" He didn't wait for an answer. "Nearly done. Just a few moments more and then it will be ready for shaping and filling. You're being very good." He went back to Paula.

It had all been arranged. His mother was Vice-Chairman of the local branch of the Jewish Association for the Blind, and once a year at the Dinner and Ball she expected Josh

40

to lend his support. She had seated Josh at the young people's table next to Paula Wiseman, daughter of Ruthie Wiseman, who was Treasurer. Both he and Paula knew why. Paula was tiny with soft brown hair, wide grey eyes and cream shoulders, which rose from a floating dress of scarlet chiffon. She was like a little kitten and as much fun. On the dance floor he had felt protective, his six feet enhanced by her five foot nothing. From behind the lottery stand, Ruthie Wiseman's eyes followed them speculatively. He saw his mother dig his father in the ribs with an eloquent elbow as they danced by.

Paula studied design at art school and was going to help her father, who manufactured dresses. They lived in a large white villa, to which Josh became a frequent visitor. Her mother fed him chicken soup and large portions of everything while her father assessed his prospects by plying him with questions about dentistry in general, his practice in particular and his plans for the future. Although knowing that everything had been set up, he allowed himself to be drawn into the machinery. He and Paula spent every available moment together and he thought he was in love. For the summer he went with her and her family to their flat in Juan-les-Pins. While Ruthie and Henry were at the Casino and her brother, Martin, was enjoying the displays of nudity on the beach, they made love in the afternoon heat. Back in England he asked her to marry him. Both families wept with joy, and he and Paula thought they had done something terribly clever.

They were taken over not all at once but in an insidious and relentless coup. It began with the ring. They found a garnet shaped like a heart, surrounded by seed pearls, which Paula exhibited with pride.

"Sweet," Ruthie said, looking at it from afar. "Not that I'm a great one for garnets."

"What about the engagement ring?" her father asked.

Josh tried to explain that that was it. Henry Wiseman took him into the study where he watched television and explained to him, as to a child, that what he had bought Paula was a nice little knickknack but that, in accordance with custom, he was expected to provide his fiancée with a diamond engagement ring of a size and quality which would reflect at the same time her worth and his good faith. If Josh wanted, he could introduce him to a man in Hatton Garden who could be trusted to provide him with just such a pledge. The pleasure they had had in choosing the garnet with its coronet of seed pearls quickly evaporated. In the interests of harmony and with a loan from his father, Josh duly provided her with an ice-cold diamond, which was worn night and day by Paula on the fourth finger of her left hand. It was assessed not so much for its beauty as for its value, and Josh was pronounced a good *shiddach*.

They found a cottage in Blackheath. Ruthie and Henry reacted as if they had decided to live in Peking. They presented them or rather Paula, for the house was in her name, with an expensive modern shoe box not a stone's throw from their own villa. In the interests of harmony, Josh pretended to be grateful and arranged with Paula to spend his free Wednesday afternoons at auction sales. Ruthie was horrified. She wasn't having her daughter living in a house surrounded by other people's old junk. She took Paula to the showrooms of friends in the furniture business, to carpet wholesalers and to kitchen manufacturers whose ranges could be found in the best department stores. To be fair, they did show Josh snippets of silk and squares of carpet from which he was invited to picture the completed sitting room or bedroom. He had his first major row with Paula when Ruthie announced one afternoon that she and her daughter had selected the marital bed.

"Don't be cross, Joshy," Paula said. "It's king size, pocket springing."

42

"I don't care about the springing," Josh said. "I suppose she tried it too?"

"We both did."

"You could have asked me to come with you."

"You were working," Paula said reasonably, "and after all they are paying for everything."

"Who needs it?" Josh said. "I just want you, Paula, not a houseful of furniture I don't even like."

There were tears in her eyes.

"Don't be unfair. Daddy's spending thousands, you've no idea what things cost, and Mummy's exhausted from all the shopping."

"Tell her not to bother," Josh said and walked out of the house.

Afterwards, aware that Paula had divided loyalties, he felt churlish and apologized.

The wedding ceremony was to be followed by a reception and dinner for five hundred guests. Shopping began in earnest for the wedding dress and the trousseau. There were to be four bridesmaids, cousins of Paula's. What with selecting their dresses (an argument which mystified him, about the respective merits of organdy and taffeta), and interviewing photographers and florists and discussions ad nauseam of menus with the caterers, Josh saw less and less of Paula. When he did, she was tired and irritable and did not want to make love.

"There'll be plenty of time for that," Paula said, "after the wedding."

"I'm not made of stone," Josh said. "I love you, Paula." He thought he did. She put her doll-like arms round him, which mollified him as usual.

"We'll make up for it on our honeymoon."

It was the honeymoon that proved the last straw. He wanted to take Paula to Athens and then to Crete to see the palace of Knossos.

"It's foolish to do all that *shlepping* on your honeymoon," Henry Wiseman said. "My partner's offered you his villa in Barbados."

They were having dinner, Josh scooping at the melon half on his plate.

"It's very generous of you," he said, "but we've settled on Greece, haven't we, Paulie?"

Paula looked at her father. "We could go to Greece another time . . ."

"I thought we'd decided . . ."

"You'll both be exhausted after the wedding," Ruthie said. "Take it from me. A nice villa, with its own pool . . ."

Afterwards, he said to Paula, "I'm not going to Barbados."

"We can't upset Daddy."

"Why not?"

"He's gone to so much trouble."

He removed her wheedling arms from his neck.

"Look, Paula, I've been very patient. Your parents have set the whole thing up—the wedding, the house, even our bed. The least you can do is to let me arrange our honeymoon, unless your mother intends coming along on that too."

"Now you're being unkind." The tears, which were never too far from the surface, flooded the grey eyes.

"Come away with me, Paula. Let's get married quietly, just the two of us."

"The invitations have gone out," Paula said, horrified. "And what about my dress?"

"Well, you can forget Barbados," he said. "We're going to Crete."

Henry sat him down and plied him with whisky.

"You have to understand women," he said in what he

thought was a man-to-man way. "If Paula's made up her mind to go to Barbados . . ."

"Paula doesn't want to upset you."

"Is that so terrible?"

In a moment of clarity, he saw the scene being reenacted down the years.

He gave Paula an ultimatum. She chose Barbados. He left Paula, Ruthie, Henry and the white villa, and took his dental nurse to Knossos. Afterwards, all things considered, he decided he had had a lucky escape.

Eighteen months later Paula married Stuart Mindel. They spent their honeymoon in Barbados and lived in the modern shoebox, where they were blessed with twin sons. Paula could frequently be seen shopping with her mother, from whom she was inseparable. Josh made up his mind to remain a bachelor.

He pressed the last plug of amalgam home into Lady South's cavity and scraped away the excess.

"All finished," he said. "Rinse, please."

5

CAROL DID NOT LIKE SEX. She never had. The rows about it had become woven into her life with Alec, and lately they had begun to undermine the fabric of the marriage.

Whenever he wanted to make love, she managed to find a different excuse. Exhaustion—Lisa had been giving her a rough time, not leaving Debbie alone for a minute and constantly provoking quarrels; sunburn when they were on holiday; indigestion. At first Alec had been light-hearted, cajoling and persuading: making love would relax her; she was only tired because she was tense; it would help her digestion. Whoever heard of sex being a cure for indigestion?

Last night he had seemed at the end of his tether, setting off a row that had been smouldering since the weekend.

"Look, Carol, I just want you. I love you. I need you. Don't you understand?"

She did not; she just wanted to put her head under the covers and sleep.

"You're driving me away," he said.

"It's because I'm pregnant."

She enjoyed being pregnant, loved the big, fat comfortable feeling of it; not the other.

It had never been any different except perhaps in the first few months of their marriage.

It was not that she did not love Alec. Over the years she had tried to explain. There had been tears and recriminations, anger and reconciliations. He did not understand. All that probing and pawing with the lights on, sometimes in strange places, not even in bed, not even in the bedroom; she would rather die than tell anybody. All she wanted was to lie in the dark with her head on his chest and his arms round her, not gymnastics.

"I'm tired, Alec."

"You're always tired," he said. "You weren't tired on Saturday at your mother's."

"It was Mummy's tea," Carol said. *"Rosh Hashanah!"*

"I'd rather spend it quietly in my own home and not waste an entire afternoon listening to your Auntie Beatty squabbling with Auntie Dolly and both of them rabbiting on about their ailments. I have enough of that with the patients all day."

"That's why you've been sulking."

46

"I've not been sulking. I've been thinking."

"What about?" He appeared to have forgotten about the love.

"I think we should move . . ."

She sat up, a silhouette against the lamp.

". . . to the country. Just the four of us; five. We could be alone. We might be able to work things out."

"The country! What on earth would I do in the country? And what about Mummy and Daddy?"

"You're married to me, Carol."

"You know they adore the children."

Her mother came round every day, her father several times a week, to see Debbie and Lisa.

"They'd still see them."

"It wouldn't be the same."

"No."

She liked her little house in the row of little houses only a few blocks from her mother; she liked her friends, the shops she was familiar with, the synagogue where the children went to classes on Sundays. She wrapped the sheet more tightly round her, afraid, suddenly, for her world.

"Think about it, Carol. I don't want to leave you. I love you and I want us to have a chance . . ."

"I don't know what you're talking about."

He took her hand. "I think you do."

She was crying now. "I could have a miscarriage. It isn't fair."

"It's my baby too."

"You wouldn't think so. Threatening me like that! I'm going to tell Daddy." She reached for the telephone. "He'll make you . . ."

"You'll do no such thing!" He pushed her arm away more roughly than he had intended.

"You hit me!" she said, clutching her arm in an exaggerated embrace.

47

He inspected it, rubbing it gently.

"I'm sorry, Carol. I didn't mean to hurt you. You provoke me. I'm on duty tonight. If you won't make love, let's go to sleep before I get called out."

But she would not let him off so lightly. Now thoroughly awake, she took from her armoury the well-worn brickbats concerning the excessive and unnatural sexual demands he made upon her and hurled them at him; in self-defense he retaliated with her dependence on the family she seemed never to have left.

Debbie, wakened by the noise—the walls were thin— came to see what the shouting was about.

"See what you're doing to the children!" Carol sobbed. Alec put her back to bed.

By the time she had run out of steam it was after midnight, and it was one o'clock before Alec could quiet her and get her to go to sleep lying stiffly in his arms.

The telephone rang in the small hours. Carol heard him say, "What does the pain feel like, in which part of the chest?" and "I'll be along shortly." She wanted to reach out to him to say she was sorry. She did nothing, watching him put his trousers on. Then he was gone. By the time he came back she was asleep again.

In the morning they scarcely spoke. There were dark circles under Alec's eyes. When her mother phoned, she was crying slow tears of self-pity.

Kitty's weekend began on Wednesday, when it was necessary to start thinking about the cleaning, shopping and cooking which must be completed before the commencement of the rest day. Sabbaths and Festivals might represent oases of peace and interjections of tranquillity in Sydney's life, but for Kitty they signified additional demands upon her energy and time.

" 'Many daughters have done worthily, but thou excellest them all.' "

Thus Sydney expressed his appreciation of his wife's loyalty and devotion to family and home in his Friday night prayers. Kitty reckoned that the tribute was not unwarranted. She found it hardly surprising that women were exempt from many of the positive religious duties. Her role in creating a Jewish home kept her, apart from her charity work and the Ladies' Guild, fully occupied. She was responsible for getting the flat ready for the Sabbath; for providing the two plaited loaves, the candles and the special meal, and for welcoming it like a bride. She cleared the leaven from her house at Passover, decorated the synagogue on Pentecost and the booth on Tabernacles. She prepared for the High Festivals, of which they were now in the midst, and arranged entertainments for the children on *Chanukkah* and *Purim*. She realized that, compared with her mother and her grandmother, she had it easy. The chopping board had given way to the food processor. She did not spend her life in the kitchen, kneading dough, stretching strudel and frying blintzes, all of which could now be bought prepacked. She still cooked the traditional foods associated with the Festivals—dairy foods for Pentecost, potato *latkes* for *Chanukkah*—but nowadays she could make extensive use of her freezer. However, whatever changes had been brought about by modern technology, everything still had to be planned and quantified, bought and prepared. Generally there were extra mouths to feed. Sometimes, particularly in the case of Passover, the preparations required the dedication of a Sisyphus and the strength of a Hercules. Since Passover fell in April this year and it was now only September, Kitty refused to think about it, concentrating her attentions on the forthcoming Day of Atonement. Although the Day itself was spent in fasting, she had to cook, in advance, two special meals. On the eve of the

Fast, the menu must be sustaining without provoking a thirst that would be unable to be quenched for twenty-five hours; the one following it preferably light and easily digested after a day of abstinence.

After Sydney had left for the office, she lay in bed thinking about the meals, about her family in general and about Rachel in particular.

Something would have to be done about Rachel and *Yom Kippur* if peace was to be kept.

She wondered if she would still be in her room and dialled the number.

"Max Rayne House."

"Room two three oh, please."

She was about to replace the receiver when a voice, heavy with sleep, said: "Yes?"

"Rachel?"

"What's the matter?"

"Why should anything be the matter?"

"I didn't get to bed until three . . ."

"You shouldn't keep such late nights. It's not good for you . . ."

"Look, mother, if you just woke me up to lecture me . . ."

"I wanted to speak to you about *Yom Kippur* . . ."

"What about it?"

"Your father's very upset . . ."

"We've been through all that. I told you I'm not coming."

"He hasn't been feeling all that well lately and business is bad . . . it won't hurt you."

"I told you. I don't believe in it."

"Don't start splitting up the family . . ."

"Look, mother, I've a lecture at nine-thirty."

"It's quarter past nine now. I thought I woke you up."

"I wasn't going but now I'm awake . . ."

"So you'll come then?"

"I didn't say so."

"At least for *Kol Nidre* night. It's always a beautiful service."

"I'll be bored out of my mind."

"Don't be late. We have to eat at five. The Fast begins at six-thirty."

"I'll think about it."

"Bring something suitable." She meant, to wear.

"I've got to go now."

Kitty put down the phone. That was settled. When Rachel came for *Kol Nidre,* she would persuade her to stay the night and go to synagogue the next day.

With Josh it was a different worry. There was no question of him not being there, beside his father, on the Day of Atonement—he always did the right thing—but she would like to see him settled. People were beginning to talk. The Paula episode had been three years ago. She still shuddered when she thought of it, all those wedding preparations and having to face Ruthie Wiseman at meetings and seeing Paula in the High Street with the babies which should by rights have been her grandchildren. She hadn't managed to get Josh to attend the Dinner and Ball since. She wondered if she would be able to talk him into it this year; she would have to start working on him soon. She knew a couple of nice girls that she could get for the young people's table. Some of the women on her Committee would give their eye teeth to have Josh for one of their daughters, judging by the hints. There weren't that many eligible Jewish boys around.

Carol and Alec would both take and break the Fast with them. It saved Carol doing everything herself. She wasn't all that strong, girls today didn't seem to be made like they used to be. She spoke to Carol every day, Sydney liked her to ring before he left so that he could say hello to the children. This morning Carol had sounded miserable, Kitty thought, low. Perhaps she needed a tonic or a good holiday before the baby. She would have a word with Alec. Busy with his patients, he didn't realize how hard it was for Carol with the telephone ringing all day and the two girls; it would be easier after *Yom Kippur* when Lisa started school. At least she'd be able to get some time to herself in the mornings.

Josh could not believe that he had only known Sarah for a week. In seven days she had become a part of his life without which it seemed the vital forces would drain away. To celebrate the occasion, he had given her a silver chain. She wore it round her neck. Now and again she put a hand to her throat to check that it was still there.

They were sitting in front of the electric fire in Sarah's flat. The evenings were drawing in. They had been laying out their lives before each other. When it was his turn, he told her about his family and about Paula.

"That first night, after Tim's," Sarah said, "I was really drunk. I was trying to forget."

"And the second?"

The dark sapphire of her eyes embraced him.

"I knew exactly what I was about."

"And the third and fourth?"

"I want to show you to my friends," Sarah said. "I've told them all about you. Kate's having a party on Monday before she goes to New York. They're all dying to meet you."

"Monday's the Fast."

"You told me Tuesday!"

"It starts on Monday night. We go to synagogue."

"Kate will be disappointed. So will I. Tell me about it."

He had been trying for the last five minutes.

Jews, he said, had split atoms, produced fine art, great music. They had also created a day of haunting beauty, of

52

spiritual power. He tried to convey to her something of its paradoxes; of the fasting and the prayer; of the repentance and the reconciliation; of the thirteen attributes and the five services; of the awe and the tedium, the rapport and the ambivalence; of the intervals of chanting and the periods of exaltation; of the terrible hours and the wondrous moments. He told her how they interceded for each other.

"Will you pray for me?" Sarah said.

"I'll do anything for you."

It was true. He wanted to please her. She brought out the best in him. Paula had brought out the worst.

6

RACHEL SWUNG DOWN THE STAIRCASE of Max Rayne House, stepped lightly along the hallway and knocked on the door of number 52. Without waiting for an answer, she went in.

"Hallo, Solly," she said.

He was lying on the bed listening to Mozart.

"Not masturbating or anything are you?"

"Come in and shut the door. What's the problem, little one?"

Rachel sat on his desk.

"She keeps ringing me up."

"Who does?"

"My mother. She wants me to go home for *Yom Kippur.*"

She picked up a pencil and pointed it at him.

"I'm not going."

There was no response. Only the adagio filling the room.

"Did you hear?"

"What do you want?" Solly said. "Permission?"

"She blackmails me with my father. 'He doesn't look well.' 'Business is bad.' 'Don't upset him.' He looks perfectly all right to me and business has been bad for as long as I can remember. This year I'm not going. I refuse to sit there bored and hungry while they drone on and on in a language I don't understand and which ninety-nine percent of the people don't understand either. All you hear in the Ladies' Gallery is what they'll be having to eat afterwards. It's an absolute farce. All that fasting. All that repentance. What's it about, Solly?"

" 'Yom,' " Solly said, "day. 'Kippur,' wiping away. It's the day when God wipes away all our sins, giving us a new start, a clean slate. We're supposed to feel sorry for the wrongs we've done and resolve to do better in the future."

"You don't have to starve yourself to death to do that."

"The fasting's a commandment. We have to deny ourselves many of the pleasures in which we indulge during the year. Eating, drinking, sex; it helps concentrate on the repentance."

"It has the opposite effect on me."

"You have to go back three thousand years," Solly said. "To Isaiah. 'Is not this the fast that I have chosen? To loose the bonds of wickedness, to undo the hands of the yoke, and to let the oppressed go free . . . Is it not to deal your bread to the hungry and that you bring the poor that are cast out into your house? When you see the naked that you cover him and that you hide not yourself from your own flesh?' "

Rachel looked out of the window.

"Why can't they just believe that I love them? Why do I constantly have to prove it? God, when I have children, if I have children, things will be different. If they only knew, Solly, like you know, if they only understood how deeply my Jewishness goes; deeper than Carol's, for all her *lokshen* pudding, certainly deeper than Josh's, who only does anything at all to keep the peace. He's always been good-natured, not like me. No doubt I shall be accused of precipitating all manner of minor misfortunes by my behaviour and then left to stew in my own conscience. I suppose you're going home?"

"Of course."

"To Manchester?"

"That's where it is."

She changed the subject.

"Are you coming to the Arab Society debate tonight? 'Opposing the Zionist State of Israel and supporting the struggle of the Palestine people for the liberation of their homeland.' We need all the support we can get."

"I don't suppose I've any choice then."

"Did you read the results of the public opinion poll on the Middle East?"

Solly opened his mouth, but she didn't wait for an answer.

"It was based on over a thousand personal interviews. One of the findings was that twenty-seven percent of those asked thought that Israel was an Arab country! I suppose you can't blame them in a way. I'm a bit shaky myself when it comes to Northern Ireland or Cambodia."

She slid off the desk. "I must go and rustle up a few people and mentally prepare myself for the barrage of mindless slogans prepackaged in Beirut."

"I wish you luck," Solly said.

"I'd have a better chance if the motion was proposing the sale of salt beef sandwiches and pickled cucumbers in the Union."

"See you later then."

Rachel blew him a kiss. "I love talking to you, Solly. Carry on where you left off."

55

She shut the door.

The clarinet concerto followed her down the corridor.

Sydney sat at his desk with its framed photographs of Kitty and of Josh and of Rachel and of Carol and Alec and the children, and contemplated the sales figures which were in front of him. The line on the graph sloped inexorably downwards. It was not a situation peculiar to S. Shelton (Fancy Goods) Ltd. There was a worldwide recession which had to come and it was beginning—more, it had begun—to bite. Business had not been so bad for years; he had not had such a headache for years. He wondered if the two were connected.

He opened the drawer of his desk and took out the giant-sized bottle of aspirin and flipped the switch on his intercom.

"Miss Maynard," he said, "can I have a glass of water?"

Closing his eyes, he leaned back in his chair and waited. It would not be quick. Miss Maynard had worked for him for twenty years and had been no spring chicken when he engaged her.

She brought the water and the afternoon post which she had opened.

"Nothing much," she said. "Mainly appeals; one's for lottery gifts."

"You'd think I was in business for charity," Sydney grumbled.

"I've got Cohen waiting," Miss Maynard said.

Sydney swallowed the aspirins. "How can I give him an order when nobody's buying?"

"They've got trouble with the boy still," Miss Maynard said. "They have to give him money for the drugs, otherwise he steals it. Mrs. Cohen's worse. She can't do the stairs at all now. They have to rely on a neighbour when Mr.

56

Cohen's not there. He'd like to put in a downstairs toilet but they need five hundred pounds for the plumbing."

"Everybody's got troubles," Sydney said. He held out his hand for the letters. "I want to leave early." He would pop into Carol's on the way home to see the children. With their bright smiles and their hugs and their kisses, Debbie and Lisa always managed to cheer him up. Carol would make him a cup of tea.

He riffled through the mail: Nightingale Homes, Buckets and Spades, Hebrew University.

"Send them the usual."

"What about the lottery?"

"The papier-mâché trays are sticking; give them those."

From his desk a haunted face from a Russian labour camp stared up at him, hounded, tired. He would write a letter to Alexander Khasin, telling him he was not forgotten; to the authorities asking for his release and that he be given the visa he had requested to go to Israel. It would not be the first time.

He passed a hand over his forehead. "That'll do for today. Send Cohen in."

"A Happy New Year," Cohen said, holding out his hand. His collar was not very clean and was frayed at the points. There was a button missing from his sleeve.

Once a *nebbech*, always a *nebbech*, Sydney thought, and extended his hand across the desk. "A Happy New Year. Sit down, sit down. How's Mrs. Cohen?"

Cohen shrugged. Incorporated in the shrug were the burden of the cooking and shopping and housekeeping, the necessity of carrying her up and down the stairs, the never-ending attention.

"How can she be?"

"And the boy?"

Another shrug. The boy was a registered addict, but it

57

was only a question of time before he killed himself with the extra heroin Cohen had to give him money to buy.

"What have you got for me?"

Cohen opened his case.

Sydney waited. Their association went back many years; he had danced with Mrs. Cohen at the Fancy Goods trade ball before the crippling illness infiltrated her muscles. Through photographs he had watched the progress of the young Stuart (on whom the Cohens had pinned their dreams) from childhood to adolescence.

Cohen picked up an intricate arrangement of metal rods from the miscellany he had laid out on Sydney's desk. He pulled them apart and let them clink together again by magnetic force into various shapes and patterns.

"An executive toy."

"Don't you think executives have enough problems? What would they want with toys? Business is terrible. No, that's not true, Cohen, it's worse than terrible, it's tragic." He thought of Alexander Khasin in the labour camp. That was tragic. "No," he corrected himself, "it's not tragic, it's terrible."

Cohen leaned forward. "That's just when people need distractions," he said with as much enthusiasm as he could muster. He had always been a poor salesman, his own worst enemy. "When things are bad you need something to take your mind off . . ."

"What else have you got?" Sydney picked up a gilt gadget that was a cross between pliers and scissors. He raised an eyebrow at Cohen.

"An egg decapitator."

"De . . . what?"

"Takes the top off your egg."

"What's wrong with a spoon? And this?"

"A dish. In the shape of a rabbit; an ashtray or for sweets . . ." Cohen's voice trailed away.

58

"This paper spike is a very popular line," he said. "It's the tail of a Dachshund; or you can have a lynx if you'd rather."

"I'd rather have nothing. Who wants a paper spike? This?"

"Cuff links like miniature playing cards; aces, clubs, diamonds, spades, any combination you like."

"Everybody's got buttons."

"Pepper mill and salt shaker?"

"We haven't moved the last lot."

"Champagne stopper, gilt or chrome, enamelled egg, hand-coloured, willow warbler on a tree."

"What's this?" Sydney said.

"Miniature Old English Sheepdog."

Sydney put it in his pocket. "I'll take that for the children. You can put the rest away. There's no business. The stores aren't buying. Nobody's buying. The tourists don't come anymore. If we survive the winter it will be a miracle. I'm going home. I've got a headache."

"It's the weather," Cohen said equably, putting the samples back into his case. "First it's hot, then it's cold. It's not healthy." He snapped the hasps of his bag, which had seen better days, and stood up.

"Don't be in such a hurry," Sydney said. "Sit down a minute." He took his checkbook out of the drawer and wrote in it. He tore out the check, folded it and handed it to Cohen.

"What's that?"

"For Mrs. Cohen. For the downstairs toilet."

Cohen stood up but was unable to move, unable to speak.

"You can pay me back," Sydney said gruffly, angrily almost, stopping the words Cohen was unable to utter, "when there's more business around."

There were tears in Cohen's eyes. "I wish you well over the Fast," he said, "and Mrs. Shelton."

"A Happy New Year," Sydney said, appreciating the hollowness of the words in the context of Cohen.

"A Happy New Year."

In the afternoons Carol rested while Debbie and Lisa played with the little boy next door.

She had just settled down when she heard Alec's key in the lock, his footsteps on the stairs.

"I thought you were doing the baby clinic." She watched him cross the bedroom.

"Finished. I've still half a dozen visits to make. I came home to see how you are."

"I'm fine."

He sat on the bed.

"How's my new baby?"

"I think he's going to be a footballer."

Alec pulled down the bedclothes.

"Let me feel him kick."

He put a hand on her belly, which was beginning to swell.

She tried to cover herself again, but he was stroking her gently.

She shut her eyes. "I thought I'd have a sleep while the children are next door."

He fondled the full breasts.

"Do you realize it's been two weeks . . ."

"I'm tired, Alec."

"You can sleep afterwards."

He was caressing her with both hands. Carol wished he would go away.

A car drew up outside the house and a door slammed.

Alec looked out of the window.

"It's your father," he said. "Bloody hell!"

* * *

60

Debbie and Lisa came in with him. They had seen the car. "Your front door could do with a coat of paint, before the winter," Sydney said. "Our little man from the High Street would do it; he can turn his hand to anything."

Alec did not reply.

Sydney took off the light raincoat he was wearing and hung it on the banisters, bending down as he did so to run a hand along the stair treads. "And I should let him move the stair carpet while he's here. It really needs shifting every six months, the price of carpet these days."

The girls clung to him on either side. He stepped over the magic painting books and the puppets and the doll's house on the floor, and settled himself in Alec's chair.

"Hello, Dad!" Carol said.

"I thought you wanted to sleep," Alec said.

She didn't reply. He watched her kiss her father.

"Come and sit on Grandpa's lap," Sydney said to the girls. "I've got something new for the doll's house."

They settled themselves on his knees and he told them to reach into his pockets and see what they could find. It was Lisa who found the Old English Sheepdog.

Carol opened the doll's house with its red roof and miniature windows. She liked it when her father came, when he took the children on his lap. It made her feel like a small girl again. She sensed the resentment flowing from Alec.

Inside the doll's house it looked like the aftermath of an earthquake: furniture lay drunkenly in inappropriate rooms and small people sprawled in heaps in grotesque positions.

"Debbie!" Carol said.

"It was Lisa," Debbie said.

Lisa slid down from Sydney's knee. "She's a big liar!"

"Don't use such language to your sister," Sydney said. "It's not nice."

"She's not nice!"

"Yes, she is. She's very nice. Grandpa loves her. I love you, don't I Debbie?"

"Stop it now, Lisa," Carol said. "Come and tidy the doll's house and then we can put the dog into it. You must be a big girl or you won't be able to start school next week."

"She's too much of a baby," Debbie said, making Lisa cry louder and aiming a kick at her shins.

"Now that's enough," Carol said sharply.

"I'll do a trick." Sydney took a handkerchief out of his pocket.

The front door slammed.

"What's that?" Sydney said.

"Alec."

"He'll have the plaster down, slamming the door like that!"

"He has some visits to make." He would be angry when he came back. Sydney held the handkerchief up. "Now watch carefully!"

Lisa and Debbie sat spellbound.

"I'll put the kettle on," Carol said.

"He could ring up," Alec said later, "before he comes round."

"He knows he's welcome anytime. At least he plays with the children."

"What do you want me to do, Carol? Cancel my visits and play doll's houses! And I don't need to be told when to paint my front door and move my stair carpet. I don't go round telling him when to move his stair carpet."

"He lives in a flat."

"And another thing. Tell your mother to stop interrupting my office hours to ask me if anything's the matter because you sound funny on the phone."

"I didn't tell her to."

"Come away," Alec said, "before it's too late. There's a practice advertised in this week's medical journal."

7

In the days before New Year the florists enjoyed a boom. Ten days ago Kitty had been standing amid cut bouquets and planted bowls to send flowers to Dolly in Golders Green, Freda and Harry in Bushey Heath, Juda and Leonora in Hyde Park and Leon and Beatty in Edgware. Each year the prices of the floral tributes, inflated for the Jewish holidays, became more prohibitive. Each year those who sent them complained bitterly—Kitty always saved a little and salved her conscience by not sending flowers to Mirrie, who spent most of the holidays with her. Instead she bought her a yearly box of chocolates, which Mirrie, who was unable to eat them because of her migraines, just as regularly passed on to one of the women in the shop for Christmas.

Before the Day of Atonement, when it was customary to visit the graves of departed relatives, there were flowers in the cemetery, too: dahlias and geraniums, pink and yellow and red, like poster paints in the brilliant light of the Indian summer. It was almost like being on holiday, Kitty thought irreverently as she hurried over the bridge of the miniature lake and along the paths between the headstones towards the place where her parents were buried.

She never knew why there seemed to be such an atmosphere of urgency on these pre-*Yom Kippur* visits, only that it had something to do with the awesomeness of the time of the year.

She was not alone in choosing this particular morning to make her pilgrimage. Here and there along the paths small groups of men in hats and women with head scarves hurried on identical missions.

The route which Kitty took was a well-worn one and many of the testimonies, chiselled on the simple marble stones, familiar. The Holocaust Memorial with its cry for the "orphans bereaved and forsaken"; "Malcolm Silverman . . . in everlasting peace"; "Golda Davis . . . sweet and gentle soul"; dearest grandmas deeply mourned; devoted wives; beloved husbands; and "Tracy . . . aged two years ten months, from those who loved her."

Kitty's mind was not on them. She was thinking about Sydney, worrying about him. He'd been looking very tired and drawn lately, not quite himself. Apart from the headaches, which she put down to business anxieties—people were going broke left, right and center—there was something else which concerned her. When he had given her her monthly housekeeping check, his signature had looked like the writing of an old man, the letters thin and spidery, where before they had been round and firm. She might have thought nothing of it if next day she hadn't found a slip of paper in the pocket of his suit on which he'd written his name a dozen times. Sydney Shelton. Sydney Shelton. The last being as attenuated, as spidery, as the first. She made a mental note that after *Yom Kippur* she would get him to see Lennie, their family doctor, for a checkup. Not that Sydney would agree. If she so much as suggested it, he'd say, don't talk nonsense, there's nothing the matter with me. She'd have to ask Lennie to pretend he'd come socially, popped in for a chat, and while he was there he could have a look at him. That's what she'd do. Get *Yom Kippur* over first.

"Kitty!"

Moss Shapira, whose wife had collapsed and died suddenly the day after their golden wedding anniversary a couple of months ago, stood misty-eyed in her path.

She took his hand in both hers. There were no words.

He looked old, frail.

"She was always the strong one." His head shook with the tremor of Parkinson's.

He leaned on the arm of his granddaughter, who wore jeans and looked embarrassed by the whole thing.

"Hetty's oldest," the old man said by way of introduction.

Kitty nodded at the girl.

"How are you keeping?" she asked Moss.

"How can I be?"

Kitty looked up at the sky.

"At least the sun's shining."

Moss Shapira seemed not to care about the sun. It did not alleviate his pain.

"I was the one always ill . . ."

Poor old chap, Kitty thought. It's no good to get old.

"Take care of yourself," she said, squeezing the hand which clung to hers as if it was clinging to life itself.

Leaving them, she thought she should perhaps have brought Rachel. Although she'd had enough aggravation with her over the *Yom Kippur* business, the matter, she believed, had now been satisfactorily dealt with. True, Rachel had been noncommittal on the telephone, but Kitty was sure that she would come home for the Fast and not make trouble with her father, who liked to have his family round him on this Sabbath of Sabbaths. If the immediate problem was relegated to the background, the more general problem of the company Rachel kept remained, her Patricks and her Christophers, who all seemed far from suitable. She

65

was still young, though, and given time Kitty hoped she would settle down, like Carol.

"Ester Goodkind (Nana)."

"Sir Harry Levine," beneath his mausoleum of black granite.

By the time she got to "Rebecca Levy, a woman of worth" her pace had always been slowed by the enforced recognition of her own mortality. No matter what the convolutions of one's life, here it would end, quietly, peacefully, eternally, beneath the sod. There seemed little point in either hustling or bustling. She took her time, allowing the sunshine to caress her harassed face.

The inexorable rate at which the wasteland engulfed its silent community was unnerving.

At her mother's funeral her grave had marked the boundary of the tended plots; now the rows of stones extended far beyond. Under a combined headstone, in a double bed of Hertfordshire clay, Rachel and Saul Greenberg lay beside each other in death as they had in life. Closing her eyes for a moment in an effort to call them to mind, Kitty stood before them. Trying to remember them was not easy. She made an effort to bring back the happy times, the joyous moments when they had been in full vigour. All that persisted were their last days, her father emaciated and suffering from the cancer which consumed him, her mother blue-lipped, succumbing to her final cardiac crisis.

There was a prayer for everything. Before and after meals; to consecrate a house; to be said by a sick person; for those recovering from sickness. Prayers when you rose in the morning and prayers before retiring at night. Prayers for a journey, on seeing the New Moon, on partaking of every food and fruit; on hearing thunder, at the sight of the sea, on seeing giants or dwarfs. Kitty opened the prayer she had collected at the cemetery gates to be recited when visiting a grave.

"O Lord and King, who are full of compassion, God of spirits of all flesh, in whose hand are the souls of the living and the dead, remember the souls of Rachel and Saul Greenberg who have been gathered unto their people. Have mercy upon them, pardon all their transgressions, for there is none righteous on earth, who doeth only good and sinneth not. Remember unto them the righteousness which they wrought, and let their reward be with them and their recompense before them. He maketh death to vanish in life eternal . . . the Lord God wipeth away tears from all their faces . . . and the reproach of his people shall he take away from off all the earth; for the Lord hath spoken it. He who maketh peace in his high places, may he make peace for us and for all Israel and say ye, Amen."

She put the prayer to her lips, kissing it as a token of respect. There were no tears; over the years they had been spent. She stared at the tombstone and realized, in the face of the cold marble, that there was nothing more she could do. Powerless to resurrect the crowns of her life, she took a few pebbles from the surrounding ground and laid them on the marble slab, her visiting card, evidence that she had called.

More slowly than she had come, she retraced her steps, her thoughts neither of God nor of immortality. She was composing her shopping list for *Yom Kippur* in her head.

In Edgware, Beatty was already doing her shopping. She had her list in her hand and waited with her basket on wheels in the queue outside Frost's, the greengrocer's. She had advanced, in a slow shuffle—everyone was taking his time—from the window of the hardware shop next door until she was level with the display of picture-book oranges and polished apples and honeydew melons and bunches of muscat grapes in their tissue-paper nests bearing the legend "do not touch."

To pass the time she chatted to Tilly Rosen, who stood behind her and who was her coworker in the local women's Zionist group.

"Any news of Nina?" Beatty said. "She's missed three meetings."

"According to her sister-in-law, I met her when I was getting my *challahs,* it's either shingles or a virus. In any event the doctor goes every day."

"She's a one," Beatty said, moving her basket up a few inches. "It wasn't that long since she had yellow jaundice."

They brooded silently on the ill luck of poor Nina.

"You got many coming?" Beatty said. She meant for before and after the Fast.

"All of them, *um beschrien,*" Tilly said. "What about you?"

"Eight to take and we're going to my sister-in-law to break."

"Kitty?"

"Sydney insists. He's the eldest, so he likes us to go there. I do a marble cake and the *gefülte fish* but it's still a lot of work for Kitty."

"It's a lot of work all right." Tilly helped herself to a grape from the display.

"Sweet as sugar!" She threw the pips into the gutter. "Unfortunately I'm the one always has to do everything in our family."

The queue shuffled forward.

"As long as you've got your health and strength . . ." Beatty said.

In front of her a young matron with false eyelashes, shiny plum lipstick, and trousers that looked as if she had been poured into them, had a list a mile long.

Tilly looked at her watch. "I haven't got my fish."

"I went first thing," Beatty said. "It's like a madhouse in there."

"You'd think they'd got gold scales, the prices."

68

"They make a fortune."

"Even herring. I remember when you couldn't give them away."

"It's the same with everything."

"I'm ashamed when the meat comes," Tilly said. "I take the bill off quick before the daily sees."

She was lucky to be able to afford a daily, Beatty thought. She'd been doing all her own cleaning as well as helping Leon in the shop for years now. She didn't have her meat sent either. You couldn't watch them that way. They always stuck a half pound more in than you'd asked for and charged for it.

These days you saw more and more people sidling out of the *treifa* butchers, as if they'd only been in to get meat for the dog, or buying neat little plastic-wrapped joints from the supermarket. You could hardly blame them, particularly the younger ones, for not keeping kosher.

She was inside the shop now.

She waited while the young matron indulged in a bout of flirtatious verbal fencing with Bert Frost, who was old enough to be her father, and bought potatoes and onions and carrots and leeks and turnips and parsnips and beetroot and cabbage and cauliflower and sprouts. She must be feeding an army, Beatty thought, as the young woman elbowed her out of the way to gaze at the pineapples as if she were at the Royal Academy.

When she was finished, the boy, on holiday from the local comprehensive school, carried the box which was overflowing to her car which was parked on the yellow band outside the shop.

Beatty bought potatoes, and vegetables for her soup.

"What are the tomatoes like?" she said.

Bert Frost opened a brown bag with the dexterity of a magician.

"Guaranteed!"

"Give me half a pound. Pick me out the firm ones."

Beatty watched him like a hawk. She wandered round the shop, going through the meals she had planned in her head.

Bert waited patiently. He hadn't built up his business by hurrying his customers.

"Grapefruit?" he suggested helpfully.

"He won't touch anything acid. What about the tangerines . . . clementines, whatever they are?"

"Sweet as you are, darling!"

"A couple of pounds." Beatty ignored the remark. "But not if they're pippy."

"Over or under?" Bert said, a tangerine in midair.

"Under," Beatty said. "A lettuce . . . are they today's?"

"I've just unpacked them."

"And spring onions. And I'll take some pears, if they're ready; my daughter-in-law's always on a diet. They overdo it if you ask me. A couple of Jaffas. Thin-skinned. Let me see them. And apples. From the front. A box of dates and I think that's the lot. Bananas. For the children." Her basket was full.

Bert played a tune on the cash register.

"A melon, I forgot," Beatty said.

He took one from the display testing it with his thumbs.

"Be careful, the eggs," Beatty said as he tucked it down the side.

". . . Well over the Fast," Bert said. He turned to Tilly. "What can I do for you, dolly face?"

In the Express Dairy, Rachel bought a packet of boil-in-the-bag cod with cheese sauce, a tin of beans and a packet of instant pudding, and thought of the pre-*Yom Kippur* meal they would sit down to without her; Josh and Carol and Alec and the children and Auntie Mirrie and her parents. It was the same every year, not only the meal but the extraordinary ethos of the Day itself and the effect it had on everybody.

She recalled the tension, the apprehension, which began, insidiously, to build up after New Year. Ten days of penitence; of increasing disquietude, resulting in a nervous irritability in all the participants. It was not, could not be, simply the anticipation of twenty-five hours with neither food nor drink. It had more to do with the claustrophobia of the hours in synagogue, the dragging measure of the *Kol Nidre* prayer intoned not once but three times, the coercion of the appeal, the hardness of the seats, the standing up and the sitting down, the eating to capacity of the meal before and the falling upon the food afterwards.

She did not deliberately set out to displease her parents. Neither did she want to disclaim her Jewishness. To do so would be to invalidate an important part of herself. They refused to understand that she felt passionately identified with Zionism and irrevocably with her people. She acknowledged the *Torah*, too, but believed that its message had long ago been absorbed into the mainstream of contemporary thought and had become the common property of Jew and Gentile alike; that its myriad, life-consuming injunctions were no longer relevant and the confusing and arbitrary hedges that had grown up around them, obsolete.

She had not the slightest intention of spending an entire day in synagogue, bobbing up and down like a yo-yo, begging forgiveness for sins she may or may not have committed from a God whose powers she considered were strictly limited.

She put her wire basket on the counter and added a Mars bar from the display. The comfortable, grey-haired cashier in her blue and white overall totted up her Eve of *Yom Kippur* goodies. When she had eaten them, she would go with Patrick to see the Max Ophuls film at the Camden Plaza.

71

She glanced at the total on the till and opened her purse. She was twenty years old. This year she was not going to be browbeaten.

8

On New Year the righteous had been inscribed in the Book of Life, and on the Day of Atonement the Book would be sealed.

The morning service in the synagogue's longest day began at eight o'clock, and by eight-fifteen Sydney was in his seat and would remain there until the final note of the ram's horn died away.

Although it was a day of fasting and repentance, it was also, in a sense, a festive day, bringing glad tidings of God's pardon and forgiveness and the welcome opportunity to start a new chapter without the feeling of misery for what one had done or failed to do in the past. Despite the headache from which for days now he had not been free, Sydney enjoyed every minute of it, perhaps this brief, bright hour, when the Cantor recited the liturgy to an almost empty synagogue, most of all. Only a handful of men were scattered among the pews in their white prayer shawls. Upstairs the Ladies' Gallery was empty. It was not in the spirit of the Day, Sydney considered, to lie late in bed in order to speed the fasting hours intended to be spent in prayer, confession and supplication.

In his row only two of the seats were occupied, his own and Moshe Pearlman's, his longtime synagogue friend and sparring partner. They were both wearing plimsolls, leather shoes on this day being prohibited, and their stubbled chins bore testimony to the fact that since the inauguration of this Sabbath of Sabbaths, they had not used a razor.

On some of the empty seats lay the abandoned cards of the previous night's "Joint Israel Appeal." In response to an impassioned plea by the Rabbi, the predictable proportion of the gathering had laced their cards in the appropriate holes, indicating the amount of their contributions, and handed them to the ushers. Payment would be made in the next few days by those in whom the avowed intentions of *Yom Kippur* were still fresh; a few would need polite letters of reminder; others, carried away momentarily by the oratory, would not honour their pledges at all. Of such normal admixes was Rabbi Magnus's congregation composed.

Moshe Pearlman, holding his book in front of him, was swaying back and forth.

"What did you think of the Appeal?" he said from the side of his mouth without interrupting his prayers.

Sydney cast his mind back to the *Kol Nidre* service of the previous night when the large congregation had been a sitting duck for Rabbi Magnus's eloquence. On the one hand, he considered the whole thing a regrettable and jarring intrusion into the most sacred service of the year; on the other, he appreciated its necessity. The defense burden of Israel was so great that she was unable to cope with the social problems swelling up in her midst without the life-giving support of the Diaspora.

Rabbi Magnus had given it his all—exhorting the congregation for their solidarity; castigating them, with dire references to the Holocaust, for their short-sightedness; shaming them with the vacuous truths about the present disposition of their income. ". . . Wear a little less," he had said. ". . . You can only wear one coat, one suit at a time. Eat a little less; do we not all eat too much anyway?; go less

to the cinema, the theater—you will not even notice it I
assure you, my friends . . . Whatever you intended to give,
and believe me I know you have all considered the matter
on the way here this evening, whatever it was your intention
to give, multiply it by two. It will not be a hardship.
Through your generosity Israel will strengthen her borders
and her future . . . provide homes, hospitals and schools.
The hand in your pocket will pay the price of peace! I know
you will not let Israel down. Amen!"

"It was an appeal," Sydney said, swaying but not in unison with Moshe Pearlman.

At midday the sun, which no matter how inclement the
weather had been always seemed to favour the Day of
Atonement, shone brightly, sending its rays in slanting
girders of tinted light onto the congregation, which was
almost at full strength.

All morning, in dribs and drabs, the men kissing the
fringes of their prayer shawls before putting them on, the
members drifted in. From the corner of his eye the Cantor
watched them as he enumerated the sins for which they had
come to ask forgiveness both privately and collectively.
Josh, standing next to his father, who rarely took his eyes
from the book or his mind from his prayers, thought of
Sarah, while all around him, sotto voce, the older men
beating their breasts, the congregation afflicted their souls.

". . . And for the sin wherein we have sinned before thee
by wronging a neighbour . . . by association with impurity
. . . by despising parents and teachers . . . by violence
. . . by foolish speech . . . by evil inclination . . . by an
arrogant mien . . . a wanton glance, haughty eyes, obdurate
brow . . . by envy . . . by tale-bearing . . . by a vain oath
. . . by causeless hatred. And for all these . . . forgive us,
pardon us, grant us atonement."

He was a happy man. With the advent of Sarah into his

life it was as if a mantle of grace had fallen about his shoulders. When he was with her everything felt right. It had not been like that with Paula.

If he looked up and turned his head, he could see Paula. She sat next to her mother, and it wasn't hard to guess that the passing of the years would accentuate their already remarkable physical resemblance. After the birth of her twins, Paula had acquired her mother's squat figure, her ample bosom, her face, with its perpetual air of slight dissatisfaction, set for all times in its mould. In twenty years, he thought, the metamorphosis would be complete. She would be her mother and most probably she would still be sitting there.

He had spent the whole weekend with Sarah. The fact that she had removed the silver photograph frame from next to the bed had moved him as much as her tenderness and her passion. Last night, the Eve of Atonement, *Kol Nidre* night, had been a punishment without her.

"A black fast?" she had said.

"No, white."

White robes, white reading desk, white-covered Scrolls of the Law. "Though your sins be scarlet they shall be as white as snow."

The havoc in his life, created since her coming into it, was sometimes more than he could bear. She occupied his dreams, his fantasies, his waking moments. He had become forgetful, careless, clumsy, unable to concentrate on his work. He was blissfully happy, yet at the same time fearful lest what he had found be summarily taken away. In front of him were her face, her hair, her body, her smile. Her voice, her touch, the feel of her skin, the scent of her, the sound of her laughter filled his head.

Catching Sydney's sidelong glance of disapproval for his inattention, he found his place in the prayerbook, collected his thoughts and tried to concentrate on the service. Although not religious like his father, he regarded *Yom Kippur* as the single day on which he was at one with his fellow Jews in every corner of the world, all of them with a common purpose, a common aim. He was prepared, through worship, to declare his unity and uplift his inner self.

It was while he was recounting the sins, his mind only partly occupied in their narration, that he realized, surprising himself almost, that he was going to marry Sarah. He glanced at his father, thumping his chest rhythmically beside him. "Blessed art thou O Lord, thou King who pardonest and forgivest our iniquities and the iniquities of thy people the house of Israel and makest our trespasses to pass away year by year . . ." That there would be no forgiveness as far as his father was concerned was something of which he could be absolutely sure.

Carol, sitting next to her mother, had the book open before her but did not see it. She joined automatically in the responses, but her mind was on Alec and the breakdown of communications between them. When he spoke to her now, it was about the practice he had seen advertised, which turned out to be in Godalming, well-placed, he said, for girls' schools. With it went an old house whose garden led down to a copse, backed by farmland. She could think of nothing worse. Miles from her parents, separated from her friends. She regarded the country as a place for picnics, the object of a day's drive. He anticipated many of her objections. They could have the kosher meat sent down on the train; start a small community; hold services in their house. His seriousness about it all made her nervous, unsettled. In the emotional state of her pregnancy even to contemplate such a move made her cry. She was waiting for a suitable moment to talk him out of it, to make him see her point of view, see reason. He was so distant with her, distant and irritable. She knew it stemmed from her increasing lack of enthusiasm in bed. The pregnancy seemed to have made her worse. She was no longer able even to pretend.

Perhaps when she had had the baby everything would be different. She knew that with all the breast-feeding and the getting up in the night, it would not.

". . . And for all these, O God of forgiveness, forgive us, pardon us, grant us atonement."

After the Memorial Prayer she would get the girls from the Children's Service and take them home for lunch. Too young, they were absolved from fasting.

She picked up her book.

She was not going to live in Godalming or any other Ming.

At one o'clock the synagogue was filled to overflowing for the first, last and only moment of the year, a fact that would not go unremarked in the afternoon sermon. For the Memorial Prayer, even the most loosely committed among the community made an effort to attend, some of them to shed tears for relatives who had been dead for forty years.

In the Ladies' Gallery the aisles were filled. The atmosphere was stifling, the air heavy with breath that was not sweet, exhaled through dry mouths from empty stomachs. The windows, except for one, were shut. When the front rows called for them to be opened, those at the back, complaining of drafts down the neck, shut them again. It was an annual battle in which there were no winners.

The congregation stood silently. All books were open at the proper place, all eyes focussed on the pulpit, all conversations stilled.

Savouring the long moment, Rabbi Magnus looked round him then spoke, clearly, softly, into the expectant hush.

"Lord, what is man that thou regardest him? Or the son of man, that thou takest account of him? . . ." He was well-pleased with the turnout but fully aware of its transience. "Man is like unto vanity, his days are as a shadow that passeth away . . ."

Upstairs the handkerchiefs, which had been at the ready, were put to faces, the quiet was punctuated by sniffs.

"In the morning he bloometh and sprouteth afresh; in the evening he is cut down and withereth."

By midafternoon, when the long day's service was at its lowest ebb, the size of the congregation had shrunk considerably. Those who had attended for the Memorial Prayer only had gone, their consciences assuaged for another year. Mothers with young children, of whom Carol was one, had taken them home for lunch. Those with headaches, and many without, had gone home to lie down in the hope of making the hours until nightfall pass more quickly. Some of the men, leaving their prayer shawls in white heaps on the seats, were taking the afternoon sunshine. A hard core, including Kitty in the Ladies' Gallery and Sydney downstairs, would sit it out until the end.

While the tales were told of the High Priest, how he "bathed and put on the golden garments and laved his hands and feet," even Sydney, forsaken by Josh and Alec, allowed himself some moments of relaxation, a few words with Moshe Pearlman. Without turning their heads they discussed the prevailing state of war between the synagogue dignitaries, Sydney on the side of Rabbi Magnus and Moshe upholding the rights of the Cantor; they commented on the pathological laziness and suspected drunkenness of Lucas the caretaker about which they were both agreed; they reminisced about the old synagogue on the corner of Brick Lane, which had now become a mosque.

"It was a world on its own," Moshe Pearlman said nostalgically of the East End of his childhood.

* * *

78

Upstairs Kitty's attention was slipping from the Penitential Prayers. It was hard to keep one's mind on the "burnt offerings" and the "incense" and the "lighted lamps" in the airless torpor of the afternoon. While less devout than Sydney, she enjoyed the day of contemplation, finding the Fast no hardship and welcoming the fact that it helped her to shed a few pounds in weight.

Beside her Carol's seat was empty, but she was thinking about Rachel, particularly when, from time to time, she saw Sydney shift his skullcap to a more comfortable position. It wasn't fair. He had enough problems without Rachel adding to them. She had told her daughter as much when she'd telephoned to say she wasn't coming home. Reluctantly she had passed the message on to Sydney before they sat down to eat the pre-Fast meal. He had not believed her.

Kitty had tried to console him.

"She'll come next year. Next year she'll come."

"I don't want to talk about it," Sydney said.

And he did not.

Despite the Fast that lay ahead, he hardly touched his dinner. She should have come, if only for Sydney's sake. He got so upset about these things and really it wouldn't have hurt Rachel at all. She had done her best. Now, no matter to what extent she interceded, Rachel would have to pay the price. It would be a long while before her relationship with her father would return to normal.

Realizing that she had allowed her mind to stray, she found the place.

"This day wilt thou strengthen us," she remembered saying. "This day wilt thou bless us . . ." Then she must have dozed off. When she opened her eyes, they were removing the scrolls from the Ark for the second time and the service was into its penultimate lap. To her dismay Ruthie Wiseman came from the row behind to sit beside her in the seat temporarily vacated by Carol.

"All right?" Kitty asked politely when she'd settled herself.

"I've got a shocking headache. I always get a shocking headache."

She took a baton of solid cologne from her handbag and rubbed it round the periphery of her face. She held it out to Kitty.

"No thanks."

"It's very refreshing."

"I'm fine," Kitty said. "I used to fast badly when I was a youngster but not anymore. Carol looks rotten. I told her there's no need to fast when you're pregnant but she won't even have a cup of tea. They're so obstinate."

"Paula's the same. Stuart looks after her like she was china."

Kitty wondered if this was a dig at Josh.

"Everyone coming to you tonight?" Ruthie said chattily.

Kitty nodded. She had no desire to gossip. If she was not actually praying, she preferred to contemplate in silence. Silence was not a condition that Ruthie recognized.

"You do it all yourself?"

"Beatty makes a marble cake and Freda brings the trifle," Kitty whispered, reprovingly. She did not inquire about Ruthie's arrangements for breaking the Fast.

"We always start with a big tray of hors d'oeuvres," Ruthie said, looking at her watch. "I'm going home to get it ready soon. My sister helps me, my two sisters-in-law wouldn't lift a finger, all they know is how to eat. We have chopped and fried with coleslaw, and all the salads, then a hot pudding. I'm going to make an Eve's pudding with the apple underneath . . ."

Kitty turned the page of her book and wished Ruthie would go away. It was not in accordance with the Day either to spend the afternoon making hors d'oeuvres or to cook hot puddings when all manner of work was forbidden.

"It's the portion about Jonah," she said pointedly, leaning over the gallery to see what was going on. "Mr. Gottlieb is going to read it. Every year I think it's going to be his last."

"I don't know where he gets the strength," Ruthie said. "He looks like a puff of wind would blow him away. Last year I did it with pineapple underneath for a change but they all complained so this year I'm going back to the apple."

While old Mr. Gottlieb, supporting himself with gnarled hands against the reading desk, began to recite, in a quavering and barely audible voice, the story of Jonah with its reminder of God's infinite compassion, Rachel sat in the library trying to write an essay on Nietzsche and watching the slow advance of the hands round the Roman face of the clock.

She had written two lines lifted directly from the book in front of her: "Nietzsche antedated American pragmatism. Brought up in traditional Lutheran circles he condemned old values and the entire trend of modern civilization."

In other years, straitjacketed into the constraining and meaningless rites of a day spent in prayer and fasting, she had sat sullenly next to her mother in synagogue, her mind on all the things she would rather be doing. Today, having broken loose from the tentacles of her religious and family obligations, she was not only with them in spirit, hearing in her head the old tunes, the familiar chants, but watching the minutes tick by with infinite slowness towards the end of the Fast. Not, of course, that she was fasting.

Last night, after the film, she had had barbecued spareribs and Peking duck in Gerrard Street. Back at Max Rayne, she had gone to Solly's room and sat on the bed in the emptiness he had left behind.

For a year Solly had been her alter ego. She had used him

as her sounding board as, bit by bit, she'd tried to disentangle herself from the stranglehold of her Orthodox upbringing; as a shoulder to cry on when she'd fallen out with Patrick.

They had sat up late discussing the dietary laws and the Festivals, and Solly had told her what Judaism had to say about Hinduism and alcoholism and racial discrimination, substantiating his views with quotations from the *Torah*, the *Talmud* and the *Shulchan Aruch*. Sometimes she grew angry with him both for his tolerance—nothing that she said could make him angry—and for his deep religious convictions, which she was unable to shake.

On *Kol Nidre* night she had experienced his empty room as a silent but implicit reproach. This morning, in the communal kitchen, with her mind on the sinking sensation evoked by the memory of the walk to synagogue on an empty stomach, she had defiantly prepared a large breakfast most of which had gone into the bin. Her lunch hour had been permeated by thoughts of the Memorial Prayer.

Looking at the clock, whose hands seemed to move with unusual slowness, Rachel guessed that the moment had come for the afternoon Portion, the story of Jonah and the drawing of the lots in order to see who should be cast overboard, and that old Mr. Gottlieb would be reading it. Rabbi Magnus's sermon requesting contributions of cakes and wine for the *succah* would precede the slow run up to the Concluding Service, the final lap in the awesome marathon of the long day.

She wondered whether it was within the bounds of possibility for her to turn up at the flat in time to break the Fast she had not observed. She knew that it was not. She would line up for curried eggs and tinned fruit salad in the canteen, and think of the feeling of relief brought about by the bright lights and the table laden with delicious food. At the end of the meal, when they were all replete, her mother

82

would make her annual pronouncement: "Another year over!"

From five o'clock onwards, as the autumn sun paled, the stragglers returned to fill in the gaps along the pews. Sydney looked at his watch ostentatiously as Josh and Alec, after their yearly walk, resumed their seats beside him.

In the gallery the ladies reassembled, wearing their fur coats against the anticipated chill of the evening. They had prepared their tables for the moment for which they were all waiting, the end of the Fast. Carol, looking pale, was in her place beside her mother.

Through the stained-glass windows the darkening sky heralded the last of the twenty-five long hours. The synagogue was not overflowing as it had been for the Memorial Prayer of the morning, but every seat was taken, every extra chair occupied. There was a mood of expectancy, a regeneration of the fervour that had petered out during the afternoon lull.

The chandeliers, the candelabra bathed the weary congregation in their amber light.

For the whole of the Concluding Service, those who were able and so inclined stood up; those who were neither, sat. In these final decorous moments all whispered confidences were repressed. Everyone followed the prayers.

For the last time the congregation confessed unanimously to having trespassed, dealt treacherously, robbed, slandered and acted perversely; to having been wicked, corrupted, gone astray and led others with them. In unison they repeated the verses of "Our Father Our King"; proclaimed aloud "Hear O Israel, the Lord our God the Lord is One"; declared seven times, with fervour, "The Lord is God," then waited, expectantly, silently, for the sound that would mark the end of the day of peace, of harmony and reconciliation.

83

The ram's horn was taken from its white cloth and all ears were alert for the final, wordless prayer, the haunting strain of the lover, Israel, serenading his beloved.

When it came, filling the synagogue with its heart-rending wail, it was the call to man to hear the sound of weeping humanity, to feel the unspeakable pain of the world, to resolve to do battle against oppression and subjugation. As it reached its zenith, then slowly, poignantly, died away, there was, for one brief moment, hope that the day might come when the tears would be wiped from every cheek and the sigh from every lip.

In that moment the nine hundred souls of Rabbi Magnus's congregation experienced a lifting of the heart, a sensation of peace and unity, such as they would not enjoy for another year. It was a spiritual and physical harmony which lasted until the final echoes foundered and the synagogue was still.

Into the silence erupted a full-throated cry of *"Shekoach!"* "May you have strength!" It was a vote of thanks to the Cantor, who had stood before them all day. With it the congregation was galvanized into action. There was a juggling of arms into coats, a relieved exchange of greetings, a light-hearted release of tension, a collection of books, a banging of box lids; a stampede towards the doors.

9

"WHERE'S RACHEL?" BEATTY SAID, holding her cup of tea in both hands and looking round the table as if Rachel might suddenly appear out of the marble cake.

Kitty caught her eye, glanced at Sydney to see if he had heard and shook her head in warning.

"Took the words out of my mouth," Dolly said. "I . . ."

"Another cup of tea, Dolly," Kitty said firmly, holding her hand out for the empty cup.

"I had one at home," Dolly said. "Norman made me one about four, didn't you, Norman? He insisted. My back was killing me and I didn't want to take my pills on an empty stomach."

"I don't suppose for a moment it was empty," Beatty said. "When have you fasted?"

"I can't help it if I get faint," Dolly said. "All I had was a couple of cream crackers lunchtime. You're not supposed to kill yourself."

"What did I tell you!" Beatty said. "You give in to yourself too much . . ."

"Leave her alone, Beatty," Harry said, holding out a dish. "Have another fish ball and shut up."

"I don't need your permission to speak," Beatty said. "Dolly's quite capable of standing up for herself. I'd sooner have a bit of the egg and lemon."

"Where is Rachel?" Vanessa said. Immaculate in a black

85

velvet suit and a silk shirt with a pussycat bow, she did not look as if she had been fasting all day.

"What was it like in Marble Arch?" Sydney looked at Juda.

"Not so many as usual. A lot of people go away these days."

"Bournemouth," Leon said.

"Israel more likely," Freda said. "Half the golf club's in Herzlia. What's the matter, Mirrie?"

"I'll be all right," Mirrie said, mopping her forehead with a pink tissue.

"You'd no business to fast with your migraines," Beatty said. "Drink a cup of tea with three sugars."

Kitty, standing at the sideboard, was already pouring it out.

"Go and lie down for a minute." She put the cup in front of Mirrie.

"No dear. It'll pass off."

"Norman wouldn't let me fast," Dolly said.

Beatty opened her mouth but Sydney said, "And what was it like in Edgware?"

Leon leaned forward to answer but Beatty, changing tack, said, "In and out, in and out all day, like Victoria Station. A number of people passed out. I'm not surprised the atmosphere in there. Barney Finkelstein had a heart attack . . ."

"How do you know it was a heart attack?" Leon said.

"They had to carry him out."

"Doesn't mean to say it was a heart attack."

"He was like a rag doll," Beatty said. "Anyway his lips were blue. That's a heart attack, isn't it?"

"Could be," Alec began, "on the other hand . . ."

"That's what I said." Beatty glared at her husband. "Everything he's got to argue with."

"I feel better now," Mirrie said. "Everything went black

for a minute." She looked round the table. "Where's Rachel?"

"She's not here," Kitty said.

"Where's she breaking her fast?"

"Somewhere else. More tea, Mirrie?"

Mirrie shook her head. "I thought there was someone missing."

They had eaten their way through the marble cake and the honey cake and the *gefilte fish* and the sweet-and-sour halibut, and were onto the desserts when Rachel phoned. Kitty answered it in the hall.

"She wants to speak to you," she said to Sydney, coming in.

"Who?"

"Rachel."

"I wondered where she was," Dolly said.

"I'm busy." Sydney did not look up.

"Just have a word with her," Kitty pleaded. "She rang to know how you fasted."

"I'm having my dinner."

"She particularly wants to speak to you."

"I'll have a little more of that trifle if there is any," Sydney said. "It was very nice."

"She's hanging on."

Sydney held out his plate. "Give me a bit more trifle, Beatty. Did you make it?"

Beatty took the plate. "Freda."

Sydney looked at his sister. *"Mazel tov."*

"What shall I tell her?"

"You've put sherry in it," Sydney said.

"Carmel brandy," Freda said. "From *Pesach.*"

In the hall Kitty picked up the receiver, which lay next to the pile of abandoned Day of Atonement books on the hall table. They would be put away now, until next year, in the glass-fronted bookcase.

"He's having dinner," Kitty said. "He says thank you for phoning."

"I get the message."

"Look, Rachel, I told him you were on the phone. What more can I do . . . ?"

"It's all right, Mum."

"Are you coming over this week?"

"I'll see," Rachel said. "I've got to go now."

Rachel put down the receiver of the pay phone and turned away slowly.

"Christ," she said aloud. "Bloody Christ."

She had done it to herself. It was unfair, but she had done it to herself. She was not going to be forced to do things she did not want to do. She was not a child, to be dictated to by her father, bullied. What was her misdeed after all? She had simply not observed a Festival in which she did not believe. She could chastise herself at any time, ask forgiveness for any wrongdoing; she didn't have to sit in a stuffy synagogue on any particular day preoccupied with her stomach. She didn't believe in God anyway, any observance she made was only to please her parents. She was a humanist and felt that religion was a hindrance to man's fulfilment, that the do's and don'ts of Judaism frustrated the desire for individual self-expression. She had discussed the matter many times with Solly, who argued that there was no reason why one could not be a religious humanist. "God is interested," Solly said, "in many things besides religion." Besides *Yom Kippur*, Rachel thought, going back to her room. He would not talk to her. Her father. Not for weeks. Months. It was his funeral. She didn't care. She did care. It was like a sore in her belly. A cancer in her entrails. She had done it of her own free will.

88

"I will not feel guilty," she said to her reflection in the mirror above the wash basin. "I will not!"

She splashed cold water on her face and went out of her room, locking the door. She would go over to the Union for a drink. Tomorrow Solly would be back.

They avoided the subject of Rachel, not wanting to upset Sydney. He was the head of the family, the oldest, elder brother to Juda and Freda and Dolly and Beatty and Mirrie.

"Are you having a *succah?*" Mirrie said to Leon when Kitty had sat down again.

Tabernacles. Festival of Booths. Next in the close season of Festivals. It commemorated the wanderings of the Children of Israel in the wilderness after their deliverance from Egyptian bondage, when they were compelled to dwell in huts or booths. Leon built a booth in his garden, driving in the first nail immediately after the Day of Atonement in accordance with the commandment.

"I'll start it tonight," Leon said.

It would be a temporary structure, covered with detached branches to symbolize its insubstantial nature and to emphasize the dependence of man on God's protection. Beatty would hang apples and pears and oranges and bananas from the branches of the roof, and for a week, at a picnic table and chairs, they would take their meals in it. In the Hendon garden Sydney had built his own booth. Now that they lived in a flat, he had to make do with visits to the communal one in the synagogue. In the week to come he would buy his *lulav,* the long, swordlike green bouquet made up of palm branch, myrtle twigs and willow, and the delicate *esrog,* like an outsize lemon, which he would point east, south, west and north, upwards and downwards, as an acknowledgment of God's sovereignty over the entire universe.

Appetites were becoming satiated after the hours of self-denial. The table had the air of the feasting that had gone before, half-eaten dishes of trifle and of fruit compote and the remains of the chocolate mousse to which Beatty helped herself when she thought no one was looking.

I have done it again, Kitty thought from her seat opposite Sydney, who was at the end of the table. Fed my family, his family, our family. Her efforts, in which she did not spare herself, were rewarded as usual by the shining, satisfied faces. It had all been worth it, the planning and the shopping and the hours on her feet in the kitchen. Next year there would be another baby, and perhaps Josh would have found a nice girl, just get the Festivals over and she'd start on him about the Dinner and Ball, and Rachel . . . Rachel. Kitty sighed and glanced at Sydney. She was in, she knew, for weeks as a go-between until the wrong that Rachel had done him by going out of her way to avoid *Yom Kippur* with the family, with her father, would become tempered though not forgiven, never that, for letting him down. In such matters he was intransigent. Doing right by his family, he expected his high standards to be reciprocated. It would take time for him to hold out his hand to Rachel; meanwhile Kitty would bear the brunt of his hurt, his disappointment. It would not be the first time.

Next to her Dolly put a hand to her back and wondered if it was too soon to take more tablets. When she got home Norman would make her some cocoa, she'd have it in bed with a drop of brandy after the rigours of the day. She'd get Norman to light the gas fire for half an hour, it was almost October, and, please God, she'd have a good night.

Norman wondered about the new girl in his office. Girl, well, he supposed she was about thirty. She wore a Star of David round her neck and had a big comfortable bust which he could not get out of his mind. He glanced at Dolly. If he said anything, her back would be bound to take a turn for the worse. He would tell his mother he had a business meeting next week and take Della to the cinema.

Freda, as she always did on these occasions, felt a deep sense of resentment that she and Harry had not been blessed with a family of their own. At the same time, she was grateful to Kitty and Sydney, without whom there would be just the two of them, alone in the big house, to break the Fast.

Harry speculated about his putting, which had suddenly taken a turn for the terrible. Next Sunday was Tabernacles and no golf and none the week after, Rejoicing of the Law; then, thank goodness, the Festivals would all be over and he could get into his swing again.

Vanessa had eaten too much, she always did when she came to Auntie Kitty's. At home they had a cook who produced elegant little meals which were rather dull. She hadn't taken her pill last night because of the Day of Atonement and wondered whether it mattered.

Josh speculated on how soon he could get away. He had told Sarah ten, and already it was quarter to. He wondered absurdly whether Sarah would ever be able to make halibut with egg and lemon sauce.

Sydney felt at peace, as he always did after *Yom Kippur*, with himself and his God. There were only two ripples in the lake of his content: his headache, which had not gone away even now that he had eaten, and Rachel. He looked round the table to where she should have been, in her place next to her mother, and wondered why she should do this to him.

*　*　*

Alec thought about the practice in Godalming which he was going to see on Thursday and where there would be an opportunity, he hoped, to practice proper primary-care medicine. Carol was going to be difficult, but he had made up his mind.

Carol felt the kick, kick of the baby pushing out misshapen pockets of flesh in her belly and wondered whether tonight, after *Yom Kippur,* she would put out her hand, when they were in bed, to Alec, who was angry with her, and whether she could go through with it, managing to keep awake and simulate enthusiasm for long enough to satisfy him.

Juda, Jules, drew at his cigar and wondered whether anyone would pick up an extension if he went into the bedroom to phone his mistress, whom he had neglected for the twenty-five hours of the Fast. He decided it was too risky. When he got home, he would take the dog for a walk to the call box.

Leonora wondered how Freda, opposite, could wear those dreadful clothes, always striped and clingy in some sort of knit, and was pleased at how elegant her Vanessa was looking. When she became engaged, Vanessa would have her picture in *The Tatler.*

Leon thought if he put the Russian broadtail in the window next to the jasmine mink blouson someone might be tempted to buy it for a *Chanukkah* present. He prayed for a cold snap, without which it would be another disastrous year.

Beatty, a hand to her mouth, said "pardon me" as the chocolate mousse repeated on her, and decided that she felt distinctly uncomfortable. She must go home soon to take off her corset.

Mirrie wondered if Kitty was going to say, "Take home some of the fried fish, Mirrie." She really enjoyed it, it wasn't worth frying for one; and what had happened to Rachel, fancy upsetting her father like that.

"What about some fruit?" Kitty said, looking round the table at the slumped family, the empty plates pushed away. "A nice plum, Harry? Freda, give Harry a plum."

There were gestures of protest.

"No more for me," Harry said.

"I couldn't eat another thing." Beatty clutched her stomach.

Josh looked at his watch.

Kitty sat back in the walnut chair with ball-and-claw feet and surveyed the scene, the well-fed, well-satisfied family. "Well," she said, as she always did at this point, "another year over!"

She looked at Sydney for confirmation. His face was contorted. He uttered a cry that they would all remember, and his limbs began to jerk uncontrollably.

10

For some *Yom Kippur* meant a Fast, for others a war, but for Kitty Shelton it would stick in her mind as the day that her nice, tidy little world began slowly, like a house of cards, to collapse around her.

At Sydney's cry eleven pairs of eyes spun towards the top of the table. The inch-long ash from Juda's cigar dropped onto the tablecloth. Sydney, the *baal ha-bayis*, master of the house, became the focal point for the riveted audience. His head and eyes rotated and his mouth, which moments earlier had been requesting a second helping of trifle, was twisted grotesquely. His arms were drawn disjointedly towards his shoulders, his elbows and wrists splayed out. To Kitty he no longer seemed to be breathing.

Alec, who had been poking a fork idly into the lace-edged holes of the tablecloth, was the first one on his feet. As he pushed back his chair and stood up, Sydney's body became convulsed in a series of short, sharp jerks. Recognizing an epileptic fit, Alec motioned the ashen-faced Josh to help him lift the convulsing body onto the floor. With unseeing, dilated pupils, Sydney stared at them, a meringue of white froth forming at the corner of his twisted mouth. By the time the others had recovered sufficiently to get up from the table and crowd round him, it was over. Sydney lay still, unconscious, on the washed Chinese carpet, a bronze chrysanthemum framing his head.

Kitty kneeled beside her husband.

Beatty thrust the smelling salts, which had been so useful throughout the day of fasting, under her brother's nose.

"Daddy!" Carol screamed, for the first time that evening forgetting the child she was carrying.

"Get everybody out of here," Alec said, taking his father-in-law's limp wrist with its inch of white *Yom Tov* cuff and gold cuff links between his fingers and raising his eyelids with the other hand.

"He's gone!" Beatty shrieked.

"Shut up, Beatty," Juda said firmly. "Come inside and give Alec some room."

"Yom Kippur!" Beatty said. "What a way to go . . ."

Juda propelled all 196 pounds of her out of the door. The others followed in shocked silence.

Kitty looked at Alec, afraid to voice the question which was on her lips.

"Is he . . . ?"

Alec shook his head. "He's unconscious. Get Norman and Uncle Juda and we'll take him into the bedroom."

He was a dead weight and the corridor was narrow.

Kitty said nothing as they laid him with his shoes on the pink satin bedspread.

"Will you open your eyes for me?" Alec said clearly, his face near to Sydney's.

"Sydney," Kitty said, "Sydney darling, it's me!"

"His pulse is good," Alec said. "He'll probably be unconscious for a short while."

"Shall I phone Lennie?" She didn't want to upset Alec.

"Good idea." He was not upset.

"He's a shocking colour," Beatty said from the doorway. "He ought to be in hospital!"

"Alec says . . ."

"Alec!" Beatty said.

"Go inside," Juda said, giving her a push.

"It's my brother!"

"Please, Beatty," Kitty said. "I'm trying to phone Lennie." She dialled the number and held the receiver to her ear. There was no reply.

"They go to her mother's," Beatty said.

"Why didn't you say so?" Kitty didn't take her eyes from Sydney's face.

"A person's not allowed to speak."

"I'll try the answering service," Kitty said. "They'll pass on the message."

* * *

In the living room Sydney's relatives sat with their thoughts, sporadically airing them in subdued voices.

"He was like possessed," Dolly said. "Poor Sydney, wouldn't hurt a fly."

"My morning woman used to suffer with them," Freda said. "Fits. Fortunately she only had them in the afternoons."

"Good job Alec was here," Mirrie said.

"He didn't have his case." Beatty came into the room. "Kitty's phoning Lennie."

"How should he have his case *Yom Kippur?*" Dolly said.

"Lennie will have his case," Beatty said, as if inside it there would be bottles of life and death, kill or cure. "I don't like the look of Sydney."

"You don't know from one minute to the next," Freda said. "Sitting there like a lamb minding his own business . . ."

"Eating your trifle," Beatty said. "Perhaps it was the Carmel brandy."

"How can you say such a thing!"

"Be better off calling the ambulance," Dolly said. "I've got no faith in doctors. I remember after the accident when poor Bertie . . ."

"They can control them these days . . ." Freda said. They didn't want to hear about poor Bertie. ". . . it's marvellous what they can do."

Kitty sat beside Sydney, watching his face, holding onto his hand. If anything happened to him she would be finished; he was her life.

They had been childhood sweethearts. It was a story her children had never tired of hearing, amazed at the romantic naïveté of their parents, which belonged to another age. Sydney and Kitty were unable to see anything bizarre in their single-minded devotion. To each the other's word was law. "Your father wants . . ." "Your mother says . . ."

There had been times when Kitty was accused by Rachel of not having a mind of her own. It was true to the extent that her existence was inextricably bound up with Sydney's and that each was prepared to spend his or her days in service of the other. In the early years Kitty had helped Sydney in the business. Later she had stayed uncomplainingly at home to raise her family and run the house, with unswerving adherence to his wishes. Each evening, and twice a day on weekends, she prepared a meal composed of his favourite dishes, which she cooked with love. On every Festival a feast was prepared in which the family was invited to share.

Their roles were clearly defined. She was not required to worry about the order books of S. Shelton (Fancy Goods) Ltd., and she did not expect Sydney to concern himself with the minutiae of her kitchen. His concession to the changing times was that he had now learned to make the cup of tea he brought to Kitty in illness or adversity, but apart from this the boundaries remained clearly defined. In her own domain Kitty was queen, and outside it she was prepared to accept her husband as undisputed king. He was a good man. Each week, with the regularity of the manna which God had sent to the Children of Israel in the wilderness, the check for her housekeeping money appeared on the glass-topped dressing table, the amount carefully adjusted in accordance with the prevailing cost of living. Before a holiday, when she had the family to feed, his family, there would be an appropriate increase. He was as kind as he was careful, and she never had to ask for more. Each birthday there was a piece of jewellery for her, small or large according to the vicissitudes of the Fancy Goods trade. Each Friday and every holiday he would bring a gift of chocolates or of flowers. His solicitude did not end with her. In addition to caring and providing for Josh and Carol and Rachel and herself, Sydney, as the eldest brother, took full responsibility, both financial and moral, for Mirrie and Beatty and Freda and their respective families. None of them made a major decision, and for that matter not many minor ones, without consulting Sydney, who gave every problem his full consideration. To the children he was rigid and domineering rather than kind and fair; he did not expect in others anything that he was not prepared to do himself. Duty was his watchword and he applied it to every sphere of his life. The collectors for charity knew that they would not call upon Sydney Shelton in vain. Not that he was an indiscriminate giver, which would not have been in accordance with his law; he assessed the merits of each appeal, often to the extent of examining the balance sheets, and contributed accordingly. Apart from the formal appeals he had his own personal charities. When *"nebbech"* Pinkus, as he was known, the beadle of the synagogue, went to Blackpool to convalesce following his hernia operation, it was Sydney Shelton who sent him; he provided doughnuts at break time for the Hebrew classes in an attempt to encourage more regular attendance and "Orders of Service" at Passover for the local old people's home. When the Salvation Army or the Lifeboat Fund called at the door, he did not turn them away; he gave them a token donation, but he was not interested. He acted on the principle that it was incumbent upon the Jew to look after his own, and he was horrified when Rachel confessed to having given her cast-off clothes to Oxfam.

He was Kitty's idol, and in her eyes he could do no wrong. If he had faults she was unaware of them. His word was law and every action correct. She was genuinely amazed when the children thought otherwise. Children! She still regarded them, talked about them, as children, they both did, even though Josh was nearing thirty and Carol now had a family of her own. As far as Josh and Carol and Rachel were concerned, Sydney had brought them up strictly and with two criteria. They were to observe the laws and customs of Judaism and to marry only within the faith. The single concession he made to the changing ethos was that as far as the observances were concerned, he shut his eyes to any aberrations he did not actually see. If they reached his ears, and they were careful not to let them, he did not hear. He could be both deaf and blind when the occasion demanded. Kitty herself, while agreeing with Sydney on most occasions, was prone to take a more liberal view of their transgressions. Sometimes she was torn between loyalty to her husband and the need to protect her children. If it ever came to a showdown, her allegiances would not be in doubt. She loved her children and adored her grandchildren, but Sydney Shelton was her world.

Alone in the quiet room with him, she stroked his hand, called his name, willed him to open his sleeping eyes, to come back to her from whatever strange place he was inhabiting.

Lennie came before breaking his fast. He had already visited two patients who had been taken ill in synagogue.

He put an arm round Kitty, who got up when he came into the bedroom, although her eyes did not leave Sydney's face.

"He's been complaining of headaches . . ." Kitty said. "I was going to tell you about it after the Fast. He said they were nothing . . . He's been looking rotten lately . . . He looked rotten tonight but I thought it was the fasting, he doesn't leave his seat for a moment. One minute he was all right, he asked for a second helping of Freda's trifle and the next . . ."

Going over Sydney's vital signs, Lennie let her talk, aware that she was shocked by the evening's events; that the retelling of them represented a catharsis, useful therapy for the maintenance of her equilibrium.

He fastened his case, mentally selecting his words as he felt Kitty's eyes upon him.

"Everything seems fine," he said. "He's sleeping now and will probably wake up quite shortly. Don't be surprised if he doesn't remember a thing about this evening."

"It looked like an epileptic fit," Kitty said.

"That's exactly what it was. Stay with him while I have a word with Alec."

Lennie helped himself to a banana from the fruit bowl on the dining room table and ate it while Alec described what had happened to Sydney.

"It certainly sounds like focal epilepsy," he said. "The question is, why?"

"I don't know," Alec said. "I examined him thoroughly and there are no real localizing signs. I suppose it couldn't be anything to do with Rachel?"

"Rachel?"

"She didn't come home. He was very upset. She rang up a little while before the attack and he refused to talk to her."

"Highly unlikely. Apparently he's been complaining of headaches. It's almost certain to be organic. In any case we'll have to have him fully examined. Who do you think, Francis Ballantyne, Pitman . . . ?"

"You can never get hold of Pitman. He's always in the Gulf or somewhere . . ."

"Ballantyne then. I'll fix it up," Lennie said, wondering what to do with the banana skin.

In the bedroom Mirrie, who had made tea, gave a cup to Kitty. Josh and Beatty sat on Kitty's bed, watching. Juda stood by the door.

Sydney opened his eyes.

"He's waking up!" Beatty said.

100

The eyes closed again.

"I think we should go into the other room," Juda said, meaning Beatty. "He'll wonder what's going on if he wakes up and sees everyone here."

He was too late.

Flinging aside the blanket with which Kitty had covered him, Sydney sat up in bed, looking not at his family but through them. Beatty, about to comment, was silenced by the blank expression on his face.

They watched as Sydney swung his legs off the bed and crossed the room.

"Sydney!" There was anguish in Kitty's voice. "Get Lennie and Alec," she said to Juda.

Sydney picked up the telephone and dialled.

"Sydney, what are you doing?" Kitty went to his side.

Her husband looked at her. "Ringing Maples," he said.

"But it's eleven o'clock at night!"

"I want to get Dolly an orthopedic bed."

11

"THEY BLAME ME," Rachel said. She was lying on the bed in Solly's room while he tried to read Megarry and Wade on Land Law.

He lifted his head from the book. "Rubbish."

"Not in so many words."

She had rung her mother on the day after *Yom Kippur* to discover if she was still persona non grata. Her mother had answered in the doom voice she kept for illness and for death.

"What's the matter?" Rachel asked.

"If you'd come home for *Yom Kippur* you'd know."

"Know what?"

"It's your father."

Her heart sank to her boots. She pictured him dead, mortally ill.

"What's wrong with him?"

"It was just after you phoned . . ."

"What was?"

"He was fine until then. A bit of a headache but we all had one from fasting . . ."

Rachel held the receiver and waited. She knew that she could not hurry her mother when she was composing one of her dramas.

". . . he had a good supper, two helpings of Freda's trifle . . ."

Rachel closed her eyes.

". . . she put Carmel brandy in it, from *Pesach.* Anyway I told him you phoned and he didn't say a word, but I could see he was upset and I'd just sat down again and nobody wanted any more to eat, although Auntie Beatty was polishing off the chocolate mousse when she thought no one was watching, and I said, 'Thank God another year over,' then it happened. I hope if I'm spared I'll never see anything like it again."

"Mother, what happened?"

"He had a fit."

"A fit?"

"Just after you phoned. His eyes were rolling, he was jerking about . . ."

"Is he all right now?"

"He was unconscious. Josh and Juda had to carry him

102

into the bedroom; he's no lightweight. It was fortunate Alec was here . . ."

"He's all right now though?"

"Almost an hour he was unconscious. Looked like he was asleep but Alec said unconscious . . ."

Rachel resigned herself. Her mother was not going to be rushed.

". . . I rang Lennie, I should have rung him before but because of the *Yom Tovim* . . . he hasn't been looking well . . . and there was no reply. Fortunately Beatty remembered they go to her mother's to break the Fast, but by the time Lennie came, thank God, he was coming round then, and this is the funny part, but both Alec and Lennie say it's quite common after a fit, he sat bolt upright as if no one was in the room, got off the bed and straight to the telephone. I said, 'Sydney, what on earth are you doing?' You know what he said? 'I'm phoning Maples to buy Dolly an orthopedic bed!' At half past eleven at night! Afterwards he didn't remember a thing about it."

"How is he today?" Rachel said.

"Lennie wants him to see a specialist. He's fixing it up."

"Has he gone to business?"

"I wouldn't let him go out!"

It was as if Rachel had made some outrageous suggestion.

"Is Lennie worried?"

"He was talking a long time in the dining room with Alec."

"Let me know what happens," Rachel said. "And give him my love."

"I'm not going to start upsetting him again," her mother said.

"Of course they're not blaming you," Solly said. "You're blaming yourself."

"I wish I'd gone home. It would have been easier in the long run. I didn't do any work. Just sat in the library watching the clock go round. How was your *Yom Kippur?*"

Solly put down his book and leaned back in his chair. "Good."

"It really does something for you, doesn't it? I've tried often enough. Three pages of sins, three times. . . . It's hypocritical anyway, just to go one day in the year."

"There's just a chance you might get inspiration for the rest of it."

"I went to Hebrew classes every Sunday until I was twelve. For all I learned I might just as well not have bothered. Not that I was given any choice."

"You could always blow your whistle."

"My whistle?"

"Have you never heard the story of the shepherd boy who, on *Yom Kippur,* brought to synagogue with him the whistle he used while watching his father's sheep. He couldn't follow any of the prayers, so he played his whistle. It was his way of communicating with God. The Rabbis who were present said that where their prayers had failed, the simple, heartfelt tune of the shepherd boy had succeeded in opening the gates of heaven."

"I feel hemmed in by all the restrictions," Rachel said. "What difference does it make if you turn on the light or write your name or pick a blade of grass?"

"None," Solly said cheerfully, "if you look at it like that."

"How do you look at it?"

"The restrictions belong to the Sabbath," Solly said, "which is one of the greatest things we've given to the world, to Islam, to Christianity. They apply on *Yom Kippur* because it is the Sabbath of Sabbaths."

"You don't need religion to tell you to have a rest at the end of the week," Rachel said. "I'm so pooped out by Friday evening I could hardly do anything else."

104

"It depends on your definition of rest."

"Not having to get up in the morning. What's yours?"

"A state of peace between man and nature; work then becomes any interference by man, be it constructive or destructive, with the physical world—hence your blade of grass! It's a day of leisure . . ."

"Come off it," Rachel said. "There was blue murder when Josh wanted to go to football on Saturday. That's leisure . . ."

"Of a different kind. I don't mean football or watching television, activities which take you away, as it were, from yourself. I mean reading certain books, which bring you closer to yourself. A characteristic of *Shabbat* leisure is that it should make man as human as possible."

"When I talk to you," Rachel said, "everything makes some sort of sense. All I seemed to hear at home was don't do this and don't do that. Why? Because it's *Shabbat, Yom Kippur, Purim* . . ."

Solly laughed. *"Purim?"* he said. "There are no restrictions concerning *Purim*. You've got your wires crossed."

"I'm just a nice mixed-up Jewish girl."

"Who said you were nice?" Solly said.

"You're right. If I were nice I would have gone home for *Yom Kippur*. It wouldn't have been that much of an effort."

"You're O.K.," Solly said. "I love you."

And he did, although he was engaged to a girl in Manchester who would light candles every Friday night of their marriage and go gladly to synagogue and bring up their children in the way that they should go.

"You're so lucky having all those uncles and aunts," Sarah said. "I've only got my uncle Arthur and he lives in Nairobi."

Josh thought of Auntie Beatty, Auntie Dolly, Auntie Freda, Auntie Mirrie, Uncle Juda. They had always been there. He had never looked upon their presence as being enviable before.

He was recounting to Sarah the events that followed the Fast.

"I thought you'd died of starvation," Sarah said, "when you didn't turn up."

Josh thought of his mother's laden table and smiled.

"What did you do?"

"Watched *Casablanca* for the hundredth time; washed my hair . . ."

He touched the hair.

"It's pretty."

They were in Josh's flat. All day his thoughts of Sarah had been interspersed with those of concern for his father. He had found it hard to concentrate on his work.

She sat with her legs curled beneath her on his sofa, which was covered with white, knobby tweed. She had placed her arm along the back of it and was facing him. Her soft wool print skirt, in autumn colours, the topaz shirt and long topaz earrings blended with the warm tones of her skin. He would never tire of looking at her.

She stretched out her fingertips to touch his shoulder. "You must be worried," she said, "about your father."

Anyone but Sarah would have offered false reassurances. He had the impression the sapphire eyes could see into his soul.

"I'm going to get you a drink," she said.

Josh went into the kitchen for ice. In his fridge was the bowl of jellied soup, the roast chicken, the Nescafé jar of cooked prunes Kitty had given him to take home; Sarah's was usually empty except for a bottle of skimmed milk.

She put the heavy crystal tumbler on the rosewood table between the *Journal of Dentistry* and the *Paintings of the Uffizi*, and sat close to him again.

"Tell me what to do to make you happy."

106

It was not a thing Paula would have said.

"Marry me."

"You can't marry me!"

"Why not?"

"I'm a *shiksa.*"

Josh said nothing.

"It matters, doesn't it?"

"Yes. It matters." Josh picked up his glass. It meant cutting himself off from his family. His father certainly would not speak to him again.

"I want to marry you," he said. "I've never wanted anything so much in my life. What about you?"

"I love you, Josh."

The words rang like bells in his head, round and round like a carillon.

"I suppose you could become Jewish."

She shook her head. "I can't *become* anything. I am."

There was no point in telling her about the years of study, the accounting to the *Beth Din,* the ritual bath. He stood up and looked out the window at the cars which hissed along the wet Bayswater Road. With one finger he played a few notes from the fugue which was open on the piano.

"We'll work something out." He sounded more confident than he felt. "I'll work something out."

Carol was plaiting Lisa's hair. It was to be her first day at school. School, well, the nursery attached to the *shul* —you wouldn't get that in Godalming. Debbie had started there.

"For heaven's sake, stand still, Lisa," she said, twisting the elastic band onto the end of the plait, "or we shall be late."

They were late, because of the traffic; it was only a short distance, but it was the rush hour and wet and the line of cars hardly moved. Driving was like that more often than not these days, which was one of the reasons why Alec wanted to move to the country. It took so much of his time and energy even to reach his patients.

She had agreed to go with him to Godalming. Well, not agreed, simply not replied. He had taken her silence for consent. It was after her father's attack, after *Yom Kippur*. The way Alec had dealt with the situation, taken charge, had softened her attitude towards him, removed, momentarily, some of her inhibitions.

When they'd taken the babysitter home, they had stood together in the nursery in the moonlight that bathed the rocking horse rug. Debbie in her bed and Lisa in her cot, arms raised in an attitude of surrender beneath the Bambi mobile, slept peacefully.

"Soon there'll be three," Carol whispered, tucking her arm into Alec's. Tonight he was her hero. She would be everything he wanted her to be: Nell Gwynne, Cleopatra, Madame de Pompadour. She would, with her womanly spells, magic away his weariness, his disillusionment with their marriage, his stupid notions about moving to the country.

She watched him undress, the pale, freckled body topped by the flaming red hair which Lisa had inherited. She did not turn her back on him as soon as they were in bed, accompanying her gesture with her yawns. She faced him, taking him in her arms. For a moment he resisted, surprised. It had been so long. The brief flame of her passion ignited by the spark of adulation lasted until he put his mouth over hers and caressed her body. At once she grew cold. She craved sleep, but managed to go through the motions, the manifestations of love.

Afterwards, he told her, tenderly, gratefully, "I love you, Carol."

She waited, eyes open in the dark.

108

"I love you too." She did. In her own way.

"You'll come to Godalming on Thursday?"

She shut her eyes in the darkness.

"Only to look," Alec said.

When Carol and Lisa arrived at the kindergarten, the children were already playing, dressing up and cooking make-believe dishes on a miniature stove, painting and attacking the play-dough. A small boy, wearing a lopsided crown and a pair of high-heeled satin shoes, came to stare at them.

"Hallo, Lisa." Miss Ellenbogen held out her hand. "Aren't you like your sister? Debbie must be quite a big girl now," she said to Carol. "How's she getting on at school?"

"Very well," Carol said.

Lisa had both hands behind her back, her tongue in her cheek, and was shifting from one leg to the other.

"We're going to build a *succah*," Miss Ellenbogen said, "and everyone's going to draw a picture to hang on the wall. Are you going to draw a picture for me?"

"No," Lisa said.

Miss Ellenbogen looked at Carol.

"She'll be all right when you've gone." She took the child's hand. "Come and play with the Plasticine."

12

Kɪᴛᴛʏ sᴛᴏᴏᴅ ᴏɴ ᴀ ʟᴀᴅᴅᴇʀ in the *succah,* behind the synagogue, fastening leafy branches and clusters of fruit onto its open roof.

In creating, together with other members of the Ladies' Guild, a "place to eat and drink in an atmosphere of joy," where the congregation would assemble after the service, she tried to ignore the knot of fear that had settled in her entrails. About the events following *Yom Kippur* little had been said. Sydney remembered nothing of the episode, and Kitty did not want to talk about it. It had left her with a sensation of foreboding and a small cloud, which seemed unwilling to disperse, over what had seemed an unmitigatedly rosy future. This afternoon she was taking Sydney to Dr. Ballantyne.

She had already told the Guild about Sydney and the dramatic end to the Fast in the Shelton flat. In return she had had to listen to accounts of the renal colic which had once had Myra West's late husband biting the carpet and the dramatic story of Rika Snowman's perforated appendix.

"Pass me a couple of pears, dear," Kitty said to Barbara Brill, who stood at the bottom of the ladder, "and maybe a red apple. I'll put one here for colour."

Below her, the ladies bustled about unwrapping parcels of cake and bottles of wine donated by the congregants in response to Rabbi Magnus's appeal.

"The ones who haven't got, give!" Joy Kaye read the card on the bottle she was unwrapping. "It's always the same."

"I read your niece had her baby," Kitty said, taking the apple. "How is she?"

"They had to operate at the last minute," Joy said. "Thank God she's all right."

"And the baby?"

"Nine and a half pounds!" It was said with pride, as if the more the better.

Kitty tugged at the apple, making sure it wasn't going to fall on someone's head.

"I didn't think they let them get so big these days."

"Nathan's expecting . . ." Barbara Brill said tentatively, not certain how the news of the Irish *shiksa*'s pregnancy would be received.

"What about a bunch of grapes?" Kitty asked as if she hadn't heard. "Over here?"

"Twenty-four bottles be enough for the first day?" Joy asked pointedly.

". . . after *Pesach*," Barbara Brill continued forlornly.

"That's enough now, dear," Kitty addressed Barbara Brill, who was not sure if she was referring to the fruit or the baby. "I'll be glad when this afternoon's over."

"Please God it'll turn out to be nothing," Ruthie said.

"My mother's got this frozen shoulder . . ." Myra West said by way of consolation, while removing a cake from its wrappings, ". . . this one's falling to bits . . . She can't lift her arm."

"Henry's sister's got diverticulitis," Ruthie said. "Mind you, I'm not surprised what she's got the size she is."

"There's this new slimming man," Barbara said.

"In Devonshire Street?"

"On the corner? That's the one I go to."

"You can eat whatever you like . . ."

"It isn't how much you eat . . ."

"It's what you eat . . ."

"He looks after your metabolism . . ."

"You see him twice a week . . ."

"He weighs you and measures you and gives you pills for the water."

"It's useless with all these holidays . . ."

"I've given up . . ."

"You have to get into a new pattern of eating."

"Henry says it's her glands," Ruthie said, "but if you ask me it's the gland in the middle of her face. What about a couple of pomegranates up there, Kitty?"

Kitty held out her hand. She tried to concentrate on what she was doing, on her efforts to create a place in which to "meditate and pray." At the moment her prayers were centered upon the hope that Sydney would have a good report from Dr. Ballantyne.

The waiting room was full of Arabs.

They sat by the vast table with its copies of *Country Life* and its yellow pile of *National Geographic* magazines. Sydney swung his trilby hat between his knees. The quiet was tangible. It silenced even Kitty, who sat looking at him as if he might melt away before her very eyes. His appointment was at two-thirty. By three o'clock she had invested him with a dozen different diseases.

"Mr. Shelton!"

The receptionist was faded and stooped. She looked as old as the house itself. She held the wide door open for them and on her thin legs preceded them up the stairs.

Like supplicants they sat before Dr. Ballantyne while he read the letter from Lennie.

The gas fire hissed soothingly.

"Dr. Silver has spoken to me about you," Dr. Ballantyne

addressed Sydney. "You had a little trouble the other night, I understand?"

"After the Fast," Kitty said. "The Day of Atonement. He had a lot of aggravation . . ." She was thinking of Rachel.

"It might be better if we started at the beginning," Dr. Ballantyne interrupted her. "May I have your age, Mr. Shelton?"

He questioned Sydney, listening attentively to the answers and writing in small, neat letters with his gold pen. Sydney gave him his past medical history. When he came to the headaches he had been getting and could think of nothing more to say, there was a silence while Dr. Ballantyne completed his notes.

"Tell me what happened," he said when he'd finished, leaning back in his chair.

"It was after the Fast," Kitty said. "We'd just . . ."

"I'd rather your husband told me about it in his own words," Dr. Ballantyne said. There was no reproach in his voice. "Then I'd like to hear how the episode appeared to you. In that way we shall get a better picture."

After they'd both explained about the Fast day, Dr. Ballantyne led Sydney away to examine him. He took his temperature and his blood pressure, listened to his heart and lungs, looked into his eyes and his ears, felt his abdomen, tested his reflexes with his hammer and his pins.

When he had finished, he straightened up.

"Excellent," he said. "Splendid. If you'd like to get dressed and come into the other room when you're ready."

"I want to ask you something," Sydney said, sitting up on the examination couch.

"Certainly."

"In confidence?"

"Of course."

"If you find anything the matter with me I would like you

113

to tell me the truth. Only not in front of my wife. She gets anxious. I've got a big family, you see, and I have to look after them. You understand my meaning?"

"Perfectly. You have my word that I shall be quite frank with you."

"Much obliged," Sydney said and reached for his trousers.

Sydney sat down again, next to Kitty. He squeezed her hand reassuringly while Dr. Ballantyne recorded his findings.

"I'd like you to have a few tests," he said finally, looking at Sydney. "First a brain scan . . ."

"God forbid!" Kitty said.

Dr. Ballantyne ignored the interruption. "I'll fix it up for you. Nothing to worry about. It's just a particular sort of X-ray and it provides us with a lot of information about things we have to know."

"You think he's got something?" Kitty said.

"When I've completed my investigations I shall be able to tell you more," Dr. Ballantyne said kindly.

Kitty opened her mouth again, but Dr. Ballantyne stood up.

"My secretary will ring you as soon as she's made the appointment and I'll be in touch with Dr. Silver . . ."

"Lennie," Kitty said. "We've known him for years, he's as much a friend as a doctor . . ."

She was about to tell him that Lennie was classed as one of the relatives on family occasions, how he came to their silver wedding and Sydney's Ladies' Night . . .

Dr. Ballantyne's hand was on the doorknob.

"When I have all the reports I will want to see you again. Meanwhile," he said to Sydney, "take it easy, lead a normal life, but don't do anything too strenuous, don't get over-tired."

114

He held out his hand to Kitty. "Mrs. Shelton."
And to Sydney. "Mr. Shelton."
He waited while they went down the stairs.

Norman sat at his desk thinking about Della, watching her. The office, an estate agent's in Golders Green, was open plan. He had started his working life, straight from school, with a small firm in the West End and had been looking forward to an eventual partnership, when his father died. The day after the funeral Dolly started to suffer with her back, needing constant attention. He had turned in his job, and with it his prospects, and applied for one in the neighbourhood in order to be near his mother. He was taken on by Bluestone and Blatt, the local whiz kids, where there was little hope of promotion and none at all of partnership. They gave him a desk in the far corner of the room and most of the donkey work. In the front row Mr. Stuart, Mr. Pearl, Mr. Bluestone and Mr. Blatt had their names etched in white on bronze plates on their desks. Norman had neither plate nor title. He was known simply as Norman. "Ask Norman," "Give it to Norman," "Norman will do it!" and Norman usually did.

From where he sat he had a good view of Della's back as she sat at the reception desk. Through the spaces in her lacy mauve jumper he could see her well-structured bra.

She had worked in the office for three weeks, having replaced the pert Miss Gold, made pregnant, so the gossip went, by Monty Bluestone. So far Norman had said no more to her than "Have you typed up the details of Corringham?" or "Have you got the keys of Erskine Hill?" She had not addressed Norman directly at all. Her hair was dark and flopped softly onto her collar. If he shut his eyes, Norman could picture the Star of David in her cleavage. She was typing, her nails clicking against the keys. It was lunchtime and Norman had seen to it that he was the first one

115

back. It was now or never. He approached her desk. She did not look up. "If it's about Heath Road," she said, without pausing, "I'm doing it as soon as I've finished this for Mr. Monty."

"It's not about Heath Road," Norman said.

Her hands hovered like red-clawed birds over the typewriter.

She looked up. The lack of youthful sparkle in her dark eyes was compensated for by their warmth. He tried to concentrate on them and not let his glance wander to the end of the gold chain round her neck.

"There's a good film at the Ionic."

"So I'm told."

"I wondered whether you'd be interested. Any night." Leaving his mother on her own would be a problem no matter what day he chose.

To his surprise she smiled. She wore mauve lipstick matching the jumper.

"What about Wednesday?"

Almost a week. It would give him time to work on Dolly.

"Fine. See you then."

She laughed. "Silly. I'll see you before."

"Of course." He laughed, too. It had been easier than he had thought.

13

FOR SYDNEY the incident following the termination of *Yom Kippur* faded into insignificance against the fact that he was once again the possessor of a clean spiritual balance sheet.

After the fasting and the supplication, bygones, vis-à-vis his Maker and his fellowman, were now bygones.

During the week of Tabernacles, while Kitty worried under a pall of anxiety, Sydney dwelt in a sanctuary of peace, his visits to the *succah* rewarding him with a sense of deep and abiding tranquillity.

In the synagogue Rabbi Magnus's sermon to a sadly depleted congregation concerned the temporary residence of the booth, comparing it with the ephemeral nature of life itself, and was not, Sydney felt, inappropriate. Rabbi Magnus had gone on to point out that because life was so like a dream that flieth away, there was no reason to suppose that it was of little value and should be spent in reckless living. Man was arbiter of his own existence and according to the quality of his life would he endure.

This thought, and others similar, sustained Sydney during the days of waiting for the result of the brain scan. He had, in any case, other things to think about.

In one week's time it would be The Rejoicing of the Law, the last of the Festivals for several months. It marked the completion of the one-year cycle of weekly readings from the Pentateuch. As "Bridegroom of the Law," Sydney was to have the honour of being called up to the reading desk to hear the final Portion, telling of the death of Moses; as "Bridegroom of the Beginning," his friend, Moshe Pearlman, would hear the opening chapters of Genesis read immediately from a new scroll. In this way the continuity of the *Torah* was established.

In addition to this ceremony, for which it was the custom to wear top hats and sit in the warden's box, the two "Bridegrooms" were expected to arrange a celebratory party for the congregation and to provide in the traditional manner for its young.

By the time he was due for his second appointment with Dr. Ballantyne, Sydney had bought sweets for the children as well as apples and flags, and had had them delivered, ready for the Festival, into the capable hands of *"nebbech"* Pinkus at the synagogue. The reception for the congregants had been discussed in full and was now left to the expertise of the Ladies' Guild.

It was with a clear conscience, therefore, that he put on his overcoat and hat, bade good-bye to a nervously hovering Miss Maynard and went out for lunch, after which he would go straight to Dr. Ballantyne's consulting rooms.

An epidemic of diarrhea and vomiting was winging its way round his patients on the day Alec was due to go to Godalming.

Carol was cooking lunch for Debbie and Lisa, who were playing "fuzzy felts" at the kitchen table when he came in.

"Thank heavens it's my half-day," he said. "They're going down like flies!" He looked at his watch. "We ought to leave shortly."

"I'm not coming," Carol said. "Daddy's going to Dr. Ballantyne for the result of the brain scan."

"What about your mother and Josh?"

"I want to be here. It would be a waste of time anyway. I haven't the slightest intention of moving to Godalming."

"If it's not Godalming, it will be somewhere else," Alec said. "I've never been more serious in my life."

"There are other people to consider."

"Do you think I haven't considered? If I don't do it now, Carol, while I'm still young . . . It takes time to build up a practice." He put his arm round her. "You'll be sorry if you don't come. I want you to see it with me so that we can decide together."

Carol turned the fish sticks.

"There's nothing to decide."

"Anyway," Alec said, "the countryside is looking beautiful now. It'll do you good to get out."

118

"I'm not coming. Debbie, put that game away!"

Alec took his arm from her shoulders.

"Have it your own way."

"You apparently insist on having yours. I like it here. There's nothing wrong with it."

He was not going to let himself be drawn into the circuitous and well-worn arguments.

"I'll see you later then."

"No lunch?" She put the fish sticks onto two plates.

"I'll buy a sandwich."

"Lisa, tell Daddy what you did in school today," Carol said, changing the subject.

"Beads," Lisa said. "And the *berochah* for milk."

"Daddy," Debbie said, "what's Godalming?"

Josh had extended his lunch hour to take his mother to the appointment with Dr. Ballantyne.

In the kitchen Kitty was rolling pastry, which she stamped into rounds with a fluted cutter.

"If you think I know what I'm doing . . . I'm only making them to keep busy . . . I'm shaking like a jelly inside . . ."

He kissed the top of her head.

"Have you had your lunch? There's a middle of plaice in the fridge."

"I've eaten. I only have an apple."

"What good's that to you? You can't do a day's work on an apple."

Sometimes he wondered if she realized that he was no longer a small boy. He watched her spread jam on the circles of pastry and cover each one with another in which she had made a central hole with a thimble. She had been making the same cookies for as long as he could remember. When they were cooked she would sprinkle them with icing sugar. His school friends had always enjoyed coming to tea.

"If it's not one thing it's another," Kitty said, gathering up the remaining dough and thumping it into a ball.

"What with your father and the business with Rachel, he's very upset still, and Carol . . ."

"What's the matter with Carol?"

"I'm worried about her. She doesn't look like she should and she's always crying. It's not good for the baby."

"Have you discussed it with Alec?"

"I wouldn't be a bit surprised if he's not at the bottom of it. He never seems to be around. By rights he should be coming with us this afternoon."

"I expect he's busy."

"It's his father-in-law and he is a doctor, after all . . ."

She picked up the rolling pin. "What have you been doing with yourself? Thank goodness it's the end of the holidays next week. I hope it's not going to be too much for your father being Bridegroom of the Law. After that's over, I've got to get busy with the Ball. It's going to be very good this year, the tickets have gone like nobody's business; they know we put on a good function. I'm doing the Lottery with Ruthie. You'll come this year? I'm making up a young people's table, I don't suppose Rachel . . ."

He watched her flip the cookies onto a baking tray with a nonchalance betraying years of practice.

". . . it's a long time since you've done us the honour . . ."

Since Paula.

". . . we've managed to get Frankie Vaughan for the cabaret . . ."

"I've got a girl friend, Mother."

". . . and a Mini for first prize in the raffle, with two weeks in Israel for second . . ." She wiped her hands on her aproned hips. "You've got a what?"

"A girl friend."

120

"You've kept it very quiet. How long's this been going on?"

"Not long."

"What's her name?"

"Sarah."

Kitty beamed. "Your grandmother's name, God rest her soul. Sarah Naomi. About time we had another wedding; no use waiting for Rachel with her barmy ideas, Patrick this and Christopher that." She dipped her pastry brush into a bowl of beaten egg.

"What is she? A London girl. When are we going to meet her? I've got a nice piece of brisket and I could make some dumplings. It might cheer your father up a bit." She painted the cooky circles with the egg, taking care to avoid the jammy portholes.

"Sarah who?"

"MacNaughton."

Kitty stared at him, brush in midair.

"Her father was Ambassador to Turkey."

She picked up the tray of cookies and put them next to the oven.

"I'll put them in as soon as we get back. How are you off for cookies?"

"I'm in love with her."

"I'm not interested in all your *meshugasim*. It's time you settled down. There are one or two nice girls coming to the Ball, intelligent girls . . . one's doing law . . ."

"It's not a *meshugas*. I told you I'm in love with her."

She began to clear up the table. "Then get it out of your system. That's what they all do these days, isn't it? You can't pick up a book or watch television without . . ."

"You don't understand."

Kitty took off her apron. "What is there to understand? I've got enough trouble with your father. I'll put you next to Gina Leapman's daughter. She goes to Oxford. Wins all

121

the prizes. Not Orthodox, that I don't expect, but at least . . ."

"I'm going to marry Sarah."

Kitty looked at her watch. "We ought to go. You never know with the traffic. I'll get my coat. What's it like outside?"

Dr. Ballantyne held out a warm, dry hand to Kitty.

"I'm so pleased you came early, Mrs. Shelton. Your husband hasn't arrived yet."

"This is my son," Kitty said.

"Won't you sit down?" He ushered them to chairs and retreated to the safety of his highly polished desk, where he put on his glasses and, while composing his words, gazed unseeingly at the notes before him.

"He's been right as rain since *Yom Kippur,*" Kitty said. "Since after the Fast."

Dr. Ballantyne didn't reply.

"I'm afraid it isn't terribly good news."

Kitty sat quite still.

Dr. Ballantyne looked at her. He saw before him a woman, not highly educated but strong and of good courage. She was well-dressed and wore her diamond engagement ring, a gold watch and a gold bracelet on hands that were manicured but testified to a variety of physical tasks. Her hairstyle was too careful and her lipstick too wine, matching the burgundy suit, but a spirit emanated from her, an indefinable and indomitable spirit, which he had seen before. She had inherited it directly from Rebecca and from Ruth.

"The scan revealed a tumour . . ."

Kitty's gaze did not falter.

". . . which would account for the attack of the other night and also for your husband's headaches and the other symptoms he has noticed."

"On the brain?" Kitty said.

122

Josh took her hand.

Dr. Ballantyne nodded. "Quite a large tumour."

"I suppose that means an operation? We've got insurance. Sydney's always insisted . . ."

"Unfortunately no," Dr. Ballantyne said and talked, only half his words permeating Kitty's stunned mind, about the impossibility of removing the growth, giving a variety of reasons incorporating technical details which she had not the slightest desire to understand.

He preempted her next question.

"The outlook, I'm sorry to say, is rather poor."

"I don't want you to tell Sydney," Kitty said. "There's no need for him to know. When he had pneumonia we told him it was a bad cough and then once he had these stomach pains, before Josh was born . . ." She looked at Dr. Ballantyne. "Is that all right?"

"I'll do what I can to stop him from worrying."

"In any case," Kitty said, "I'd like a second opinion."

Dr. Ballantyne nodded. "Certainly."

There was a buzz and he picked up the telephone.

"Your husband's on his way up now."

They sat in silence until Sydney opened the door.

Whatever Dr. Ballantyne decided to tell him concerning the outcome of the tests was immaterial. The results were written on Kitty's face.

In the side room Dr. Ballantyne finished his examination.

"Well?" Sydney said. "Not that you have to tell me. One look at Kitty's face, bless her . . ."

"There is an abnormality . . ."

"A growth?" Sydney said.

"A tumour."

Sydney digested the news.

"It would account for the occurrence of the other night, also for your headaches and the impaired control . . ."

123

"So you want to remove it?"

Dr. Ballantyne folded his stethoscope and leaned against the wall.

"That's not possible. The location of it is such that . . ."

Sydney wasn't listening. "How long have I got?" he said.

"It could stay dormant for years, on the other hand . . ."

Sydney was buttoning his shirt cuff. He shrugged.

"The Almighty's been good to me," he said. "You can't live forever!"

"I wish I had something more cheerful to tell you." Dr. Ballantyne looked crestfallen.

"These things happen." Sydney tried to cheer him up.

"Your wife would like you to have a second opinion . . ."

"If it makes her happy," Sydney said.

"I'll send you to Arnold Avery. He's very sound. You'll like him. Meanwhile I'll give you something a little more effective for the headaches and I'd like you to come and see me from time to time. If anything bothers you or you get any further symptoms, don't hesitate to get in touch."

Sydney put on his jacket, adjusting it at the neck.

"It might be as well to avoid any strenuous activity," Dr. Ballantyne said. "Take things quietly, don't go digging in the garden . . ."

"I don't know one end of a spade from the other," Sydney said. "Anyway, we live in a flat."

"It's called 'Peartree Cottage,' " Alec said. He could not keep the excitement from his voice. "It's absolutely secluded, hedges and trees all the way round. There's a rose garden, a pergola, an orchard, a kitchen garden and an herbaceous walk. There's also a paddock; we could keep a pony for the children. Inside there are four bedrooms, well, three and a half, one's more of a boxroom really. The office is in the village about a mile and a half away. It's ideal, Carol. There's even a heated greenhouse and a little guest wing. You could have your parents to stay."

He looked at Carol, who had tears rolling down her face.

"There's nothing to cry about!"

"Daddy's got a brain tumour."

He put the particulars of "Peartree Cottage" on the table.

"I'm sorry."

"They can't operate. The specialist explained why to Mummy but she couldn't understand all the technical details. You should have been there instead of running off . . ."

He put an arm round her. "What can I say?"

"We're telling him that his headache is due to high blood pressure. He's got some tablets to take. He must be all right until the baby. I know it will be a boy. He so wants a grandson."

"At least he'll be brought up in the countryside. You could smell the air!"

Carol stared at him. "You must be mad," she said. "I told you, Daddy's got a brain tumour. He might die at any moment and all you can talk about is moving to some God-forsaken cottage."

"I've agreed to buy it," Alec said. "And to start in the practice on April the first."

"That's Passover," Carol said, sniffing. "You know we always go to Mummy's."

14

"SHALL I COME HOME?" Rachel asked when she heard the news.

"You must please yourself," Kitty said.

You could not win. If she went home, it meant facing her father's tight-lipped disapproval over the Day of Atonement; if she did not, she must live with her failure to give moral support to her mother, sympathy to her father, at a time when it was needed. She wanted to see him. She had lain on the bed and wept for him, for herself, needing his approval. They let you go, but only so far. Like the kite she had flown on the sands at Westgate with Josh when they were children, keeping tight hold together as it turned this way and that in the summer sky. You imagined you were free, but all at once they pulled on the string. Please yourself. You could fill a book with the implications of the words. She went home and cried silently on her mother's shoulder.

"We're not telling a soul," Kitty said, holding her close. "He thinks it's his blood pressure."

He sat in his chair reading his trade journal.

"I'm sorry about your high blood pressure," Rachel said.

He looked at her for a moment and, before his eyes became guarded, it was acknowledged that the fabricated diagnosis was only a symbol in the charade that from now on would be acted out.

"Am I forgiven?" She meant for *Yom Kippur*.

"There is such a thing as *derech eretz,*" Sydney said. He meant "way of the earth." It had been drummed into them as children that it embraced the respect due to one's parents at all times.

She wanted to comfort him. He looked no different. She didn't know what she had expected to see.

"I don't believe in all that fasting and praying."

"Josh does the right thing."

"There's more than one way to be a Jew. I'm not Josh."

"You knew I'd be upset."

She knew. "I'll come next year."

He looked at her.

She guessed that she had blown it forever as far as the Day of Atonement was concerned.

"Can we forget it then?"

"If you think you did the right thing." He cast her back into the slops of her own conscience.

"We missed you," Sydney said and went back to his journal. It was the only concession he would make. It would take time before they were back on the old footing. Rachel wondered if there would be enough and why he had to be so unyielding.

Kitty wheeled her basket slowly along the tree-lined road towards the High Street. Generally she enjoyed her expeditions to the shops. A week ago she had stocked up light-heartedly for Tabernacles, and now, with The Rejoicing of the Law before her, at which her husband was to be honoured, her feet felt like lead. Something for dinner, a vegetable and a sixty-watt bulb, she kept saying to herself to keep more unpleasant thoughts from her head. She had left her list in the kitchen.

Outside the kosher butcher's she met Ruthie Wiseman with her shopper-on-wheels of tartan cloth. They stopped, facing each other, basket to basket. Their images were reflected in the window among trays of wine-red liver and ox hearts laid out beneath the hanging salamis and the conjuror's strings of beef sausages. The shop was empty. Next door, where they sold ready-breaded pork escalopes, tastily threaded kebab skewers and tiny, bacon-larded *poussins* ready for the oven, there was always a queue.

"I've been meaning to ring you," Ruthie said. "What did the specialist say?"

"Blood pressure." Kitty's eyes were dark with pain.

"What's he given him? Tablets?"

Kitty nodded.

"Thank God they didn't find anything else."

"Thank God." Kitty said and changed the subject. "How are the children?"

Ruthie knew she meant the grandchildren.

"Lovely, bless them. We're going down to Bournemouth tomorrow for a week and taking them with."

"You'll have your hands full." Kitty's response was automatic. She did not care about Ruthie's grandchildren.

"Paula's got a marvellous Swiss girl; she's coming to look after them. It'll give Paula a bit of a break."

"I'm going in here." Kitty pulled her basket towards the doorway of the kosher butcher's.

"Another holiday," Ruthie said. "It's nothing but eat. I shan't be sorry when they're over. Give Sydney my love. Tell him to take it easy."

"Love to Henry," Kitty said.

She watched while the butcher in his bloodstained overall cut two steaks from the ball of the rib and put them on the scales, which showed the outrageous price per pound, the weight and the total in flashing scarlet figures. She was not surprised there was a queue next door. It was the price one paid for adhering to the laws enumerated in Leviticus and Deuteronomy, for distinguishing between permitted

128

and prohibited animals and obeying the injunction concerning the blood.

"We've some nice fresh brains." He pointed to a heap of them.

Kitty looked at him in horror.

". . . beautiful braised."

Bella, on the cash desk, had been there forever. Sometimes Kitty wondered whether she was permanently attached to her high seat behind the till.

"What about the weekend?" she said to Kitty. "Remember we're closed till Tuesday."

How could she not remember.

"My husband's Bridegroom of the Law." She said with pride.

"*Mazel tov.* What about a nice pickled tongue?"

"I'll have a fowl," Kitty said. "And a set of giblets and a knuckle of veal."

"No veal. It's a short week. What about a knob of shin?"

For the traditional Sabbath soup.

Bella wrote the order. "Family well?"

Kitty's heart was too heavy to talk about Sydney. It was easier to nod affirmatively.

The cash register pinged. "That's the most important thing. As long as you've got your health."

She handed Kitty her change and the till slip. "I wish you good *Yom Tov* if I don't see you."

"And you." Kitty put her purse back into her handbag.

"All the best," Bella said. "Look after yourself."

Crossing the road to the greengrocer's, Kitty was only half aware of the traffic and its hazards.

She had not got used to Sydney's tumour. If she made the effort to think about it and all that it implied, other thoughts, trivial and unassociated, got in the way. She found she was wondering whether to have the three-piece suite cleaned or leave it until Passover. Sometimes she told herself quite categorically that he could become increasingly incapacitated, helpless and blind, or even die at any moment. She did not believe it and found that while she convinced others that the trouble lay with his blood pressure, she was also rapidly convincing herself.

She bought a pound of carrots to go with the steak—she would make some *tzimmes*, which Sydney loved. Glancing unseeingly into the windows of the boutiques, deserted now that everyone had bought their new clothes for the holidays, she trundled her basket home. If she passed faces that she knew, she did not see them. When she opened the door at the flat and switched on the light, only four of the five curved gilt arms were illuminated. She had forgotten to buy the new bulb.

She could think no further than Sydney.

Sydney was not afraid of dying. Although he valued his life dearly, the strength of his faith enabled him to prepare with equanimity to give it up. He thought it not unreasonable that a God who took the harvest of the ground at some point also required the ingathering of men's lives. He hadn't quite the sublime faith of a Rabbi Elimelech, who actually rejoiced when he knew he was about to enter the higher worlds of eternity, but he was not prepared to allow an atmosphere of gloom to pervade the time which was left to him. Whatever days remained he was determined to live well and to make no delay in putting his affairs in order.

He sat at his desk dictating to Miss Maynard. In front of him was the bottle which contained his new, stronger painkillers. Miss Maynard saw to it that there was always a glass of water within reach. Although he was dictating, she was not transcribing his words into shorthand. It was a skill which she had never mastered. Over the years she had perfected her own singular method of speedwriting, which suited her well enough and to which Sydney was indifferent. He preferred to have one loyal Miss Maynard, whose note taking was slow and whose typing erratic, than a dozen dolly girls who demanded inflated salaries, vouchers for lunch, and were unable to spell the most commonplace words.

He was not a poor man. He had worked hard all his life to build up his business and had not dissipated the rewards in high living. Whatever profits were not ploughed back into S. Shelton (Fancy Goods) Ltd. had been widely and wisely invested. He was now attempting to dispose of his worldly acquisitions in what he considered a fair and proper manner. When he had clarified his thoughts, with the help of Miss Maynard, he would see his solicitor.

They had been at it for some time. He had made provision for Mirrie, Dolly, Josh (provided he married within the faith), Rachel (likewise), Carol, his grandchildren, and for numerous small bequests to such people as *"nebbech"* Pinkus and Miss Maynard herself, which tactfully he omitted from his dictation, and was now well into the charitable organizations he favoured with his support.

"How far have we got?" he asked Miss Maynard.

She turned back a page of her spiral notebook.

"British O.R.T., Children and Youth Aliyah, Nightingale Homes, Buckets and Spades, East End Jewish Scholarship, Friends of the Hebrew University, Hammerson House . . ."

"That will do for the moment," Sydney said. "Take a letter."

Miss Maynard flipped over another page. She had never married, but loved her employer with a blind and dogged devotion. In her more fanciful moments she thought of herself as the Virgin Mary, the Virgin wife without the Christ child. She did not ask him why he was preparing a new will. In the first place, although she had been in his service for so long, she considered such a question pre-

131

sumptuous. In the second, she knew her employer well enough not to need to be told of the outcome of his visits to the doctor, and in fact had already shed tears both at home in her tiny flat and in the lavatory at the back of the second floor to which she alone had the key.

"To Doctor Alexander Khasin," Sydney said.

"USSR. RSFSR. Moscow B 306. Uralskaya Ul. 6 Coro, 2, Apt. 47.

My dear Dr. Khasin,

This week in our synagogue we celebrate the Festival of The Rejoicing of the Law. We have been told that not only have your Hebrew books been taken from you but that you have been removed from your dear family, your wife Anya and two small daughters, and imprisoned in a faraway place on the flimsiest of fabricated pretexts.

I am writing to let you know, dear Dr. Khasin, that during the Festival of Joy, for which I have been appointed Bridegroom of the Law, we shall be making the customary seven circuits in the synagogue. Each of the verses which accompany them and which we sing ends with the cry: "Answer us on this day that we call."

The "call," both of myself and our congregants, will incorporate a fervent and sincere prayer to the Almighty for the release of yourself from the bonds of tyranny, for the safety of your wife and the well-being of your daughters, who even at their tender ages are veteran campaigners for the human rights we are all fighting for.

Together with every thinking person in the free world, and more especially in the Jewish Community, of which I am proud to be a member, I applaud your courage and will include in my prayers the sincere plea that you will soon all be freed to join your parents in Israel.

Last week's Festival of Tabernacles brought home to us the interdependence of all nations meant by God to live and work together like members of one large family, in harmo-

132

ny, mutual helpfulness and peace. On the eve of this closing Festival of the Season of Festivals, I salute you, my brother, and assure you most sincerely that your family has not forgotten you.

I remain, etcetera, etcetera . . ."

Sydney looked across at Miss Maynard. "You'll have to ask at the post office about the stamps."

15

In the Rose Sugarman hall, the Ladies' Guild was preparing for the party that Sydney and Moshe Pearlman were providing. *"Nebbech"* Pinkus and Lucas the caretaker had put up trestle tables in long vertical lines stemming from a horizontal one, and the ladies had covered them with white cloths. Paper plates had been set out on either side of the tables, and Barbara Brill and Rika Snowman were folding a pile of red paper napkins into triangles. They looked up as Kitty came through the swinging doors into the hall.

"Here comes the bride!" Barbara Brill's voice was shrill. Rika silenced her with a glance and went over to greet Kitty.

"What did the specialist say?"

The other ladies left their napkins and the sprays of fern they were pinning to the tablecloths and the teaspoons they were counting and the wineglasses they were polishing, and gathered round her.

Kitty's heart was heavy. The shock of what Dr. Ballantyne had told her and the numbness that accompanied it had

133

worn off, and the reality of his words had left an abyss in the region of her stomach. She tried not to think of the truth. "Keeping busy" was a favourite remedy but, energetic and caring as she was, there were moments, sometimes hours at a time, particularly during the night, when a chill descended on her which nothing could dispel. She tried to dismiss it as if it were a mirage, a bad dream; to put back the clock to an earlier time when her horizon had been unclouded, but there was no way round or through or over. Her Sydney had an incurable and progressive condition which could remove him from her side at any time. A few short weeks ago she had joined with the choir in reciting the solemn passage concerning who was to live and who to die in the coming year. She had not thought then that for the latter group God had very likely selected Sydney.

Rika Snowman, Barbara Brill and the other ladies were waiting. They wore aprons and were holding bundles of forks, a cucumber dish, a few carnations. They were good women, family women, feeling women.

"Blood pressure!" she said to the poised semicircle which surrounded her.

They relaxed.

"Thank God," Nita Cooper said. "They can give you tablets. You always have to take them."

"Brain scans!" Joy Kaye said. "Frighten the life out of you!"

"He mustn't get excited." Barbara Brill was adamant.

"Like they'll listen, men!"

". . . don't take a blind bit of notice."

". . . like babies you have to watch them . . ."

"And when they've got a cold in the head they think they're dying. Leslie had forty-eight-hour flu for three weeks; a real *matzo* pudding he made out of it. It went round the whole family but when it was my turn I couldn't even stay in bed."

134

"What about the flags and the sweets and the apples for the children?" Kitty said. There was still the party to get through.

They were in cardboard boxes at the far end of the hall. Kitty put her coat on a chair and rolled up the sleeves of her woollen dress.

She opened up the carton containing the sweets and began to divide them into individual paper bags. If she concentrated very hard on what she was doing, she might be able to forget for a while about Sydney.

Sarah had cooked dinner in Josh's flat. Now they were playing backgammon to the accompaniment of Bach.

"It would make no difference," Josh said, hitting the white man, which was Sarah's, "if you were Princess Anne and Princess Margaret rolled into one. Our children would not be Jewish."

Sarah threw a double.

"I wouldn't even be able to take you to see them," Josh said. "Not my father, at any rate. Certainly not now."

"I know them already," Sarah said, making a point on her board. "Carol, Rachel, Alec, Auntie Beatty . . . All I can produce is Mama and I don't suppose she's going to be absolutely over the moon. Diplomatic people are very cliquey. You'll have to come up with me sometime, to Leicester. You're very attached to your family."

"I can live without Auntie Beatty; not without you." He made a bad throw and landed on the point she had made.

"I thought times had changed, that all these racial and religious boundaries were being eradicated."

"If you said that to my father he would come back with the mockery, made by such ideas, of the sacrifice of Isaac and the Exodus and Masada and the stand of Judah Maccabeus against the Greeks and the *Yom Kippur* war . . ."

He took his red man back to the beginning.

135

"Josh . . ." Sarah looked at him, the dice suspended in her hand. "We don't need to get married you know . . ."

"I'm not going to let you go."

"I'm not going anywhere." She let the dice fall but did not look at them. "I love you."

"I'll take you to my Uncle Juda's," Josh said. "I can talk to him. How would you like that?"

She leaned forward across the table.

"I'd like anything with you."

"I'm so lucky, Sarah." His mouth met hers.

"Me too."

There was no more backgammon.

When it had finished, the Double Concerto switched itself off.

In the front half of the "knocked-through" living room of Leon and Beatty's semidetached in Edgware, Leon, with his feet up on the mottled tiles of the mantelpiece, in which was an inset electric fire, was watching television.

"It's half past seven already," Beatty shouted from the kitchen, where she was drying the teacups on a blue "milk" tea towel. "Freda and Harry will be waiting."

They were to have dinner together, as they often did. This time at a new restaurant Freda had discovered, in Borehamwood.

"So they'll wait," Leon said. "It's *The Two Ronnies*. You didn't tell me we were going out."

"I told you a dozen times," Beatty shouted, putting the cups on the pull-down "Easiwork" table. "I'm not surprised you don't hear you have that thing on so loud. It's a wonder you've still got the use of your legs."

"Whatd'you say?" Leon said.

"I said . . . Oh never mind," Beatty shouted. "I'm going up to put some lipstick on. I'll fetch your jacket."

136

"Five minutes!" Leon called, chuckling to himself. "It's very funny this week."

In Bushey Heath, Harry, in his navy blue blazer, was running his razor over his chin for the second time that day.

"What time have you booked the table for?" he asked Freda, who was painting her eyelids with frosted green shadow to match her knitted two-piece.

"Quarter to eight."

"No hurry," Harry said, looking at his quartz digital watch, the razor still buzzing in his hand. "Leon's bound to be late."

By the time *The Two Ronnies* had finished and Leon had watched the announcement of programs for the following evening, Beatty had been standing in the hall with her Persian lamb jacket on for ten minutes. When they pulled up behind Harry's midnight blue Jaguar in the accommodation road in Borehamwood, it was eight o'clock.

"It was *The Two Ronnies*," Beatty said by way of explanation to Freda and Harry, who were waiting in the booth for four. "You know Leon!"

"It's a wonder he hasn't got square eyes," Freda said. She took her handbag off the banquette next to her to make room for Beatty.

"Doesn't seem a bad place." Beatty looked round at the newly painted walls with their prints of the Doge's Palace and the Grand Canal and the potted plants. "Quite a few people."

"It's only been open a couple of weeks," Harry said.

"Plenty of fish," Freda said, looking at the menu. "They've even got salmon."

"Frozen," Beatty said. "No good this time of the year."

All four of them adhered to the dietary laws, not so strictly that they did not eat in restaurants but when they did, they selected only the permitted foods, shutting their eyes to any infringements that might be going on in the kitchens.

The waiter stood by them with his note pad.

"I can recommend the scampi today. And the crab cocktail; very fresh. Avocado with prawns . . ."

"We don't want any shellfish," Harry said firmly.

"Consommé, made in our kitchens . . ."

Beatty glanced at Leon. Consommé meant meat bones.

". . . melon with Parma ham."

"No ham."

"We 'ave a very good *quiche lorraine* . . .?"

"What do you recommend in the way of fish?" Harry asked.

"Turbot, halibut . . . everything is very good . . ."

"I'll have the sole," Beatty said and nodded at Leon. "And grilled plaice for him, on the bone."

Freda and Harry ordered the plaice and all four, the avocado pear with *vinaigrette* sauce to start.

When the fish came, Beatty picked up her knife and poked at it.

"Don't go away," she said to the waiter. "What's this?"

"Sole *bonne femme,* madame."

"Sole *bonne femme* is with mushrooms."

"White wine sauce and mushrooms," he agreed.

Beatty pointed with the knife. "What's this then?"

The waiter leaned over her shoulder and looked at the pale pink semicircles which decorated her fish.

"Shrimps, madame."

"It's supposed to be mushrooms."

"And mushrooms, madame."

Beatty lifted up the plate and thrust it at him. "Take it away and give me one without the shrimps. And don't just scrape them off. I want another one. Tell the headwaiter."

It turned out that the sauce was ready-made, the shrimps an integral part of it. Anxious to please, they cooked Beatty

138

a sole *meunière*. When it came, she was still muttering that she had never heard of sole *bonne femme* with shrimps.

From the trolley they ordered four different desserts. Four pairs of eyes watched as the generous portions were served. Four spoons were taken up simultaneously and crossed like swords. Beatty reached for Harry's *profiteroles,* Harry helped himself to Freda's *gâteau,* Freda dug into Leon's *crème caramel* and Leon aimed for and speared a piece of strawberry *flan* from Beatty's plate.

"Not bad," Beatty said, "not bad at all." She exchanged her scraped plate for Leon's, who had given up halfway.

"I keep thinking about poor Sydney."

"Didn't put you off your dinner," Harry said, pushing his plate away and lighting a cigar.

"It's only blood pressure, thank God," Freda said. "He's always suffered with it."

"What did he want a brain scan for then?" Beatty said. "They've only got two or three in the country. They don't give them to everyone with blood pressure."

"Just to make sure, I suppose," Harry said. "You've got to have a look."

"Well, Kitty sounded very funny to me," Beatty said. "And Dr. Adler's wife, she's having a bit of velvet let into her broadtail, said you can't get a fit from blood pressure."

"Much she knows," Leon said.

"She knows. When Austin was little she knew he had whooping cough before the doctor even saw him!"

"Kitty would have told us if there was anything," Harry said. He leaned back while the waiter cleared the table and served coffee.

"No cream for me," Beatty said. She put a hand inside her waistband. "I'm trying to lose a bit."

The waiter put down a saucer with four wrapped chocolate peppermints and four squares of Turkish delight.

Beatty's was the first hand out. "They do try," she said.

139

"I like a bit of nosh to finish up with." She removed the silver paper, took a bite of the chocolate and stared at it meditatively. "You mark my words; I couldn't sleep last night, worrying. I don't think he's been looking well for a long while."

"He's never said anything," Freda said.

"You ever heard Sydney complain?"

"I'll ask Josh," Harry said.

"You can ask as much as you like," Beatty said, taking the last peppermint, which should by right have been Leon's.

"They give you heartburn," she said to him. "Have one of the Turkish delights. If they don't want to tell you anything, they won't."

"If Kitty says it's blood pressure, it's blood pressure," Freda said. "Be thankful."

"I suppose we could give the specialist a ring," Harry said, looking at the end of his cigar. "Make some sort of excuse . . ."

Beatty stared at him. "He's a very big man," she said. "You don't ask him questions!"

Leon, anxious not to miss *The Old Grey Whistle Test,* looked round the edge of the booth for the waiter so that they could get the bill. His head spun back as if he had been stung. He beckoned the others to come closer. When the four heads were together, he said:

"Don't look now, but who do you think I've seen in the corner?"

As one they turned, Freda and Harry leaning sideways.

"No, not there. The other side. By the far door."

The heads swung round.

"Norman!" Beatty said.

Harry took the cigar out of his mouth. "With a girl!"

"She's not such a girl," Freda said.

Beatty burped and put her hand to her mouth. "Pardon me! I wonder if Dolly knows!"

16

Although Norman had started off with sweating palms, the evening had been a good one. It was a long time since he had taken a girl out.

All day, as he answered queries concerning three-bedroomed houses with garages and modern flats near to the station, he watched Della's back. The transparent lacy jumpers she usually wore had been replaced by a frilly white blouse with ruffles at the neck in honour, he presumed, of the evening. He was disappointed. Apart from the blouse she was the same. She talked to him as usual, smiled at him as usual, distinguished him in no way from Mr. Stuart, Mr. Bluestone or Mr. Blatt. While all day he struggled to keep his mind on his job rather than on the evening ahead, he searched for some sign and, finding none, wondered if she had forgotten.

His mother, as was to be expected, had woken scarcely able to move.

"You'll have to give me a hand," she said pathetically, when he had taken her her morning tea. "I can't even turn myself over!"

He opened the curtains and pulled her up while she bit her lip and rolled her eyes in agony until she was leaning against the pillows he had stacked at the head of the bed. He gave her her glasses and the newspaper and her bedjacket, which he helped her to put on, and switched on the heater and went down again to the kitchen for a Marie cooky, and put out her five morning tablets in three assorted colours.

"I hope I'll be able to get myself out of bed," Dolly said, leaning back against the pillows and watching Norman from the corner of her eyes. "I've been in pain all night."

"Do you want me to ring Dr. Levy?"

"What can he do? He comes in for two minutes, he doesn't even take his coat off, and runs away again." She looked at Norman's navy blue suit.

"What have you got your best suit on for?"

"I told you. I've got this important client this evening. I have to show him a few properties."

"In your navy blue suit?"

"He's very important. Saudi Arabian. A prince!" he said, suddenly inspired.

"What does a prince want with Golders Green?"

"Hampstead," Norman said. "Winnington Road."

"I thought Mr. Monty did those himself."

"He's going to the opera." Norman sighed, his invention was running out.

"I expect I'll be all right. If I don't get so fixed I can't move."

"Well, you've got my number, and Dr. Levy's, and Mrs. Goldberg's." She lived next door.

"A lot she cares."

He moved the telephone so that it was within her reach.

She was right. There didn't seem to be many people who had a lot of sympathy with his mother. She really did need him.

"You'll feel better when the tablets work," Norman said. "You know you're always stiff first thing in the mornings."

"They upset my stomach."

He handed her the bottle of antacid tablets.

"Take a couple of these with them."

"If I take any more tablets, I'll rattle."

142

Norman looked at his watch. "I have to go."

"I'll manage," Dolly said weakly. "What time will you be back?"

"I'll try not to be too late."

He kissed her forehead, smoothing her hair. "I'll ring you at lunchtime. There's a good play on television tonight."

"If I can get myself downstairs."

When he shut the front door behind him, it was as if he'd stepped out into a new world.

The film had been a mistake. At least he thought it had. It was called *Hooper's Rides,* and he knew that it was about the West Coast of America and some of its glorious scenery. The rides, he had imagined, would be on horseback. In actual fact, Hooper drove an old Dodge and had a bet with a college friend about how many girls he could lay in the course of his three-week vacation in California. The scenery, it was true, was breathtaking: Malibu Beach and Monterey, Yosemite in all its glory, Death Valley and Big Bear Lake. The symbolism was not subtle. For every mountain there was a breast, for every lone pine and giant redwood a sweating close-up. There were grainy shots of sand and of skin, of undergrowth and tangled hair, of smooth rocks and undulating thighs, of natural clefts and heaving buttocks, caverns and parted lips, pounding surf and climaxes in a dozen different places, innumerable different ways.

For the first half hour, Norman sat rigidly, not daring to look at Della. He felt himself personally responsible for Hooper's promiscuous behaviour and was prepared to die from shame and embarrassment. When he steeled himself to turn round, he found that she was laughing at Hooper's escapades with the rest of the audience, and tears of merriment were running down her face. He opened the popcorn he had brought and took her hand while they shared it. By the time Hooper, not in the least fatigued by his adventures, had arrived back in college to claim his wager, Norman's arm was round Della, and he was enjoying the closeness of a woman, which he had not done for ages, and his palms were no longer damp.

It was Mr. Monty who had told him about the restaurant in Borehamwood. Because he had eyes only for Della at their table in the corner, he did not notice his Auntie Freda and his Uncle Harry, his Auntie Beatty and his Uncle Leon in the booth against the wall.

When he stopped the car in Kingsbury, Della said she couldn't ask him in because her elderly parents were light sleepers and she didn't want to disturb them. To his astonishment, she leaned forward and kissed him on the mouth softly and gently and with unmistakable promise. She thanked him for a beautiful evening and, before he could recover, had opened the door and disappeared into the block of flats. He did not drive off immediately. He sat in the deserted, tree-lined road and thought how very good it was to be alive and that tomorrow morning he would see her again. In a night Golders Green had become Paradise; Bluestone and Blatt, Estate Agents, the Garden of Eden.

He crept in but not quietly enough. He did not want the mood, which he experienced so rarely, to be shattered. It was. Into a thousand pieces. By his mother. By Dolly.

"Norman?" The voice was chockablock with admonition, with recrimination, with complaint. "Thank God you've come home. I'm frozen stiff, and my throat's parched."

He noticed in the kitchen that she had ironed a clean shirt for him to wear tomorrow, cooked some dried fruit for her breakfast, washed the tea towels. He filled the kettle and switched it on.

"The whole day I've been in bed," she called. "Not a soul to do anything."

He disposed of the bones of the mackerel she had grilled

144

herself for supper with what looked like mashed potatoes and spring greens. She was fussy about her vitamins.

"I'll be up in a moment," he answered. "I'm making you a nice cup of tea."

It was The Rejoicing of the Law and Sydney was determined to rejoice. He sat in the seat of honour, in the warden's box that faced the congregation, his black silk hat proudly on his head. He was a happy man. He was in a building that he cherished, among people whom he loved, and he knew that if he lifted his eyes to the Ladies' Gallery, he would meet the ever-vigilant ones of the female members of his family, including those of Rachel, who had come to synagogue as it was only right she should. His behaviour towards her had paid off. It was all very well for Kitty to call him hard, inflexible, but he had proved to himself time and time again that such an attitude worked. Being lax did no good. One could see the results of the permissive generation in the anarchy and violence all round. Children had to be taught their duty, if necessary the hard way. It never did anybody any harm. Had never done him any harm. He had no use for soft options. They did not enter into his scheme of things.

Next to him, similarly dressed, sat Moshe Pearlman, who, after Sydney had been called to the reading of the final chapters of the Pentateuch, would be summoned immediately to its new beginning. Sydney wondered whether perhaps the Almighty himself had selected this particular year, possibly his last, to dignify him with this special office. He was not a believer in coincidence.

The atmosphere in the synagogue was relaxed, the decorum of the Sabbath and other Festivals absent. As the morning progressed, the service would get both noisier and merrier. Those who were not in favour stayed away. It was a moving sight to see the children holding their paper

145

flags, upon which were inscribed words speaking of the greatness of the Law they had inherited and which they would in turn pass on to their own children. Sydney looked tolerantly upon the whisperings, upon the comings and goings, upon the spontaneous outbursts of song and the public consumption of the apples, which were impaled on top of the flags until the temptation to eat them proved too great. He looked fondly at Debbie and Lisa next to Alec and felt a sudden dejection at the realization that there was every chance he would not live to see them grow up. They would manage without him. Grandfathers were dispensable. He dismissed the thought and with it the desolation. If it was the will of the Almighty . . .

At the signal from *"nebbech"* Pinkus, whose perambulations he had been watching from the corner of his eye, Sydney, together with Moshe Pearlman, stood up and opened the low door of the box. It was time for the seven circuits. Some said the circuits corresponded to Abraham, Isaac, Jacob, Moses, Aaron, Joseph and David, one for each; some, to the seven heavens; yet others, to the circumvention of Jericho at the time of Joshua. Whatever its origins, the custom on this day was to circle the synagogue seven times carrying all the Scrolls of the Law.

By the time Sydney reached the reading desk, experiencing some difficulty with the steps that led up to the platform, the Ark was opened, revealing in brilliant light its cache of silver-adorned scrolls. Facing them, he inclined his head briefly, and the handing out began.

To Rabbi Magnus was given the largest and most important-looking scroll, and after him came the Cantor. The Bridegroom of the Law and the Bridegroom of the Beginning took careful hold of the next in size—they were not lightweight—and hoisted them into comfortable positions on their left shoulders. After them it was the turn of the members of the Board of Management, who were waiting patiently, then the senior congregants, and so it went on until the humblest and the smallest *Sefer Torah* was allotted and the Ark was empty.

At a sign from Rabbi Magnus, the choirmaster in the curtained gallery above the Ark flipped his tuning fork and the choir struck up. One by one, with their precious burdens, the scroll carriers stepped down into the main body of the synagogue. Like the Pied Piper of Hamelin, they were joined on their way by the children with their flags, who emerged from the pews, propelled by encouraging pushes from their fathers. Swaying from side to side, the ragged procession made its way down the aisle. The first circuit had begun.

Looking down from the gallery upon the disarray, listening to the discord with its undertones of chatter and the intermittent cries of small children, Rachel felt more disenchanted with the scene than usual. Next to her she was aware that her mother, smiling, was following every step, every movement of her father with proud eyes. It seemed a lifetime ago that she had herself been one of those small children. Dressed in her uncomfortable best, she had made the circuits with Josh, holding tightly to his hand and waiting eagerly for the end of the morning and the sweets. Josh, she remembered, had, for the benefit of the ladies distributing them, invariably invented a small brother, in some years afflicted with measles and in others with mumps, according to his imagination, and invariably had come away with double rations.

The Rejoicing of the Law. According to Solly, it was among the first laws of the world, and throughout the ages the greatest of legislators had borrowed freely from it; it was essentially just, free and humane. The ancient and tribal rites being performed beneath her seemed to denigrate, by their undignified disorder, anything that the religion might have to offer. She felt no pride in the shambles, the cacophony.

The seven circuits, accompanied by the chanting, proceeded. She thought she would die of boredom as the scrolls were transferred slowly, tediously to other shoulders at the end of each lap in the interests of democracy. She switched off, as she had learned to do when she was into meditation; it was the only way to endure the long morning. In so doing she missed the high spot of her father's day when he was called to the reading of the final chapters of the Law in his capacity as its Bridegroom.

She stood up and sat down mechanically in the appropriate places and may even have exchanged words with her mother, with Carol. She came to only as Moshe Pearlman was summoned to the reading desk and the recitation started of the verses of the new scroll. The first words of Genesis winged round the synagogue, and skimmed the stained-glass windows, unifying the congregation:

In the beginning
God created the heaven and the earth.

To Rachel, it was the Primal Scream.

17

"YOU'VE BEEN TAKING A GIRL OUT," Dolly said. She had chosen her moment and taken him unawares. Beatty had passed the news on more than three weeks ago, and Dolly had been watching Norman ever since. Not that Beatty had meant to interfere. She said so. She had merely called in to see Dolly on her way home from shopping in Golders Green where she had been trying to buy a pair of shoes.

The two of them had sat in the kitchen discussing Dolly's back, to which Beatty was unusually sympathetic, listening with patience to the latest blow-by-blow account of its vagaries as if it were a soap opera. When her sister seemed to have exhausted all the possibilities of the offending portion of her anatomy and had started to drink her coffee, by now cold, Beatty said, "Went out to eat last night. New place in Borehamwood."

"Lucky," Dolly said. "I never get out for a meal. My back . . ."

"With Freda and Harry," Beatty continued quickly. "They had some very nice fish. Sole *bonne femme* I asked for but I finished up . . ."

"I can't afford sole," Dolly said. "It's the only fish I'd give you a thank-you for . . ."

"You'll never guess who I saw there."

"Where?" Dolly had got sidetracked by the sole.

"Borehamwood," Beatty said. "They were sitting in a corner behind a potted plant, one of those Swiss cheese plants . . ."

"I'll put the kettle on," Dolly said, bored. "My cup was stone-cold."

She stood up, a pained look on her face and a hand on her back.

"Norman!" Beatty said, as if she were pulling a rabbit out of a hat.

"What about Norman?" Dolly stood up straight, attentive now, holding her cup with two hands.

"Behind the Swiss cheese plant," Beatty said, patiently.

"You talk in riddles, Beatty," Dolly said.

"If you listened for a minute, you'd hear what I'm telling you. Norman was in the corner. We saw him, all four of us. Ask the others if you don't believe me."

"Norman doesn't eat in restaurants. He comes home."

Beatty shrugged. "Maybe he's got a twin."

"Last night did you say?" Dolly was incredulous.

Beatty nodded.

He had been showing the Arab prince a house in Winnington Road!

"He wasn't alone," Beatty said, turning the screw.

Dolly relaxed. He must have taken the prince out to dinner to clinch the deal.

"With a girl!" Beatty played her trump.

Dolly sat down again, the coffee forgotten.

"What do you mean a girl?"

"What do you mean what do I mean? A girl's a girl. Not that she was such a girl anyway, thirty, thirty-five, big-busted . . ."

Dolly stared at her.

"He never saw us," Beatty said. "Too busy!"

Dolly didn't move.

"I'll put the kettle on for you," Beatty said as if butter wouldn't melt in her mouth. "Then I must be going. It's early closing and I've got a pair of kippers for Leon's lunch."

"What were they doing?" Dolly said.

"Having dinner as far as I know. He's entitled to a night out, isn't he?" she asked innocently, shrugging into her tweed coat with the vast checks. "There's nothing wrong in having dinner."

"He has dinner here. With me."

"Maybe he wanted a change. I wouldn't have mentioned it if I thought you were going to get all excited . . ."

"Who said I'm excited . . . ?"

"I just thought . . . anyway, never mind, forget it!"

"A Jewish girl?"

"I told you, they were behind the Swiss cheese plant.

150

Why don't you ask Norman?" She kissed Dolly. "Look after yourself. Don't come to the door; it's very raw outside."

That was three weeks ago. Dolly had bided her time, watching Norman like a cat a mouse, awaiting the moment when she would pounce. In the second week there were two nights he didn't come for dinner. In the third week, on Monday, it was after midnight. In the morning when she put his shirt into soak, there was mauve lipstick on the collar. She waited until Friday night when she'd lit the candles and he'd made *Kiddush* for her. He wouldn't lie over the candles.

"You look tired, Norman," she said when she'd served the soup.

He stretched. "Busy week!"

"It's all that night work."

"Property boom," he said. "They're going mad for it."

"You've been taking a girl out!"

The soup ran off Norman's spoon in a golden rivulet as it stopped halfway to his mouth.

"Now look what you've done over the clean cloth!"

"What are you talking about?"

"You've no need to lie to me, Norman. Beatty told me. She saw you. So did Freda and Harry and Leon. In Borehamwood. Having dinner. The night you told me all that tommyrot about the Arab prince. It's not as if I mind you taking a girl out, although Beatty said she's not such a girl, I don't even mind washing all that filthy lipstick off your collars. It's the lying upsets me and you know if I get aggravated it starts my back off. You've got your own life to lead. I don't know why you have to tell me a pack of lies."

Norman sighed. They had been so careful. He would ring Beatty's neck. He put down his spoon. His appetite had gone. He waited for the inquisition.

"What's her name?"

"Della."

151

"Jewish?"

He nodded.

"At least that's something. Better than the last one. What's she do?"

He told her about Della before she destroyed the magic of the last three weeks. When he'd finished, she said, "God knows why you have to go sneaking off like that. It's not like you haven't got a perfectly respectable home to bring her to. Unless of course you're ashamed of her?"

"She's the nicest person I've ever met," Norman said, stung into defense.

"Well, perhaps I'll have the honour of meeting her myself," Dolly said. "I suppose she does know you've got a mother?"

"I don't want to talk about it anymore," Norman said, his face white.

"Perhaps it's me you're ashamed of."

He raised his voice. "I said I don't want to talk about it!"

"There's no need to shout," Dolly said. "I don't think this girl's a very good influence." She picked up the plates and in the kitchen poured the remains of Norman's soup down the sink.

Josh took Sarah to dinner with Uncle Juda. It was Friday night.

When the Filipino houseboy let them in, he was explaining to her the significance of the metal tube, the size of a cigarette, affixed on the right-hand side of the door.

"A *mezuzah*," he said. "You'll find one on every Jewish house. It's a symbol of God's presence and a sanctification of the home. Inside it there's a piece of parchment on which is written the first two paragraphs of one of our special prayers."

"Where's yours?" Sarah said.

Josh did not reply. His father had brought him a *mezuzah*

back from Israel, but he had never got round to putting it up.

In the drawing room the picture lights illuminated a fairy-tale collection of paintings. Uncle Juda was smoking a cigar, Leonora, busy with her needlepoint. Cushions round the room testified to her industry. Her Welsh Corgi slept at her feet.

"Josh has always had impeccable taste," Juda said, greeting Sarah.

He had an eye for the ladies. Josh could see that he approved of Sarah by the way he contracted the muscles of the spare tire which rolled gently over his initialled belt.

The room was furnished with period chairs with matching footstools, Chinese leaf screens, inlaid tables and china cabinets all neatly in place on the Aubusson. There were arrangements of flowers that looked unreal but were not, and above the overmantel, a portrait in oils of Leonora. Josh always felt he was in a museum.

His Uncle Juda had started selling "antiques" from a market stall when he came out of the army. After that he had gone on to dealing in property, and his father sometimes hinted he had not been scrupulously honest. When he had made his fortune, in single-minded pursuit of which he worked day and night, he married Leonora, and together they travelled the world in search of the rare and the beautiful. What he did with the wealth he had amassed no one in the family knew. "Well, he can't take it with him," his mother was apt to remark when Juda gave less than anybody for one of her good causes or refused to support a play or a concert. He was strange in many ways, both he and Leonora, but Josh had always liked his uncle and aunt and valued their opinion.

"How's your father?" Juda had the sherry decanter in his hand and had half-filled Josh's glass. "No more blood pressure?"

153

He didn't wait for Josh to reply. "Probably too much fasting." He dismissed the subject. He could not tolerate illness.

"Working hard?" He handed Josh the glass. "No good, a one-man business." He always said it. "You don't want to go bending over that chair looking into people's mouths five days a week for the rest of your life. I tried to get your father into property, when he was a young man. Wouldn't hear of it. Look at him now, *shlepping* away in that lousy office day after day. 'The apple doesn't fall far from the tree,'" he said in Yiddish.

From the corner of his eye Josh could see Sarah in conversation with Leonora.

"You serious about this girl?" Juda said.

Josh nodded.

"Your father's not going to like it." He always came straight to the point. "Seems a nice girl. Different class altogether from that Paula. Never did take to her. What are you going to do?"

"Get married."

"Didn't think you had it in you. Rachel now . . . Want me to have a word with Sydney?"

"It wouldn't make the slightest difference."

"Obstinate cuss. Always has been. Let me know if there's anything I can do."

When they went in to dinner, Juda stubbed out his cigar, carefully, so that he could relight it the following evening. Abstention from smoking was one of his two concessions to the Sabbath, that and the ritual of Friday night.

The table, beneath the Venetian chandelier, could have seated fourteen. Five places were laid on the white, drawn-thread cloth. The Sabbath candles were George III. They were already lit but would not be blessed by Leonora, who acquiesced but did not participate in the proceedings.

154

Vanessa, straight from the beauty parlour, joined them for dinner.

Sarah sat on Juda's right hand with Josh next to her. There was an oasis of tablecloth between them.

Josh signalled to her to stand up for the Benediction and put his skullcap on his head.

Juda poured wine into the silver cup and recited the blessings on the inauguration of the Sabbath. Josh did not look at Sarah, who stood behind her chair, holding onto it, her head bowed.

When he had finished, Juda removed the embroidered cover from the two Sabbath loaves and broke off a piece, which he divided into smaller pieces, sprinkling each with salt. He handed one to Sarah, who looked at Josh.

"The blessing," he said, "over bread."

". . . *ha motzi lechem min ha-aretz*," Juda said and, removing his skullcap, sat down.

The thin soup did nothing to dispel the chill of the high-ceilinged room. Juda was careful with the heating and rationalized his frugality by declaring that too high a temperature was not good for the furniture and the paintings.

The plates were cleared, as if by magic. Josh knew that Leonora had a bell beneath the table near her foot.

Fried fish, garnished with parsley and lemon quarters, was brought in on a silver platter.

When they were all served and Leonora had started, Sarah picked up her knife and fork. Almost immediately she put them down again. She leaned over to Josh in horror.

"My fish is cold!" she whispered.

Josh smiled. "It's supposed to be."

She eyed it uncertainly and began again.

When he had eaten all that he was able to with his knife and fork, Juda picked up the remains of his fish with his fingers and sucked the sweet flesh from the bone. He had no pretensions. He surrounded himself with the visible

155

fruits of his success largely for the benefit of Leonora, but he never forgot that where he had been raised there was no dining room and the large family had eaten at the table in the kitchen, the focal point of the house, on which his mother cooked and round which they sat to eat and to talk and to work and to pray.

They had syllabub with tiny triangles of angelica on top from eighteenth-century jelly glasses. Afterwards Juda put on his skullcap again and opened the prayerbook. The Filipino, in his white jacket, retired discreetly.

When Juda started to sing in his rich baritone—he had been in the synagogue choir as a boy—Sarah looked at Josh.

"Your little hat!" she whispered.

He took it out of his pocket. Only he and Juda recited the prayers. Leonora sat impassively at the head of the table with her manicured hands folded. Vanessa looked bored and kept glancing at the face of her watch, which was so tiny that she had to squint.

Juda had talked to Sarah throughout dinner, assessing her, Josh knew, like some newfound commode, measuring her against the yardstick of his experience.

On the way back to the drawing room, where the coffee was waiting on a silver tray, he said to Josh, "I wish I was twenty years younger." It was his blessing.

He sat at one end of the room watching the television set, which was concealed in a drum-fronted chest, and Josh and Sarah talked to Leonora against the sudden spurts of canned laughter. Vanessa had gone out.

When it was time to leave, Leonora took him aside.

"She's quite charming," she said. "Bring her to see us again."

It was the nearest he would get to family approval.

In the car Sarah said, "I don't think I could ever be Jewish."

156

"All those prayers?"

Sarah laughed. "No," she said, "the cold fish!"

18

DELLA AND DOLLY sat opposite each other in the faded armchairs in Dolly's front room while Norman poured the tea.

"Norman has to do everything for me," Dolly said, "because of my back. I couldn't manage without him."

"He told me you suffer with your back, Mrs. Glicksman . . ." Della said.

"Suffer with it! You don't know the half of it. Some days it's as much as I can do to . . ."

Norman handed the tea round to the accompaniment of Dolly's monologue. He had warned Della. She seemed to be listening intently to the diatribe.

"You're a very courageous woman," Della said when the flow of complaints had stopped. "Pain in the back can be most distressing . . ."

Dolly stared at her. Nobody had ever called her courageous, had never commiserated. She looked with suspicion at Della. There was only concern on the face she had been prepared to dislike from the first. She had to admit it was a kind face despite the unfortunate mauve lipstick.

". . . there are some new analgesics on the market," Della was saying. "I can't remember what they're called but if you like I could inquire."

"I don't go out much," Dolly said, "not in the winter. Norman would have to get them."

"I'll find out the name," Della said. "You never know till you try."

Slightly mollified, Dolly handed the cookies to the alien presence Norman had introduced into the home.

"I always used to make my own," Dolly said, "but I can't stand in the kitchen anymore . . ."

"I expect you're a jolly good cook," Della said. "I can hardly boil an egg. I live with my parents and my mother does it all."

Dolly sniffed, revising her opinion.

"They both alive then?"

"Yes."

"Lucky. I'm a widow. My poor husband, Norman's father that was, was unfortunately killed in an accident." She realized she had found a receptive listener.

Norman watched Della with pride. She was the best thing that had ever happened to him. Each day his first waking thought was gratitude for his good fortune. Their problem at the moment was that in the evenings they had nowhere to go where they could be alone. They could not spend their lives in the cinema; the car was not private and was unsatisfactory for what they had in mind. It was a problem that for both their sakes would soon have to be resolved. Between Della's desk and his own in the office stretched a powerful and magnetic line across which they sent unobserved and loving communications. He found it increasingly hard to keep his mind on his work.

"I expect your father's retired," Dolly said.

Della laughed. "Not at all. He's a collector for the Welfare Board. He likes the exercise. He'll keep on until he drops."

"Door to door?" Dolly said, horrified.

"That's right."

A charity collector. What good was she going to be to Norman?

When Della had gone (she wouldn't let Norman take her home), Norman braced himself and returned to the front room. He collected the tea things in silence, waiting for the first salvo.

"Quite a kind girl," Dolly said, which for her was praise indeed. "Getting on a bit though, isn't she?"

You could hardly call her a girl was what Beatty had said.

"In what way?" Norman brushed imaginary crumbs from the sofa.

"Been round a bit. What I mean is . . ."

"Yes?" He picked up the tray.

"She looks the sort of girl who knows a thing or two!"

"I expect she does." He deliberately misunderstood her.

"Could do with losing a couple of pounds. I'm surprised she doesn't fall flat on her face. I wonder why she never got married. You mustn't let her throw herself at you, Norman. I recognize that sort, it's a question of anything in trousers . . ."

"I'll wash these things up," Norman said, striving to contain himself, "then I'm going out for a walk."

"How long are you going to be?" Dolly said, surprised.

"Not very long." Only until he cooled down.

"Then we'll watch the television," Dolly said, dismissing Della from her mind, "just the two of us."

"I think I've redeemed myself," Rachel said, "after sitting in *shul* for that nonsense with the apples and the flags. The bit with the scrolls is enough to put anyone off for life."

"It depends whether you're on the inside or the outside," Solly said.

"I know where I am. What's in that tin?" She pointed to Solly's shelf.

"Fruitcake."

Rachel opened it. "Can I have a bit?" She helped herself. "My mother made it."

"I can taste the love. Is Miriam going to spoil you?"

"I daresay."

"Tell me how it feels from the inside. How you can tolerate all that repetition?"

Solly took a piece of the fruitcake, giving Rachel the almonds from the top.

"Imagine a carriage in a tube train . . ." he said.

"What line?"

". . . Circle. It's empty except for a fellow with his arm round his girl and the guy opposite. The fellow says, 'I love you.' The girl replies, 'I love you.' They say it a million times between Mansion House and Notting Hill Gate. Nothing else. Just 'I love you' over and over again, till the guy sitting opposite is ready to scream; he's never heard such boring, tedious nonsense.

"For the fellow and his girl, though, it's different. What they have to say to each other is stimulating, full of meaning which is incomprehensible to the onlooker because he doesn't have their special knowledge of the situation, their involvement with each other, their unquestioning love. The guy can't wait for his station to come up so that he can get out. The couple would be happy going round and round on the Circle line repeating the same phrases for ever. It's a matter of perspective."

Rachel lifted her chin and poured the remaining crumbs from her palm into her open mouth.

"Solly boy, your mother makes a good fruitcake. It's all right for you; you're the one with the girl. You try being the guy on the other seat for a bit. I'd flip my lid before Embankment. I could only stay in *shul* at all by switching off. I completely missed the big moment when my father was called up."

160

"No one asked you to go."

"Do they have to ask? Do they have to keep telling me to find a nice Jewish doctor like my sister and settle down? Every time I look at Carol, whose idea of heaven is living near to the kosher butcher, I feel sick. They really think my goal in life should be to spend all my waking hours doing housework, looking after small children, going to *shul*, making fruitcake." She looked at Solly.

"I didn't say a word," Solly said.

"I'll do things now," Rachel said. "For my father. Because he may not have long to live. That's how they get you, you know, the whole time. He knows about his tumour."

"I thought you weren't going to tell him."

"We haven't. Everyone's sticking to the 'blood pressure' bit like mad. But I know that he knows and he knows I know he knows. We've always been close."

"Maybe he'd like to discuss it with you. Perhaps it would be a relief?"

Rachel shook her head.

"You know the name of the game. I have to hide my feelings about religion, Josh has to hide Sarah, Carol has to hide that she's fighting with Alec, all so that they won't be 'aggravated.' " She looked at her watch. "And if I don't go and meet Patrick, there'll be a bit of 'aggro' there. It's a wonder you get any work done at all with me around."

"Give Patrick my best."

Solly put the cake tin back on his shelf and opened the door for her.

As she passed he caught the fresh tang of her body, and she felt the brush of his bare arm, below his rolled-up shirtsleeve, against hers.

When she was outside, she turned and asked in a voice that sounded not quite natural to her own ears, "There aren't any more Festival things before Passover, are there?"

"You don't know?" Solly said. He held her gaze until she lowered her lids.

"If I did I've forgotten."

"Only *Chanukkah.*"

"I don't mind that. It doesn't count and we get presents. When is it?"

"The week before your Christmas."

"Touché," Rachel said softly. "Tell your mother to make another fruitcake!"

The weakness in Sydney's leg grew worse. Kitty bought him a cane. From time to time he saw Dr. Ballantyne. He went alone.

"There seem to be no changes, other than the leg," Dr. Ballantyne said. "I think we can say you are in a period of remission."

Sydney put a hand to his head.

"Perhaps it's stopped growing."

Dr. Ballantyne looked at him, impeccable in his white shirt and City suit. Only the circles beneath his eyes spoke of the headaches and of the pain-killers.

"Nothing is impossible."

"You have to trust the Almighty," Sydney said. "Doctors! What do they know?"

He looked at Dr. Ballantyne, realizing what he had said. "No offense . . ."

"Don't worry," Dr. Ballantyne said. "You're probably absolutely right. I wish I had your faith."

"It's not exclusive," Sydney said.

Dr. Ballantyne wrote up his notes. "I'll see you again in January. You can enjoy your Christmas."

"We don't celebrate Christmas," Sydney said. "We have *Chanukkah.* It's a family festival. We light eight lights, one each day, in a special candlestick. They bring a message of hope to all those in despair."

162

From his face Dr. Ballantyne could see that it did not occur to Sydney to count himself among them. Over the weeks he had come to respect the valour, the fortitude of this patient, to learn with interest something of the religious beliefs which upheld him. He watched Sydney manipulate himself out of the chair, and went down with him in the lift, walked with him along the narrow corridor.

Outside it was snowing, the first snow of the winter. It drifted unhurriedly onto the cars and the people in soft, fat flakes.

When Sydney got back to the office, Cohen was waiting. He watched as Sydney limped in with his cane.

"What's the matter?" Cohen said, surprised.

"I've got blood pressure," Sydney said.

"In your leg?"

"It affects it."

"I'm sorry. I didn't know. You got pills?"

"Plenty."

"All those stairs can't be good for you. Not thinking of retiring?"

"What would I do sitting round at home?"

There was no answer. "I came to thank you," Cohen said. "We've got the downstairs toilet. My wife doesn't know herself."

"My pleasure. What's with the boy?"

Cohen's face closed.

"It's his birthday tomorrow," he said bitterly. "Twenty-one years old. They only give him a few weeks."

"You managing?"

Cohen knew he meant the heroin.

"The price has gone down. By half. It comes in from Iran." He shrugged his shoulders. *"Metzia* for the kids!" He opened his case and Sydney ordered a gross of paper-

163

weights and some corncob holders for the dying boy. He was running the business down.

"Look after yourself," Cohen said when he was leaving. "Maybe you should see someone else. I'm not a doctor but I never heard of anyone having a bad leg from blood pressure."

As the snow from his shoes melted into a puddle under his desk, Sydney took out his thoughts and examined them. Having arranged for the disposal of his worldly goods to the best of his ability and fully aware of his physical condition, he felt that he was living on borrowed time. At the beginning of each day, when he woke up and saw the light coming through the window, he gave thanks to the Almighty; at the end of each, he thanked Him again. Sometimes he had the sensation that he was in the world but not of it; problems, at business and with the family, while no less real, had assumed less importance; he had distanced himself from many day-to-day issues.

He had taken Rabbi Magnus into his confidence, and they had had many discussions about why, when life was so sweet and desirable, one was in constant danger of having it summarily taken away. The problem was not new. The first man and woman had stood outside the barred gates of Paradise wondering why they had been given what they were doomed to lose; even the Psalmists, who came so near to God, had been similarly torn with doubt, overwhelmed at times by despondency. He and the Rabbi spoke of how nothing in the material world could be destroyed, however fragile; that matter could only change form. By the same token, there would inevitably be a cessation of life as it was known—a change and a passing but no death for the soul. The mechanics of the transformation Sydney was prepared to leave to God. He found it difficult to imagine a place where the needs of the body no longer existed; where there was no sitting, standing, sleeping, no death, distress or

164

laughter. The prospect did not frighten him. Sometimes when his headaches were bad, he quite looked forward to it.

He felt sorry for Kitty. He had tried on a few occasions to let her know that he had no illusions about his condition. She would not have it. With a mental shrug he decided that if that was what she wanted he was content. He understood that it was her way of facing the future, her means of coping. They loved each other with a fierce loyalty, but often hid the tenderness they felt behind a jocular and admonishing facade. Sometimes when he woke in the morning, he found Kitty's face close to his, her eyes, which he remembered when they had not been set in a fine cobweb of lines, clouded with anxiety.

"What are you looking at?"

"Looking to see how ugly you are!"

Love spoke a hundred different languages.

19

CAROL, SIX MONTHS PREGNANT, sat dejectedly cleaning her eight-branched candlestick. Tears, now never very far away, were running down her face. The situation between herself and Alec had gone from bad to worse. The point of deadlock had been reached. Deaf to all her protests, he had gone ahead with the house in Godalming, which she had resolutely refused even to see. The arrangements for the transfer of his practice had been made. In vain she had pleaded. The new baby would be only a couple of months old; her father was sick and she wanted to be near him; Passover, with its family *Seder* nights, fell in April; she was happy where she was. Excuses, Alec said. It was true. She had no intention of moving, certainly not to the country. If he insisted on going ahead, he would go alone. It was as simple as that.

She had enlisted the help of her mother, who summoned Alec to the flat one morning.

"How can you walk out on her?" Kitty said.

"I'm not walking out, whatever Carol may say. I love her. You know I do. And the children. And you don't really think I want to be separated from my new baby? If you would only come and see the house, you and Carol, you'd be delighted. It's peaceful, there's space, the children can roam round . . ."

They sat with coffee at the kitchen table. Kitty put a hand on his arm. "Alec dear, I'm very fond of you; you know I am. Your poor mother's dead, God rest her soul, so I have to talk to you like a mother. There's nothing wrong with the country. I used to like a drive on a Sunday when Sydney was feeling better. Nobody enjoyed the countryside more especially if it was a nice day, only now the traffic's got so terrible you're better off at home. But it's not for you. It just isn't. You've got *Shabbos,* you've got Festivals . . ."

"We'd be changing our address, not our religion. And it's only Surrey. Anyone would think I wanted to take her to the North Pole."

"How about Hebrew classes for Debbie and Lisa?" Kitty said, ignoring him. "If it turns out a boy what about his *Bar Mitzvah?*"

"That's in thirteen years! He's not even born yet. Anyway, we don't know it's going to be a boy."

"Thirteen years isn't such a long time. You realize that as you get older. You have to think of all these things. Listen to me, Alec. I'm a bit older and a bit wiser. It's not for Carol. She wouldn't be happy in the country. And what do you know about the country?"

"I know I'm going to like it, and Carol would get used to it. And if she didn't after a fair trial, I'd be willing to discuss coming back."

Kitty decided it was time for her trump card.

"Her father hasn't got very long."

Alec covered her hand with his. "You know how I feel about Dad. It isn't really very far away, you know."

"It's not the same as round the corner."

Alec was silent. He could not refute the statement, which was one of the objects of the exercise.

"Don't be obstinate, Alec," Kitty said. "She won't go with you."

"She would if you told her to."

"I'm not interfering. It's Carol's life. She must please herself."

"I'm not leaving her," Alec said. "Just Swiss Cottage."

"What's wrong with Swiss Cottage?"

Alec looked at his watch. He had calls to make. This was not the time or the place or the person to whom he could say it wasn't just Swiss Cottage but Carol's frigidity, and that in a different environment where they had more room to live, to breathe, free from the parental eye, where he would have to work less hard, would have more time for Carol, for the children . . .

". . . so be a good boy," Kitty was saying. "You don't want Carol to break her father's heart."

The conversation had been useless. Everything had been useless. Each day Carol expected him to relent and each day he made some practical move that entrenched him more firmly along the road to Godalming. By day they scarcely spoke. At night Carol refused even to lie close to him unless he agreed to drop his crazy ideas. They slept on opposite sides of the bed.

Debbie was watching, her face concerned.

"I'm not crying," Carol said, wiping her eyes on a piece of papertowel. "It's the polish. I'm getting the *menorah* ready for *Chanukkah,* making it nice and shiny."

"It's not a *menorah,* it's a *hanukkiah,"* Lisa said. "We've got one at school and I'm making you one out of cardboard for a present. I'm painting it."

"I thought it was supposed to be a secret," Debbie said. Lisa looked crestfallen.

"I didn't really hear," Carol said. "What would you like me to buy you for *Chanukkah?"*

"A piano," Debbie said.

Carol smiled. "You know we haven't any room. We all have to squash up a bit to make room for the new baby."

"Daddy's going to buy me one when we move to the country."

Carol looked at her.

"And I'm going to have a pony!" Lisa said.

Josh bought two dolls for his nieces. A dark-haired one for Debbie, a blond for Lisa.

They were sitting on the piano.

"They're for *Chanukkah* . . ." he told Sarah.

"Not another one!"

"Just a minor Festival . . . a bit like Christmas. We light candles, one each night in celebration of the rededication of the Temple after the Syrians were defeated under Judah Maccabeus. We all go home for the last night, when all the candles are lit and the children get presents."

"It sounds lovely," Sarah said. "I wish I could come."

The floor in Kitty's living room was littered with toys and with games. On the last night of *Chanukkah* she made one of her teas. Each year Sydney gave the children a traditional spinning top, with which they played forfeits, a silver coin

168

and a carefully chosen gift. It was hoped that in this way they would not feel too left out by the frenetic preparations for Christmas which they saw going on round them.

Full length on the floor, Robert, his chin in his hands, read his new comic book and Lisa and Debbie played with their dolls.

On the sofa Carol held her arm out for Vanessa to admire her *Chanukkah* present from Alec. It was a bracelet of amethysts, her birthstone, and had been chosen with love.

Kitty picked her way over the bodies, collecting the abandoned wrapping paper.

Sydney sat in his chair, watching them contentedly although the vision in one eye was not as good as it had been and his headache was bad. Surrounded by his family, he thought with affection of the simple home ceremony he was soon to perform, perpetuating the splendid loyalty of the Maccabees. He liked to recall how, by their unyielding demands for right conduct and moral living, they had arrested the paralyzing influences of their day; how their souls, shining like beacons, had flooded the dark valley of the years with their blaze of glory, which would be perpetuated by the candles he was soon to light.

"I can see three stars," Kitty said, pulling aside the curtain, "and the children are getting tired."

The baby, Jeremy, began to cry as if in confirmation. Beatty took him from Leon's lap.

The branched candlestick with its full complement of coloured candles stood ready on the table.

Sydney picked up his cane.

"Uncle Sydney's going to light the candles," Beatty said, pulling at Robert.

"Give me the baby a minute," Mirrie said, taking him from her, feeling the warmth of him. There was not much warmth in her life.

The family grouped round, the men wearing skullcaps.

169

Robert lit the first attendant candle, then gave it to Lisa, who, with her hand held by Debbie for safety, lit the others with its flame. Red and green and blue and yellow. She went along the row of dead, pale wicks until their flickering orange haloes proudly proclaimed the miracle of the Temple lights which burned for eight days, although there was only sufficient oil for one.

Sydney recited the Benedictions; then, inviting those who loved him and whom he loved to join him, he led the singing of the *Chanukkah* melody known to Jews the world over. They all participated with varying degrees of tunefulness, making up in enthusiasm for what they lacked in harmony.

After the second of the five stanzas, Rachel, who had been standing by the door, left the room, not because she considered the ceremony, with its eight-branched candlestick, a relic of early pagan rites, but because the sight of her father singing so lustily and with such obvious enjoyment reminded her that it was very likely the last year he would live to do so. She could not bear to watch him.

20

"TURN IT AND TURN IT AGAIN," the Sages said, "for everything is contained in the *Torah.*"

Every Monday throughout the winter, no matter what the weather or the difficulty he was having in walking, Sydney attended, as he had for years, Rabbi Magnus's discussion group. Together with other synagogue members and anyone else who was interested, they pondered the *Talmud,* the repository of thousands of years of wisdom, which, with its unique blend of philosophy and logic, history and science, Law and legend, was Judaism's most important book. At various times throughout the ages, it had been reviled, slandered and consigned to the flames by the enemies of his people, who were well aware that without its perusal there would be little chance of survival.

Sydney did not find it incongruous that he should spend some of the precious time that remained to him in study. "It is not our business to finish the work," the *Talmud* itself said, "but neither must we desist from carrying it out." Enjoying the elucidation and revelling in the debate, Sydney had no intention of giving up his Monday nights. No matter how disinclined he felt to make the journey from home to synagogue, he knew that at the end of the evening he would return home stimulated and inspired. Often, meditating upon what he had learned and attempting to incorporate it into the daily conduct of his life, he was able to forget, for long periods at a time, the bleak prospect of his future.

The discussions were held in the Simon Baron Hall, where the heating was insufficient in the interests of economy and the wooden folding chairs formed an untidy semicircle on the dusty floor. Sydney greeted a few of the regulars who had already arrived. Ignoring their glances of compassion for his deteriorating physical condition, he put his hands in the pockets of his overcoat and waited for Rabbi Magnus.

While he waited, he considered the precious, and most probably short, span of life that remained to him and the contingency plans he had been busily putting into action. The material side of his affairs had been dealt with. He had had long meetings with his solicitor and his accountant, and was satisfied that when his moment came to depart the earth, everything would be left in order. Josh, whom he had appointed his executor, should not find his task too difficult. It was now the question of the *Kaddish* which concerned him. He had tried to tackle Kitty on the subject.

"If I were to die," he'd said to her, attempting to sound casual, "do you think Josh would say *Kaddish* for me?"

"Don't talk about such things," Kitty said with more lightheartedness than she felt. "You're not an old man."

"I didn't say I was going to." He let her off the hook. "I said 'if.' "

"What made you think of such a thing?"

"I just wondered."

"Josh is a good boy."

"He doesn't like going to *shul* much."

"I'm more worried he doesn't settle down . . ." Kitty said, changing the subject and not allowing herself to be drawn.

He could not bring himself to tackle Josh directly.

Death itself did not alarm him, but he believed, albeit irrationally, that the daily recitation of the Memorial Prayer by his son for eleven months following his demise might redeem his soul from the torture of Gehenna. He was wondering, not for the first time, how to go about setting his mind at rest upon the subject, when his ruminations were interrupted by the arrival of the Rabbi.

Apologizing for his lateness, Rabbi Magnus handed out a pile of Xeroxed, Hebrew-printed sheets to those assembled, rubbed his hands, put on his glasses and dropped his eyes to the open book on the table before him.

"Two men are travelling in the desert. One has enough water to survive until he reaches civilization. If the water is divided between the two, both of them will die en route. What should they do?" Rabbi Magnus paused. The question, his audience knew, was rhetorical. He pointed a finger at them.

172

"The *Talmud* Sages argued the point extensively, but the conclusion that was accepted as *Halachah* . . ."

Losing himself in the problems of the relationship between justice and compromise and the question of the Law versus private moral considerations, Sydney forgot such minor preoccupations as the hardness of the chairs, the coldness of the hall, Josh and the *Kaddish,* and the changes that were taking place beneath his skull. He followed the text on his lap and concentrated on Rabbi Magnus.

There had been girls before but nobody like Della. Della was different. She didn't grumble at him like his mother for never doing enough, chastise him like Uncle Juda for his lack of initiative, tease him like Uncle Harry for his bachelor status, goad him like Auntie Beatty for being tied to his mother's apron strings. She simply accepted him as he was. It was unbelievable; he could not believe it.

Norman knew that as far as appearances were concerned, he was nothing to write home about. The occupants of the front desk at Bluestone and Blatt brought it home. They wore costly imported suits from shops he had never heard of, had their hair "styled" at unisex hairdressers, adorned themselves with gold jewellery and drove fancy cars about which they never seemed to tire of talking.

Because of other, more pressing commitments, Norman had not had a new suit for years; his barber would have died a thousand deaths rather than admit women to his tiny shop; his only item of personal adornment was his father's watch; and he could boast about his car only in that it was serviceable enough to take his mother out on a Sunday. He never ceased to be amazed that from all the men available Della had chosen him. She had taken him to meet her parents. They were cheerful and practical, like Della. They had little and wanted nothing. Her father pounded the pavements in all weathers, knocking at reluctantly opened doors, collecting for charity. Her mother, who took in small sewing jobs, made butter cake and tasty meals in her little kitchen for Della and her father when they came home, and she gossiped with her clients as she kneeled on the floor to pin their hemlines. Both she and her husband made a fuss over Norman. They were thrilled with him.

Dolly was a different story. He had his mother's disapproving face to contend with each time he went out with Della, every time he brought her home. Her back pained her in direct relationship to the number of occasions on which he and Della were together.

Happy as they had been in each other's company for the past months, Norman was filled with trepidation when he decided to ask Della to marry him. Although Della had made no secret of the fact that she was fond of him, he could not really accept the obvious. No one had ever loved him, wanted him, for himself. He had the inescapable feeling that as soon as he mentioned marriage, Della would laugh, run away, disappear into the air. He could not imagine anyone except his mother, about whom he had no illusions about his role, wanting to spend their lives with him. He was not, as Auntie Beatty was fond of saying, exactly a *"metziah";* but then perhaps Della was not looking for a bargain.

After the cinema he and Della usually had coffee at Lindy's at a table which they had made their own. Having made up his mind to propose, Norman had been in a state all day. He had felt sick, ill, elated, excited, apprehensive and despondent in turns. By five-thirty he had exhausted himself by the range of his emotions and had slept right through the film.

"Are you all right, Norman?" Della said, holding his hand across the pastries. "Not sickening for anything?"

She scraped up the last of her *mille-feuille.* The fork, when

174

she took it from her mouth, was smeared with mauve lipstick.

Norman nodded, unable to speak.

The waitresses were pushing in the chairs, resetting the tables, getting ready to close. He could not contemplate another day of suffering.

"Will you marry me?" he said.

He waited for the laughter, for the instant dismissal of so outrageous a proposal.

Della, who had been expecting the question for some time and had long ago made up her mind what she would answer, looked into his eyes.

"Will that be all?" the waitress asked, her pencil poised over her bill pad. She wanted to go home.

"Of course," Della said. She was talking to Norman.

"Pay at the desk." The waitress put the bill beneath the sugar bowl.

"Do you mean it?" Norman said. "I'm not exactly a 'metziah.'"

"Who told you that?" Della said. "You're wonderful, Norman, and I love you."

He could not believe it. He wanted to kiss Della, to hug the tired waitress. He grinned at the unsmiling cashier.

In the car he said, "Let's not wait too long. We're not chickens."

He took her happy face in his hands and leaned towards her, eager to make up for lost time.

After he got home, he decided to get the confrontation with Dolly over with there and then. "Della and I are going to get married," he said when he took Dolly up her night-time tea and a cooky from the fancy tin he had bought her for *Chanukkah.*

His mother picked up the biscuit and handed it to him with a shudder. "I can't eat that," she said. "I'd be up all night with indigestion!"

175

"Did you hear what I said?"

"I'm not deaf!"

"Well, haven't you anything to say?"

"I warned you," Dolly said. "I could see she was out to get you."

"I asked her to marry me," Norman said.

"I don't doubt it. She's been working on it hard enough. Take her away for the weekend, I'll manage; then you'll get it out of your system."

"I love her," Norman said, more angry than he had ever been with his mother.

Dolly looked round the room.

"I suppose I could move into your room and give the two of you this one, not that there'd be much space for my things."

"We shan't be living here," Norman said. "There's a new block of flats in Hendon . . ."

"What about me?"

"What about you?" High on love, Norman hadn't exactly dealt with the problem of his mother. He could only cope with one thing at a time.

"I'm not moving. Anyway I don't like flats."

Norman was silent. The flat had only one bedroom.

"I doubt if Della would want to live here," he said.

"I wouldn't mind if she wanted to change the curtains. I never liked them much. I bought them when everything was still on coupons."

"Is that all you've got to say?" Norman asked, as if he'd really expected anything else.

"Foolishness!" Dolly said. "For the life of me I can't see what you want to get married for."

176

21

THE TELEPHONE LINES BUZZED between Bushey Heath and Hyde Park, Edgware and Golders Green.

"Norman?" Beatty said. "Pull the other one!"

"What's wrong with Norman?" Dolly asked huffily.

Beatty was silent. They all thought of Norman as a good-natured, asexual, permanent unpaid housekeeper to Dolly.

"You still there?" Dolly said. She was in her element. Ringing up the family. Shocking them. For the moment it took her mind off the problem of her future. She had tried not to believe it, but Norman had bought Della a ruby ring on which he had spent, if you asked her opinion—which he hadn't—far too much, and booked the Rabbi and the synagogue and paid a deposit on the flat in Hendon.

"So who is she?" Beatty asked.

"How do you mean, who is she?"

"I mean, is she anyone?"

Dolly pretended not to understand. "Her name's Della. Della Berkowitz."

"Not the Berkowitzes used to . . . ?"

"No."

"What is she, young?"

"Thirty-three."

There was a silence.

"What's the matter with her she hasn't got married? Or has she?"

"No."

"Thirty-three," Beatty said. "Where did he meet her?"

"She works in his office."

"Good-looking?"

Dolly thought of the puddingy face, the mauve lipstick.

"Lovely, a lovely girl."

"You pleased?"

"Why shouldn't I be pleased?"

"When they getting married?" Beatty changed tack.

"After *Pesach.*"

"So soon?"

"What've they got to wait for?" Dolly said.

"*Mazel tov* anyway," Beatty said.

She put down the receiver and lifted it up again straight away to phone Freda.

The last weeks of Carol's pregnancy had not been happy. With a heavy heart, with her mother, she had sorted vests, washed diapers and blankets, which, although put away clean from Lisa, had the smell of storage. When she took them out of the dryer in the garage, Alec said, "In Godalming you could hang them in the garden."

He had gone ahead with his arrangements. He brought home parting gifts from patients grateful for his services, each one knocking another nail in the coffin of her despair.

"What are you going to do?" Kitty said.

"I don't know."

She did not.

"Daddy's the only person could make him see sense."

"It's too late," Carol said. "He won't change his mind now."

They had all had a go at Alec, persuaded by Kitty; Juda and Leon and Harry. He was polite but adamant. He was moving to Godalming. Carol could come if she chose.

"Good job the house is in your name," Kitty said, thinking unspoken thoughts of divorce. She was attaching new organdy frills to the old crib in Carol's nursery.

"Alec isn't like that," Carol said.

"How do you know? You didn't know he'd run off and leave you. When I think of those poor children . . . if only I could tell Daddy. I have to be strong for both of us. What with watching him go downhill every day and Josh's *shiksa* . . . I thought at least you and Alec . . ." She looked at Carol. "There's no point crying. You've cried enough. Don't think about it. Get the baby over first. Maybe when Alec sees it he'll alter his mind."

"It's too late, I told you." Carol sniffed.

"It's never too late. There's always a way . . . stop crying . . . it won't do the baby the least little bit of good."

When the pains came, in the middle of the night, she stretched out an arm to Alec on the far side of the bed.

They got dressed, bumping into each other with excitement as they moved round the room. Carol looked in on the sleeping children and the crib, freshly trimmed, and woke the girl who had come to look after Debbie and Lisa, telling her where they were going. At the door Carol stopped. "I'd better phone Mummy."

"If you do," Alec said, "she can take you to the hospital."

Carol hesitated, hugely swollen, her face white from sleep.

She opened her mouth to plead, but a contraction engulfed her body in its strong arms. She allowed Alec to lead her towards the car.

All night he sat with her, sponging her hot face, helping her with the breathing she had been taught to ease the pain, encouraging and consoling. It was like old times, the two of them together, waiting for the child, no stupid talk of the country. In the morning his hand was sore where she had clung to it.

Alec looked at his watch. It was time for his office hours. "Don't leave me," Carol said. She did not mean just now. Her eyes followed him as he went to the door.

"I've cancelled my appointments," he said when he came back.

She thanked him with her smile and got on with her labour, which was advancing to its final stage.

I love him, Carol thought between the pains. There was no world outside the room with its ghostly figures, coming and going, no Godalming; he had not mentioned it once.

Suddenly the discomfort she had been suffering all night was as nothing against the torment to which, open-mouthed, she now surrendered.

Morris Goldapple appeared in a green mask. The peace of the long night was shattered by lights and trolleys and cots, murmurs that she did not understand, and words of command. All eyes focussed on her nether regions, hands busy, pushing, pulling. The pressure became intolerable. She thought that she would die. Morris Goldapple's voice was soothing, calm with authority. He had seen it all a thousand times before. There was a sticky sensation of warmth between her legs. Somewhere a child cried. A bundle, warm and wet, with thin arms and legs, tiny fingers, lay on her stomach.

"It's a boy!" Alec said, his face beneath the flame-red hair illuminated by a radiant smile of pride.

Carol lay back.

"Daddy will be so pleased!"

Sydney dragged himself into the room, not letting Kitty help him. Carol, glowing with her achievement, waited in her clean sheets to present her son.

Kissing her, they held her close for the thing she had done.

180

Kitty delved into her handbag. "I didn't bring you flow-ers, darling. You'll get plenty; it drives the nurses mad."

She put a paper bag down on the locker. "I brought you a salmon sandwich. It'll do you more good."

They stood spellbound over the cradle.

"He looks exactly like old man Solomons," Kitty said.

Carol had thought that with his skin, which was almost white, and wisps of red hair he resembled Alec.

Sydney gazed at the tiny, perfect replica of humanity and was unable to speak. This scrap, this bundle, with the rov-ing eyes and the searching fingers represented his contri-bution to eternity, his footprint upon the sands of time. He looked out of the window so that no one would see the tears that had welled up in his eyes. It was the first time that he had cried. He knew Carol was waiting for him to speak.

"What are you going to call him?" To his relief his tears receded. This was Carol's moment.

"David. After Poppa Greenberg, God rest his soul," Kitty said, running a finger over the baby's downy head.

"How about Gideon?" Gideon Solomons was Sydney's late father. Sydney would go to synagogue and make a blessing for the child. He wondered if they would name the next one after him.

"Gideon David!" Kitty said. "Yes, Gideon David, that would be nice. Or David Gideon, whichever you like . . ."

They have decided, Carol thought. They have already decided.

"Alec wants to call him Mathew."

"Where is Alec?" It was the first time they had asked.

"Gone to fetch Debbie and Lisa."

"David Gideon Mathew," Kitty said. "What a mouthful! Tell him to bring the girls over to me. They can help me with the baking."

181

"His name's *Mathew*," Carol said, "and Alec's taking them to the zoo."

"And he that is eight days old shall be circumcised among you; every man child in your generations."

At eight o'clock, because of Alec's morning office hours, the family was assembled in Carol's living room at one end of which was the table laden with food, prepared by Kitty and Freda, for the feast after the ceremony that would initiate the infant, Mathew, into the "Covenant of Abraham."

"It always gives me the shivers," Beatty said. "I remember when Austin . . ."

Freda, next to her, did not want to hear.

She looked across the room to where Dolly sat in a chair with a reborn Norman on its arm.

"Give a *kik* at Norman," she said behind her hand to Beatty. "He looks like a young man again."

"Tell you the truth, I didn't think he had it in him," Beatty said.

"I don't think Dolly looks too well."

"When is she well?"

"No, seriously. Look how pale she is."

"A bit *shwach*," Beatty said. "All the excitement. And she's not used to getting up so early. I was in the middle of telling you about Austin's *bris*, I remember . . ."

Lennie Silver, who was performing the circumcision, looked at his watch, called for quiet and motioned everyone to stand.

They turned to the door. At the threshold Kitty stood with the child, in a long, frilled robe that had been her mother's, on a white pillow.

Sydney, who was the godfather and whose privilege it was to hold the baby during the ceremony, sat on a chair, waiting to receive him. His condition had not improved.

182

The concern of his family for his increasing disability tempered the joy of the occasion.

Josh took the child and set him on Sydney's knees as Alec looked on.

The men, in their skullcaps, clustered round.

The women, at the back, did not look.

They heard the loud murmurings of the prayers and suffered, each as if it were her own child, in the still moment when Lennie removed the baby's foreskin in a swift and practiced operation.

They heard the boy named with his Hebrew name, Matityahu Gideon David, and above his affronted cries, the blessing:

"Just as he has entered into the covenant, so may he enter into the Law, the marriage canopy and into good deeds."

They joined, thankful that it was over, in the final "Amen" and lifted their heads to see Josh drink wine from the cup and put a few drops from his finger into the open mouth of the indignant Mathew.

They made a path in their midst for Kitty, who advanced importantly to take Mathew to his mother, who waited upstairs, ready with the comforting breast.

"Kate's organizing a skiing party," Sarah said. "They've rented a chalet in Klosters. Would you like to go?"

They were having breakfast. She had moved in with Josh. Her great-grandmother's patchwork quilt was on his bed.

"Good idea," Josh said. "When?"

"First week in April."

"It's Passover," Josh said. "We have two special nights when we all get together at home."

"Couldn't you give this one a miss?"

"Not this year . . ."

"Your father?"

183

He nodded.

"Does everyone come, Auntie Mirrie, Auntie Beatty, Uncle Juda . . . ?"

Josh smiled. "Everyone. You go to Klosters."

She took his hand across the table.

"Not without you."

"When I look in the mirror," Josh said, "I sometimes wonder what it is you see in me."

Sarah stood up and put her cup in the sink.

"What's this holiday about?"

"Freedom and human rights," Josh said. "The liberation of the Jews from slavery under the Pharoahs. Each one of us regards himself as if it were he personally who had been set free."

Sarah sat down again, her hands beneath her chin, her morning face attentive.

He described for her the *Seder* table, with its ritual and its symbolism, round which they would all sit. He told her about the children's questions and the father's replies. Of the recitation of the story concerning the deliverance of the past and the Messianic hopes of the future. He tried to convey the sensations evoked by the wine-marked books that were passed down from generation to generation and recalled the blood-stained pages of Jewish history; the sense of timelessness as they gathered yet again round the *Seder* table. To his surprise he realized that he was trying to communicate to Sarah feelings which he had not known were inside himself. He was interrupted by the telephone.

When he heard his mother's voice, he knew it could not be good news, especially so early in the morning.

"It's my Auntie Dolly," he said when he sat down again. "She's had a stroke."

22

Although he blamed himself, Norman was not to blame. Sitting in the bedroom armchair, watching his mother as she slept, he was possessed by the unreasonable idea that had he not been out with Della at the time, it would not have happened. According to Dr. Levy, the stroke could not have been foreseen. Norman was not so sure.

Before leaving the office on their cinema night, he had telephoned his mother as usual.

"I'm not feeling at all well," Dolly said in answer to his inquiry. Her voice was heavy with accusation.

"Take a couple of your tablets," Norman said.

"The tablets are for my back. It's not my back."

"What's the matter then?"

"I don't know. I just don't feel well."

"What do you think it is?" Beside him Della was putting the cover on her typewriter.

"How should I know? I'm not a doctor."

"Do you want me to come home?" Norman asked, avoiding Della's gaze.

"I'll be all right," Dolly said. "You go out with your young lady. Enjoy yourselves."

"I won't be late," Norman said.

"Don't worry about me."

He had been looking forward to the film, but could not concentrate on it.

185

Afterwards Della said, "Shall we skip coffee?"

She was fastening her coat, bathed in the neon lights of the cinema from which wafted the odour of onions and hot dogs.

Norman stood transfixed on the pavement.

"I think you should go home," Della said gently. "You didn't enjoy the film. You kept fidgeting."

He touched her waist. "I want . . ."

"Go home, Norman. I'll see you tomorrow."

It would be another week before they could have the whole evening.

He found Dolly in a crumpled heap at the bottom of the stairs. Dr. Levy had come at once.

"That's what happens when you cry wolf," Beatty had said on the phone. "When you're really not well, no one takes a blind bit of notice!"

Luckily the stroke had been a mild one, but it left her with a useless right arm. She was to stay in bed for two weeks.

The district nurse came every day, someone from Home Help in the afternoons. Mrs. Goldberg next door let them in. Other than that, there was Norman. He was her right hand. In her left she had a cane with which she banged on the floor when he was wanted.

"I'm glad it happened to me and not to you," Dolly said as he brought her supper, helping her with it, then settling her down at night.

There was only one consolation.

She had forgotten about her back.

Carol usually assisted her mother in getting ready for Passover. Because of the new baby, Rachel came instead.

When Alec arrived to say good-bye, they were in the kitchen.

"What about *Seder* night . . . ?" Kitty said, making a last-ditch stand. ". . . I thought at least we'd all be together

186

for *Seder* night. As it is, Dolly won't be coming and I don't suppose Norman will want to leave her on her own."

"I'm sorry," Alec said.

"It's Carol you should feel sorry for . . ."

"I've done my best," Alec said. "She's made up her mind."

"If Sydney was well, believe me you wouldn't . . ."

"Let him go," Rachel said.

Alec kissed his mother-in-law with affection.

There were tears in Kitty's eyes.

"I don't know why he has to be so obstinate," she said to Rachel when he'd gone. "A lovely wife, two lovely girls, a new baby . . ."

"If you want me to help you with the things . . ." Rachel said, "I've got to go in a minute."

The task of preparing for Passover was a formidable one, but Kitty did not shrink from it. For the eight-day period all bread, cookies and any other product that might contain leaven had to be banished from the home; thin *matzos*, typifying the cakes baked hurriedly by the exiles from Egypt, would be eaten in their place.

For the past few weeks, when she had not been running over to Carol and the baby and, more recently, to Dolly, Kitty had washed curtains and carpets and paint, turned out cupboards and drawers and relined them with paper, prepared her kitchen in accordance with the specific injunctions.

Now she stood on the step stool in her pantry and took the groceries that Rachel handed up to her from the boxes that had been delivered. *Matzos* in their cartons covered with Hebrew writing; *matzo* meal, which she would use in place of flour for cooking; orange juice and chocolate that came from Israel; jam and marmalade and tea and coffee, whose production had been especially supervised.

Rachel looked round the kitchen at the old-fashioned

187

china that had been her grandmother's and came out once a year for Passover; at the mammoth black saucepan and the cheap cooking utensils that replaced for a week the ones in everyday use; at the cake tin, "Cries of London," that would shortly be filled with the traditional macaroons and coconut cookies; and at the blue and white cups in which the taste of the tea would take her back to the earliest days of her childhood. For as long as she could remember, Passover had meant the family *Seder* nights with their noisy songs and seemingly endless narrative. She looked at her mother's face, tired, streaked with dirt.

"Why do you do it?" She asked the same question of her every year.

Kitty did not answer; she was not well versed in the rationales of the *Torah*. She did it because her mother had done it and *her* mother before her. She did it because she felt intuitively that the security of Judaism rested upon her loyalty to preserve the traditions of the past, and because it was expected of her. She arranged the containers of cinnamon and ginger and mixed spices, thinking how neat the pantry looked and that it would be nice throughout the year to have it as uncluttered with bits of this and jars of that one never used.

"You haven't given me the potato flour," Kitty held out her hand.

Rachel looked in the empty boxes.

"There isn't any. That's the lot."

"Hand me the big dish then. Every year they forget something! As if there isn't enough to do!"

Rachel handed her the giant oval dish, relic of the days when families of ten and twelve children had been the norm. There was no room for it in modern cupboards. It lived for the week at the top of the larder. Her grandmother's special Passover china, she presumed, would be handed on to Carol. There was no place for it in either her life or Josh's.

By the time *Seder* night came Kitty was exhausted. When everything was ready, she bathed and put on her black dress and her pearls. The knowledge that she had done her best, that all was as it should be, and that her part in the proceedings was for the time being over, revived her.

In the dining room she checked the table with its special requirements. Wine, which was sure to be spilled on the white cloth before the evening was over, and *matzo;* a dish of salt water; a hard-boiled egg, which she had held over the gas flame until its shell blackened; parsley; a roasted shank bone; bitter herbs; and the sweet paste she had made from wine and dried fruits to represent the mortar that had been used for the bricks during the time of slavery in Egypt.

Without Dolly, who, thank God, was on the mend, without Norman and without Alec, the table would be depleted. In Hendon, where the dining room was bigger, they had had twice as many.

Content with her handiwork, she moved a spoon here, aligned a chair there, enjoying her brief moment of tranquillity, and waited for her family.

Mirrie came first, bearing a rubber plant, followed by Freda and Harry with a bottle of Israeli liqueur from which, after its contents were drunk, they said you could make a lamp. Josh brought Passover chocolates, and Miss Maynard from the office, who came every year and loved it, a pineapple. Juda and Leonora arrived empty-handed, and Rachel, who rushed in at the last moment smelling of tube trains, a primula, which had seen better days and over which she swore the man in the market had cheated her.

It was the night of the children. Lisa and Debbie, excited as kittens, had brought their large, illustrated books from which they would try to follow the service. As the youngest,

Lisa would ask the four questions. She had been practicing all week. In a few years it would be the turn of Mathew Gideon David.

When they had found their places at the table and stood by them, and their places in the books, and when even Lisa had stopped fidgeting, Sydney picked up the silver wine cup in an unsteady hand and began in his fluent Hebrew to inaugurate the service.

After the sanctification of the wine, he washed his hands in water from the jug Kitty had provided and they sat down. Leaning against his cushion, Sydney held up the *Seder* dish with its symbolic contents, and in the manner of his ancestors he began to read the *Haggadah* to his family.

"This is the poor bread which our forefathers ate in the land of Egypt . . ."

Kitty allowed herself to relax, her thoughts to wander. She was aroused from her reverie by the sound of Lisa's sweet, childish voice asking the four questions. Sydney followed the words in his *Haggadah* lest she stumble, the aunts and uncles nodded encouragingly, Kitty watched her granddaughter with pride. Even Debbie, keeping the place for her sister with her finger, could not find fault. When she had finished, Lisa began the translation: "Why is this night different from all other nights . . . ?"

When the congratulations on her performance were over and the flush had subsided from her face, Sydney picked up his book and began to recite the answers to the questions she had asked and to relate the Passover story in accordance with the commandment. He told how their forefathers had been slaves in Egypt and of their hurried departure; he enumerated the plagues, from blood to the death of the first-born; he showed them the roasted shank bone, representing the paschal lamb, the *matzo*, the bread of affliction, the bitter herbs recalling lives embittered by bondage.

As the story unfolded, Sydney was careful to bring home

to his family its contemporary significance, and included a special prayer for their fellow Jews whose freedom under oppressive rule was threatened because of their beliefs.

The men followed his reading closely, echoing his phrases. Debbie and Lisa looked at the pictures in their books to help pass the time. They saw Miriam casting the infant Moses into the waters of the Nile, the frogs and the lice and the wild beasts of the plagues; the miraculous division of the Red Sea. They joined in the blessing over the *matzo* and the sweet *charoseth*, of which they each had two helpings. When they tasted the bitter herbs, the tears ran down their faces but they did not complain. It was time for the festive meal.

Afterwards the family sang the old songs to the old tunes. Because of his headache and the fact that he was getting tired, Sydney left the conducting of the songs to Josh.

"It Came to Pass at Midnight" and "Build Thy Temple Soon"; "Who Knows One, and Who Knows Two . . . ," up to thirteen, ending in discord and merriment. The room grew warmer and the voices louder and Debbie more flushed and excited and Lisa more sleepy as they drank the obligatory four cups of wine.

Making a supreme effort as master of the house and ignoring the consuming pain above his temple, Sydney called eventually for silence and for a measure of unity in the final song. *"Had gad-yo . . ."* His voice was firm but lacking in some of its former vigour.

They all joined in, even Rachel, as they sang enthusiastically and noisily the legend of the kid that the father bought for "two *zuzim*," starting with the first verse and adding one line each time until finally,

> . . . *came the Holy One, blessed be He.*
> *He destroyed the Angel of Death,*
> *Who slew the slaughterer,*
> *Who killed the ox*

191

That drank up the water
That extinguished the fire
That burned the stick
That hit the dog that bit the cat
That ate the kid,
Which father bought for two zuzim.

"One only kid, one only kid." Sydney closed his book.
"Had gad-yo . . . o . . . o . . . o, had gad-yo!"
He looked at the gathering round his table. They
removed the skullcaps from their heads, rubbed their eyes.
His glance met Kitty's for a fraction of a second over the
guttering candles. There would not be another *Seder*.
Lisa jumped up, and the fifth cup of wine, which had
been poured but not drunk, spread in a purple pool over
the white cloth.
"Lisa!" Debbie shouted.
"Leave her alone," Kitty said. "Somebody had to do it."

23

"IF ALL THE ALMOND PUDDINGS were laid end to end they
would cover the Sinai Desert and probably taste like it,"
Rachel said, thinking of the meal her mother had served on
Seder night. "There's so much food in the kitchen you'd
think there was going to be a total stoppage of all dock
workers for the next three months."
She sat with Solly on the steps, enjoying the warmth of
the spring sunshine on their faces. It was the first day of
term and they had not met since Passover.
"After the destruction of the Temple," Solly said, "eat-

ing was viewed as part of a whole way of life and of worship of the Creator . . ."

"We seem to do an awful lot of worshipping then."

". . . the table became the Altar. Each man's table was said to atone for him and inviting poor guests to meals could compensate for the material and selfish aspects of eating, giving it a dimension of sanctity."

"If you could see my Auntie Beatty filling her face with cinnamon balls you wouldn't talk about dimensions of sanctity!"

She changed the subject. "How's Miriam?"

"She sends her love. We're getting married in August."

"*Mazel tov.* Choral and floral?"

Solly ignored the jibe. "Will you come?"

"I'm going to India with Patrick."

"I shall miss you next year."

She turned to him, her face with its halo of curls silhouetted by the sun. "You won't have time. You'll be so busy in your 'semi' with your mortgage and your washing machine, providing for Miriam and, please God, as they say, all the little Finegolds, that you'll forget all about me."

He ruffled her hair. "Impossible."

"When we were children," Rachel said, "we used to go to Westgate for our holidays with the aunts and uncles. We had the same house every year and took all our own pots and pans. We had a hut on the beach; Mummy and Daddy used to sit in it huddled up. It always seemed to be raining. I can still smell the seaweed, they called it 'ozone,' and feel the wet sand between my toes. They're paralyzed with fear at the thought of my going to India; they look at me as if it were outer space. To be perfectly honest, Solly boy, I'm a bit paralyzed myself, although I wouldn't admit it to anyone but you. I have this enormous urge . . . Udaipur, Bombay, Jaipur, on to Kashmir and Ladakh, we've been planning it for months. Then I hear their voices . . . 'What will you do in the middle of nowhere if you have a puncture/sunstroke/appendicitis?' I think they lace the chicken soup with their ghetto terrors from your earliest days."

"You'll be all right," Solly said. "Think of me, when you have your dip in the Ganges, sweating away at my Articles, stuck in an office from nine until five."

"Think of me," Rachel said, "screaming for help, all alone on the Rooftop of the World, longing to touch England."

"You'll have Patrick," Solly said. "Anyway, it'll still be here when you come back."

Since Dolly's stroke, Norman and Della had stopped going to the cinema. Dolly's condition was stable. She could get about, slowly, and her speech was improving, but she had not regained the use of her right arm. She had gone to bed.

Norman and Della sat facing each other on the moquette armchairs. The electric-fan heater, which warmed the air to an uncomfortable dryness, was the only sound in the room. They were discussing Norman's decision. He had made up his mind. Dolly could not be left.

"She needs me," Norman said. "There's no Home Help on weekends."

Della said nothing. She had seen it coming. She lit a cigarette, staring at the worn carpet, the curtains which hung unevenly at the bay window.

"The house is big enough," Norman said.

"That isn't the point."

"We can have Mother's room. She offered it. I'll redecorate it exactly as you like."

Della's smoke drifted upwards towards the fringed lampshade.

"I can't see why we can't live here," Norman said. "It

194

would be a lot cheaper. We'd have the garden. It's not a bad house . . ."

"What about the flat?" Della said, holding the ashtray on her lap. They had spent weeks getting it ready.

"We'll sell it," Norman said. "Everyone wants those flats. You're making things very difficult."

"Perhaps I am."

"I thought you loved me."

Della leaned forward and held out her hand.

Norman didn't take it. "What do you want me to do? Walk out and leave her, practically helpless . . ."

"There are places . . ."

"Della, it's my mother—can't you get that into your head?—not some stranger . . ."

"You have your own life, Norman. Our life."

"It wouldn't be for very long . . ." He met Della's penetrating glance. "If you'd just explain why . . ."

There was a bang and the ceiling shook as if it would come down. The bang was followed by a short tattoo.

Della raised her eyes in the direction of the sound.

"I expect she wants her cocoa," Norman said.

Della got up. "I think I'll go."

"Look, don't get angry."

"I'm not angry."

"I won't be long," Norman said. "I'll just settle her down for the night, then we can . . ."

"I'm tired, Norman," Della said.

The banging was renewed.

". . . I'll be as quick as I can."

She had her coat on, picked up her handbag. The banging stopped, not with any finality.

"Give your mother my love."

They stood in the narrow hall, their images reflected in the oak mirror.

"Norman!" Dolly's voice was querulous.

"I'm coming, Mother!" He took Della's coat lapels, pulling her towards him until their faces were close.

"Sure you won't change your mind?"

Della looked at her watch.

"It's Monday tomorrow. I'll see you in the morning."

She could see him going downhill but never spoke about it to him nor he to her, keeping up the pretense. They had always smiled, Kitty and Sydney, at the old men sitting with their canes on the wooden bench on the corner of the High Street. Now he was one of them. Not old, just tired from dragging his leg, needing to rest. He waited while Kitty did her shopping. He did not go into the office much now, leaving Miss Maynard to cope as best she could. When he did go, he took a taxi; he had given up driving. Sometimes Miss Maynard found it difficult to understand what he was saying. Kitty understood him. She had had a lifetime of practice. She spoke for him, would have breathed for him if she could.

On Pentecost, for the first time, Sydney did not go to synagogue. The Ladies' Guild had decorated it as usual with lilies and giant hydrangeas, but when the holiday came, Kitty, who had stayed at home with Sydney, was not in her seat. It was customary to provide dairy foods. She made a cheesecake that turned out as heavy as her heart. She had not lost her touch, just forgotten the quantities in her anxiety, in her distress. He would not let her help him; he had always been an independent man. She died a thousand deaths watching him struggle with his shoelaces in the mornings; sometimes it took him half an hour. She told him that people these days wore shoes without laces and offered to get him some. She'd thought he hadn't heard, although there was nothing wrong with his hearing. Then he said, "What would I want with new shoes?"

She tried to get on with her life. She threw herself into

196

the planning of the winter program for the Jewish Association for the Blind: "Women in Israel," a talk by the wife of the Israeli Ambassador; a brunch; a dinner at the House of Lords; a Legal Brains Trust; and a visit to the Queen's Gallery to see the Royal Collections of Sèvres Porcelain. She surprised herself by her ability to go through the motions, planning and arranging and finalizing and sending copy for the Diary of Future Events, to the quarterly broadsheet, which kept members posted. She was never without her bright smile, her breezy manner. Among themselves, the Committee said she was "marvellous"! Many of them had seen Sydney, leaning on her arm and on his cane, on their way to or from the High Street. They formed their own opinions about his condition, but took care not to cross the barrier of taboo Kitty had erected. Any inquiry concerning his health was met with a "mustn't grumble" and a change of subject. Blood pressure was now seldom mentioned.

When they were alone, she and Sydney spoke of the future as they always had: the fortnight in Rimini planned for August—they were taking Dolly to give Norman a break. They greeted each milestone of Carol's baby as if the little Mathew had won an Olympic medal instead of returning a smile, gripping a finger. They spoke of the breakup of Carol's marriage as if it were inevitable. Kitty was already planning to get a few older, eligible men along to next year's Ball.

In the mornings she was afraid to leave Sydney on his own in the bathroom in case he fell, but despite her pleadings he always locked the door. He pretended not to notice, or chose to ignore, the small things that she did for him. She got his clothes out of the cupboards, the suits were heavy; she took the telephone to his chair in the evenings when he was wanted; she read the television programs aloud; lately she had begun to cut up his food. He acknowledged none of these services other than with his eyes. She was not looking for acknowledgment.

Alec sat on the bed, holding Mathew against his shoulder and talking to Carol. "The orchard's white with blossom. You can see it from every window. Each morning when I look out I wish you were there. Sometimes I imagine I can see Debbie and Lisa running over the lawn. I have to shake my head. I'm getting to know the patients. They seem to like me. The whole place knows about you and Debbie and Lisa and Mathew. This house is too small, Carol, all those stairs . . ."

"I couldn't now. Not with Daddy . . ."

"We could come up on Sundays."

"What about Friday nights? He lives for the children."

He wasn't going to be drawn. He moved Mathew onto his other shoulder. "I'll put him down."

"He needs changing," Carol said.

"I'll do it. It won't be the first time."

Carol lay back against the pillows and looked round the room. It was small, boxlike. The houses were terraced. When your neighbour sneezed, you had to stifle the urge to say, "Bless you." Mathew's cries could, she knew, be heard on either side. Alec had shown her photographs of the bedroom in Godalming. It was long and low with three windows looking out onto the lawn and onto the orchard. There were a swing and a wishing well and, in the fields beyond, cows and horses. It had been lonely without him. Some nights she cried. She spent hours on the telephone, talking to her friends, her mother. She could not manage without them; she could not manage without Alec. Often she tried to think the problem through, but, busy with Mathew, she gave up halfway. There had been no talk of divorce. Her mother tried to draw her on the subject. Alec phoned every night to speak to Debbie and Lisa; he made

198

no attempt to brainwash them with the delights of the country.

He came back into the room and leaned against the door, looking at her. She had to admit that he appeared fitter, younger, less harassed; there was a healthy tint to his pale freckled face. She recognized the look in his eyes and began to fasten her nightdress.

"Don't do that."

He was unbuttoning his shirt, taking off his trousers.

"Mathew's crying."

"He'll stop."

They hadn't made love since before the baby.

He got into the bed and took her in his arms, kissing the swollen breasts.

"It's so lonely at nights, Carol. Just the stillness, the occasional owl. I'm surprised you don't hear me thinking about you, wanting you."

She only thought about how tired she was and Mathew's next feed. One ear on the crying baby, she turned to her husband, wondering if, after so long, things would be any different.

He left at six, having to go back for his morning's appointments. Mathew was still sleeping. Sometimes if his last feed was really late, he did not wake until nearer seven. Carol stretched out her arm to where Alec had lain beside her. The bed was still warm. Nothing had changed, but afterwards she had enfolded him as she enfolded Mathew, holding him to her soft body as if he were a baby, her baby. When he left, he kissed her eyes, her mouth, her neck. She had put her arms round him. She felt better than she had since before Mathew, in love with the world, with Alec. If she opened her window, she imagined seeing an orchard white with blossom instead of the pseudo-Georgian terrace of the houses opposite, breathing air that was sweet instead of petrol fumes.

199

Mathew's cries contracted her womb. She gathered up her thoughts. Today was Friday, and she would take the children to school. Already Lisa knew the blessings for bread and wine and fruit and thunder, and on seeing beautiful trees and a rainbow in the sky. She retained what she had learned and had begun to participate in the Children's Service to which Carol took her every Saturday. She would come back and feed Mathew, give him his bath, then go out again for shopping and coffee with a friend. They would talk babies, comparing notes, until it was time to fetch Lisa and bring her home.

Most days her mother came at lunchtime. Today she would bring food she had cooked for the weekend, to save Carol the trouble. She would look after Mathew and Lisa while Carol rested in the afternoon; collect Debbie from school, bringing her home for tea and her Hebrew lesson. Mr. Binstock was coming. Tonight Carol would take the girls to her parents for dinner. Friday night was the high spot of their week. Grandma's dinners, the Sabbath sweets, the weekly gifts her father brought for them. It was the life she had been brought up to, not owls, not orchards. Mathew filled his lungs with air and howled angrily. She swung her legs out of bed. Her day had begun.

24

By the time the call came, Josh had given an engagement ring to Sarah, and Della had given hers back.

Norman sat with his head in his hand, staring at the circle of platinum with its ruby stone as if mesmerized. He could not believe it, could not. He had been so sure that he could convince her, win her over, that it was only a question of time. She had returned the ring on Sunday night. It was now Tuesday. He had not been to work, telling them he had flu; he felt as if he had.

Sunday night kept going round in his head. Della had looked as if she had not slept.

"It's no good, Norman. There's no point in talking anymore. It's not going to work."

"It'll work, Della. I know it will. I promise you."

"I've been over and over it. There's no room for two women in one house."

"For the time being . . ." He did not convince even himself.

"I don't know how to say this, Norman." Della opened her bag. "But you've been the best thing that has ever happened to me. It's been marvellous. It really has." She took out the velvet box with the ring they had chosen together in Golders Green and put it on the table.

"I just want to say thank you, for everything. And you're a marvellous person, Norman. And I love you. And . . . I'm giving in my notice tomorrow. It'll be easier for both of us. I can get a job anywhere. I might go away for a bit . . ." Her voice broke. ". . . I don't really know yet . . ."

She shut her bag and kissed him on the mouth.

"I'm going now, Norman. Please let me go. My mind's quite made up. There's nothing you can do . . ."

He did not stop her. He just sat there and listened to the front door slam as if it were in another country. He felt when she walked out as though she had taken his life with her.

"Who slammed the door?" Dolly called.

He went up to her. "No one."

"I heard the door slam."

"Della."

"What'd you say no one for, then? Where is she?"

"She's gone."

"That was quick."

"We're not getting married."

"The engagement's off!" There was surprise in the lop-sided face. "It wouldn't have worked. Too headstrong. Too headstrong for you, Norman."

In his room he had wiped the lipstick from his mouth and put the handkerchief with its smear of mauve into a drawer.

Dolly was watching him watch the ring. He had spent all day staring at it as if, like the frog in the fairy tale, it would suddenly change into a human being, into Della.

"It's not a bit of good sitting there brooding," Dolly stated.

Norman said nothing.

She waited. "And there's no point in taking it out on me. It's not my fault. I did everything I could. Offered you my room. It's a nice room. Gets all the sun." She glanced at the ring. "Why don't you put it away, Norman? It's not going to bring her back. You'll make yourself ill the way you're going on. What are you thinking about?"

He was wondering whether he had been wrong to let Della go, whether he should have found a home that would take his mother. He had heard that the nurses were cruel in these places, pushing and dragging the patients round, shouting at them. He couldn't have lived with himself, never mind Della.

"You don't know what it's like not being able to do things for yourself," Dolly said, looking at her hand which lay like a limp rag in her lap. "It's very frustrating. I wouldn't mind a coffee when you've got a minute. And one of those cook-ies Freda made, with the cherries on. And you can put the television on while you're up. Better than sitting here talking to myself. Juda's going to get me one of those things you can put it on from your chair; then I shan't have to bother you."

Expressionless, Norman got up to make the coffee.

"You don't know when you're well off," Dolly said to his retreating back. "That shocking lipstick! I don't really care for that type of person. Anyway, she couldn't even cook!"

Josh was debating whether to put in an alloy or go for gold on the second molar of his twelve o'clock and thinking about Sarah. He had bought her a ring. A sapphire for her eyes. After he had put it on her fourth finger, he remembered Paula.

"Would you have preferred a diamond?"

She held the sapphire, which was fiercely blue, up to the light where it sparkled deeply. "Diamonds are for call girls and rich wives. I don't remember saying I'd marry you."

"Say it now."

She looked at him. "Heaven help me, Josh, both of us. I can't do anything else."

She took him to Leicester to see her mother, who was wearing a tweed skirt and Wellingtons and spreading manure on the roses. A cigarette hung from the corner of her mouth.

She looked Josh over as if she were considering him for a horse race.

"Sarah's a big gel, she must do as she pleases." It was her only reference to the subject.

They lunched off kippers and whisky in the vast old kitchen with its butler's pantry. The dogs took a fancy to Josh and kept jumping up while Sarah's mother said, "Down George, down Albert," but not very enthusiastically.

After lunch, dead-heading the daffodils, she asked him why he thought the azalea leaves were curling up and dying. He told her he was a dentist and knew nothing about

203

azaleas, but she appeared not to hear. When they were going, she took off her boots and ran her fingers through her hair and said she had to dash off to a Red Cross meeting.

"We'll let you know about the wedding," Sarah said.

Her mother looked blank for a moment.

"Oh, the wedding," she said vaguely.

Josh thought it extraordinary, as if she had ten daughters, not just Sarah.

He decided on the alloy and, taking the filled syringe from Jacky, squirted some of the liquid into the air.

"You'll just feel the needle going in," he said. "It might sting for a moment, then it will go quite numb." He selected the exact spot with his finger and gently pierced the mucous membrane.

Jacky was making frantic signs to him from the door.

"Your mother's on the phone," she whispered. "I think it's urgent."

"We'll just leave that to work," Josh told the patient reassuringly, nodding to Jacky to keep an eye on her.

"I'll be back in a moment."

For Kitty the day had begun like any other. They were not her days now, with Sydney, dashing hither and thither as she had previously done, but days adapted to his pace, Sydney's pace. The summer had come early and the bright sun filtered by the London mist shone through the net curtains, pointing an accusing finger at the grime. Such tasks, washing the curtains, cleaning the paint, seemed unimportant. Her main concern was Sydney. It was her morning for the High Street. In the old days she would have been there and back. Now it was an expedition, taking Sydney. By the time he had bathed and dressed and she had helped him on with his light coat, his foulard scarf—the sun could be deceptive and he felt the cold sitting on the seat—

204

his hat, half the morning had gone. He leaned heavily on his cane and sometimes swayed when he walked, would have stumbled were she not holding his arm. Looking at him, she saw a man ten years older than her husband, a man who was old and sick. She saw it in the eyes of the neighbours, in the eyes of the porter as he opened the doors of the lift for them.

"Morning!" He touched his cap and leaned forward to help Sydney. "Lovely day again!" He was gentle as a nursemaid. "Bit nippy out of the sun."

It took them ten minutes to walk to the traffic lights, five to cross the road. A summer throng poured out of the tube station and hurried in the direction of Lords. She looked protectively from side to side in case, in their hurry, the crowd bumped into Sydney.

"It's a wonder there's anybody left running the country," Sydney said slowly.

Two denimed youths skipped and hopped past Kitty on the pavement, jogging her arm as they went.

She left him on the seat, outside the bank.

"I won't be long."

"Take your time. I haven't got a plane to catch."

She fiddled with his scarf. "Warm enough?"

"Too warm."

"You want me to undo your coat?"

He shook his head. "Don't fuss."

The boutiques, with their colourful window displays, were woven into the fabric of the High Street at calculated intervals so that you could not go to the butcher's or the baker's or the greengrocer's without passing them. The dress caught her eye. It looked like silk but most probably was not, a shirtwaist with a red and navy pattern on a cream ground, the skirt an accordion of pleats. She stopped in front of it for a moment, seeing herself in it, imagining the look, the feel, how it would fan out when she turned; she could wear it with her navy shoes, later with white or cream . . .

"I saw Sydney . . ." Ruthie Wiseman touched her shoulder. She was pushing the twins in the pram, the brown Rolls-Royce of prams with the monogrammed cover.

She followed Kitty's gaze. "Too fat-making, pleats!"

Perhaps for you, Kitty thought, looking at her powerful hips in the jersey two-piece that must have been a size eighteen. She decided to try it on after the butcher's if only because of Ruthie. She looked at the pudgy-faced twins, who were the image of Stuart Mindel and who might have been Josh's.

"Growing up," Kitty said, as if it were remarkable.

"How's Josh?" Ruthie said.

"Fine."

"Nothing doing there yet?"

She would have a field day if Kitty told her about the *shiksa.*

"He's not in a hurry." Kitty looked at her watch. "I mustn't be too long . . . Sydney."

"I saw him on the seat," Ruthie said. "I'm taking them for a trim. Paula's in bed with sinus."

She walked off with her wide hips towards the hairdresser's.

In the butcher's Kitty bought veal for *schnitzels,* watching as they were cut by the tall blond youth who looked as if he should have been a pop star, not behind the counter in a kosher butcher's shop. She asked for a marrowbone to make some soup for Sydney. He was eating so little.

Bella played a short tune on the cash register.

"Four fifty if you please, Mrs. Shelton."

Kitty took out her purse, reminding herself that she must go to the bank.

She took out a five pound note. "It doesn't go anywhere."

206

"Not today." Bella picked up the note
"We'll have to give up eating meat."
She punched out another tune. "Fish is no better."
She gave Kitty her change. "As long as you've got your health and strength . . ."

Bella realized she had said the wrong thing. "How is Mr. Shelton?" she said quickly.

Kitty's face took on the expression, which had come down to her through the generations and spoke more loudly than the words she could not formulate, that things could have been better.

"At least the weather's a bit more cheerful," Bella said. "Cold out of the sun, though. You have to be careful."

Kitty shut her bag, picked up her parcel and turned to leave.

"Look after yourself," Bella said. "Take care!"

She went to the bank, where the cashier greeted her by name; the greengrocer's, where they picked out the tiny new potatoes that she liked; and to the baker's, where she bought fresh rolls for lunch.

Hurrying back to Sydney, she saw the dress from the corner of her eye; she had forgotten it. She stopped. It wouldn't take a moment. If she left it until another day, it might be gone. She pushed open the door.

"Mrs. Jonelle here?"

"Mrs. Jonelle's in Paris," Mr. Jonelle said. Their name was Joseph, but they had almost forgotten. "Can someone else help you, Mrs. Shelton?"

"I'm in a bit of a hurry," Kitty said, "but I wondered about that dress in the window . . ."

"Certainly, madam . . . Zelda please!" Zelda came forward with her big bust, her glasses hanging round her neck from a chain.

"Zelda, Mrs. Shelton would like to see the Louis Gerard dress in the window."

207

"Certainly, Mrs. Shelton. It's the last one. I'll get it out for you." She cast an experienced eye over Kitty's figure. "It should be your size. People have been going mad for them. We can't get enough."

She tried it on in the little cubicle, wondering why it was always so hot in dress shops.

"It's gorgeous!" Zelda said before she was even properly out. She put the hanging glasses on her nose. "They're all wearing pleats this summer. They're not the pleats that make you look big; you know what I mean, some pleats are terrible, I can't wear them myself; those pleats I can wear."

Kitty looked in the mirror. "It's a bit tight . . ." She put a hand to her chest.

Zelda stood behind her and smoothed her bosom. "Don't worry about that. Everyone's had to have it let out. It's such a useful little dress. You can go away for the weekend and come up for a function, so fresh—you need something fresh in your wardrobe when the summer comes —with navy shoes, even red shoes . . ." Her imagination was carrying her away.

"I don't wear red shoes," Kitty said.

"You can even wear it in the winter under a fur."

Kitty turned to one side and to the other, watching the pleats swing. It was a nice dress, a comfortable dress.

Zelda put the knife in. "It looks gorgeous," she said. "Gorgeous. Believe me! You know I wouldn't tell you. You look like a million dollars."

"Do you think it's a bit young?" Kitty asked. "I don't want to look like mutton dressed as lamb."

"With your figure! You should see some of the women come in here! You don't have to think twice."

"How much is it?" Kitty said.

"You know the story," Mr. Jonelle said. He had come to *kibbitz*, his arms folded. "If you have to ask the price you can't afford it!" He put up a hand to stop Kitty's protestations. "It's a joke!" He lifted up the ticket from the belt of the dress and peered at it as if the price weren't printed on his mind.

"It won't break the bank. Eighty-five pounds. Next year it'll be more. That I can promise you."

"For a little day dress!" Kitty said.

"Feel the material," he begged, picking up a piece of the skirt. "It's like a slub; almost a silk. You can wash it, do anything with it. I couldn't repeat it if I wanted to."

Kitty looked at her watch, worried now about Sydney.

"I'll think about it."

Mr. Jonelle shrugged. "I can't promise you it'll be here."

"I'll take it," Kitty said.

Mr. Jonelle and Zelda relaxed perceptibly.

"I'll call the fitter," Zelda said, "about that little inch."

"What about the hem?" Kitty said, turning. "Do you think it's a bit too long?"

"I wouldn't touch it," Zelda dropped her glasses.

"They're wearing them long," Mr. Jonelle said.

He was asleep on the bench in the sun, propped up between a fat lady, who sat with her knees apart so that you could see her long bloomers, and a man Kitty recognized as Abe Feldman, who had recently had his gall bladder out.

"Pity to wake him up," Abe said, raising his hat to Kitty. "Having a lovely doze."

She woke Sydney gently, and while he blinked his eyes in the sun, she inquired after Abe's missing gall bladder. She held her shopping in one hand and Sydney's arm with the other, and they started the slow trek back. She would give him a roll for lunch with some smoked roe. He liked anything savoury.

When they got in, she took off his coat and hung it in the hall cupboard, putting his hat and his scarf on the shelf.

"I think I'll lie down a moment," Sydney said, heading with his cane for the bedroom.

"I'll help you with your shoes." She followed him.

He sat on the bed, not protesting as she undid the laces, pulled off the shoes, helped him out of his jacket and into his blue cardigan.

"Have a rest until lunch, darling," Kitty said, putting his jacket over the back of the chair.

He got his legs onto the bed and stared at her in horror as if she had said something strange.

"Are you all right?" she said, worried suddenly. He did not usually rest in the mornings.

He fell back on the bed, his eyes still staring.

"Sydney!"

25

LENNIE SILVER CAME STRAIGHT AWAY, but there was nothing he could do, nothing anyone could do. A massive brain hemorrhage, Lennie said. He had died immediately.

It seemed strange in the flat, Sydney lying on the bed, cold. Sydney was cold. Kitty could not believe it, going back over the morning in her mind as if it would yield some clue. Sydney's coat, the porter, the bench in the sun, Bella in the butcher's, the bank, the new potatoes, the dress . . .

There was a cup of tea in her hands—she wasn't sure how it had got there—and Lennie was waving a piece of paper, the death certificate. She'd heard of an "A" certificate, for the cinema, or an "X" certificate, never of a death certificate. He left it on the hall table, next to the coupon for washing powder that had come through the letter box, and went to fetch her neighbour, Addie Jacobs, from across the hall. Addie came in her bedroom slippers, smelling of fried fish, and embraced Kitty, crying, as if she would never let her go. Kitty was surprised; they had never been particularly friendly. Addie wiped away her tears with a yellow Kleenex, and Kitty thought she should have been the one who was crying, not Addie, who, after all, had hardly known Sydney more than to say good morning to; but she did not feel like crying, did not feel like anything. Addie said, "Who shall I phone?" and Kitty said, Josh and Carol, no, not Carol, she'll get a fright and the milk will dry up, and Juda and Beatty, no, not Beatty, she'll start carrying on over the phone; just Josh and Juda, and they can get in touch with the others.

She sat in the bedroom, watching Sydney who, in death, looked better than he had for months. She sat watching him, waiting for him to wake up. Addie brought her the two fresh rolls with the smoked roe, and some coffee, but she couldn't touch them, only the coffee, which she took back into the kitchen to drink, it being forbidden to eat or drink in the presence of the dead; trust Addie not to know.

It seemed no time at all before Josh was there and Juda, filling the flat with his cigar smoke, and Leonora and Mirrie, all pale with shock and embracing her wordlessly, wetting her face with their tears. For each of them, she recited the chronicle of the morning's events, not forgetting the fresh rolls and how Sydney had fallen asleep on the bench; then Kitty, normally so bustling, so busy, sat there while Mirrie and Leonora hovered and Josh and Juda discussed what was to be done.

They took off their jackets and gently lifted Sydney off the bed and laid him on the floor in accordance with the custom. Kitty looked the other way.

"What about the funeral?" Josh asked his uncle. He was inexperienced in such matters.

Juda looked at his watch. "It's too late for today; we'll have to fix it for tomorrow. You'll probably have to give them something to get the time you want. Leave the Burial Society to me; I know the Secretary. Has he got a plot?" he said to Kitty.

They both had. Sydney was not a man to leave such matters to chance.

Josh left for the Registrar's Office with the death certificate, and for the synagogue to fetch Sydney's prayer shawl in which he would be buried, and to tell Carol. Juda rang Rabbi Magnus.

While he was phoning, Beatty and Leon, who had closed the shop, arrived; and Freda and Harry, who had been on the golf course.

"My poor darling Sydney!" Beatty embraced Kitty. "What happened?"

Kitty went through her story like an automaton, then Juda put his head round the door to say he was off to the Burial Society to try to arrange the funeral for the morning. Beatty said, "You can't have it in the morning, Austin's up north. Brenda can't even get hold of him until tonight."

"Rabbi Magnus has a wedding in the afternoon," Juda said.

"Austin would want to be here," Beatty said. "He was very fond of Sydney, and it's very awkward for Charles. Angela says he's in court all day tomorrow."

Kitty listened to them argue as though it were no concern of hers. Josh left Beatty in midsentence, protesting about her "boys," but she fired a parting shot: "Has anyone phoned *The Jewish Chronicle*, otherwise it will be too late for this week?"

"And the *Telegraph*," Harry said. "You go off, Juda, I'll see to it."

212

Beatty rolled up her sleeves and covered the mirrors throughout the flat with white napkins and lit candles in the room where her brother lay on the floor. Freda sat on the chair by the hall table and phoned Miss Maynard at the office and Moshe Pearlman and Harvey Frankel from the Board of Management and the more remote echelons of the family to tell them the news. Kitty listened to her voice. ". . . Yes, yes, it was sudden; no one expected it; a sudden hemorrhage," as if she spoke of a stranger, no one remotely connected with herself.

While they were busying themselves, Norman arrived with Dolly, who said she would have come sooner but had to wait for Norman, she was helpless on her own. Addie Jacobs, who was enjoying the excitement on a Wednesday, went back to her flat.

"If you want anything," she said to Kitty, "you know where I am."

"How's this?" Harry showed her the announcement he had written out.

Beatty looked over his shoulder. "Put 'Darling husband of . . .' 'Another angel in heaven,' 'A prince of a man,' something like that."

"Not likely," Kitty said.

"I'll do an announcement of my own," Beatty said huffily, "for the *J.C.* From me and Leon and Angela and Brenda and the boys."

The smell of onions frying drifted into the room. Mirrie had taken over the kitchen and was making a casserole. Kitty sat still, empty, in the midst of the activity round her. A sudden thought came into her head.

"Has anybody told Rachel?"

Rachel cried, on Solly's shoulder. She telephoned Patrick, but Solly was there. He put an arm round her, comforting her silently, letting her weep.

213

"He was still angry with me," Rachel said.

"No."

"Yes. It's not been the same since *Yom Kippur.*"

"It's your imagination."

She shook her head. "And now he's dead. I'm afraid."

"What of?"

"Going home. I don't want to see him. I've never seen anybody dead."

"You don't have to. Would you like me to come home with you?"

"I'll be all right." She blew her nose.

"I'll come to the funeral. Will you ring me? And the prayers."

"What prayers?"

"The *shivah.*"

"Oh God! I'd forgotten about that. Do I have to do it?"

"It will be expected."

"Sit on those hard chairs for a week? With Auntie Beatty and Auntie Dolly . . ."

"And your mother and Josh."

"And all those crowds of people coming every night, talking among themselves as if it were a cocktail party and not taking a blind bit of notice of us. I'd never survive. Do you think they'd be very upset if . . ."

She caught Solly's eye.

"I prefer to mourn in my own way. Anyway I'm in the middle of exams."

"You'll have to see your tutor and explain."

"Seven days. He'll think I'm off my rocker. When Mary's mother died, she went home only for the morning. I went with her. When we left, her father was cleaning his car."

"You happen to be Jewish."

"It's archaic."

"It's recognized as a very practical way of dealing with

bereavement. By the time the week is up, the worst is over. People suffering a loss need to be told what to do."

"They only come for the social bit, all those people. I bet half of them won't even have known Daddy."

"Your mother won't be alone."

"I'd have stayed with her. I'd better go. Oh God, if you knew how I hate this, Solly."

She stood outside the front door of the flat, with its *mezuzah* and its spy hole and its four locks against the burglars who were so prevalent in the district, and tried to summon up courage to ring the bell. Her mother's bell, not her father's. Her father was dead. She did not want to go in. All the family would be there. She didn't know what to say to anybody, what she was supposed to do. It was dark and warm in the hall. She had a sinking feeling in her stomach. It had been with her all the way from college. She was frightened.

Beatty opened the door and pulled Rachel to her.

"My poor *sheppsele*, my poor *sheppsele!*"

Rachel squirmed to get away.

"Where's Mummy?"

"In *there*."

"With . . .?"

"With your father." Beatty blew her nose.

"I'll tell her you're here," Freda said. She was the most sensible one of the lot.

Rachel faced her mother in the corridor. She looked as she might have on any other day, not all dishevelled with a red nose from weeping, like Auntie Beatty. They moved together wordlessly, and it was Rachel who cried.

"Don't, darling," Kitty said stroking her hair. "It's all right. It was so sudden. He didn't feel anything. Do you want to see him?"

"I can't," Rachel said. "I'm sorry."

"He just looks . . . peaceful."

Rachel shook her head, wondering what they'd think of her. She stood there not knowing what to do, then followed the smell of cooking into the kitchen.

Auntie Mirrie was cutting up apples, Auntie Mirrie would not fall upon her.

"Hallo, darling," she said to Rachel, more feeling in her words than in Beatty's suffocating embrace. "I'm making a strudel. Come to help me?"

In the evening, in their black hats, black as beetles, the men from the Burial Society came, bringing the low wooden chairs on which the mourners would sit for a week, bringing the prayerbooks for those who would come to comfort them. Soft, quiet, respectful in their shabby suits, they set the chairs in a row in the lounge, nine of them for the widow and the children, the brothers and the sisters of the deceased. They stacked the prayerbooks in piles on the cocktail cabinet which lit up, displaying the cut glass, when you opened it, and they left a black-edged printed message of sympathy from the synagogue, its Rabbi and the Board of Management, on the mantelpiece. When they had finished, as respectfully as they had come, they crept respectfully away.

Rachel looked at the row of wooden chairs with the stunted legs and sat down to try one.

"Not now!" Beatty said, shocked. "Not till after the *levoya.*"

"After the what?" She would not be able to stick Auntie Beatty for a week.

"The *levoya,* the funeral. Then you start sitting."

Rachel looked round the room at the family. They were waiting, doing nothing. There was nothing to do. She got up from the chair. How was she supposed to know? She sat on the sofa next to her mother. Norman was in with her

216

father, in with the body, which was not to be left alone. She took her mother's hand.

"Has anyone got a decent black hat?" Freda said into the silence. "Mine's more like a little bit of nonsense."

"Wear a headscarf," Beatty said. "Everyone wears a headscarf these days. You got a black dress, Kitty?"

"If I have, I have, and if I haven't, I haven't. It doesn't matter."

"For the funeral at least!" Beatty said. "You want me to bring some tights in the morning? They've got them in the sale in Golders Green. I was looking for 'Marzipan,' but I know they've got the black."

"It's not necessary," Kitty said.

"I'm not going to the funeral," Dolly said, snivelling into her screwed-up handkerchief. "I can't take it. Anyway, I can't stand up . . ."

"I can't stand up either. I make myself!" Beatty said.

Dolly opened her mouth, but Mirrie came in to say dinner was ready.

Round the table in the dining room they had Mirrie's casserole. Only Kitty and Rachel could not eat, putting down their knives and forks after a few mouthfuls.

"You've got to keep your strength up," Beatty said, justifying the gusto with which she was emptying her plate.

Harry and Freda talked of the mixed foursomes they would be missing; and Juda told Josh of an auction at Sotheby's and how much a Botticelli had fetched, bemoaning the fact that it had gone to America. This led Leonora on to talk about Maine, where she was going in the summer, and Beatty saying she wouldn't give you a thank-you for Maine, give her Bournemouth any day, where you knew what was what. Mirrie said Bournemouth always made her go to sleep, too relaxing, and that she preferred Brighton only there was nowhere to stay anymore, meaning a kosher hotel. Freda said that they were planning to go to Israel, which led to a heated discussion about the giving up of the Sinai to Egypt and the occupation of the West Bank. Listening to the argument go back and forth, Rachel thought, "They've quite forgotten Daddy, quite forgotten what they're here for," and met her mother's eye.

The family stayed, the men taking turns keeping vigil in the bedroom until the two men from the Burial Society came in their shabby black coats to lay out the body. They nodded to the family and followed Juda into the bedroom, closing the door.

Their work was set out clearly. They did no other. They would prepare the body in accordance with the minutiae laid down in the laws and customs of Israel. When it was ready they would wrap it in the prayer shawl which the deceased had used during his life, praying that his soul should be so adorned in the Garden of Eden.

After they had finished, one of them came into the lounge.

"Where is the son?"

Josh stood up. The man went towards him and, taking the lapel of his suit, made a slit in it with the knife he carried. He stood waiting.

"Tear it a bit further yourself," Juda told him. "You have to 'rend your garments.'"

Beatty held out her hand for the knife and advanced on Kitty.

"Do your underslip," Dolly said. "You don't want to ruin a good dress. What about Rachel?"

All eyes turned to Rachel.

Beatty advanced with her knife.

"Stay away from me," Rachel said.

"You've got to tear," Beatty said.

Beatty looked at Kitty. "Leave her alone," Kitty said.

Rachel ran out of the room. As she left, she heard Beatty saying, "Shocking behaviour!"

218

26

Rachel stayed, sleeping with her mother in the spare bedroom. In the night she heard Kitty tossing restlessly. You could hear the sounds of the traffic on the main road.

"Go to sleep," Rachel said.

"I can't sleep and I can't cry."

Rachel got up to fetch water and gave her mother the tablets Lennie had left; she would need all her strength.

Auntie Beatty arrived at ten in the morning, all in black. Hard on her heels came Barbara Brill and Ruthie Wiseman and other members of the Ladies' Guild, bringing sympathy and boxes of cookies and cakes which they had made. They took over the flat.

"You've got to make a table," Beatty said, "for when they come back from the *levoya*. I've got a list somewhere. Someone can go across the road."

"I'll go," Rachel said.

Beatty looked shocked. "Not you! You're an *ovel*, it's your father! One of the women will go."

"I want to go."

"She can bring some fish," Mirrie said. "For supper."

"Take the car," Kitty said. "The keys are in the hall."

Rachel was glad to get out into the normality of people going about their business, going to Lords.

In the delicatessen she consulted Beatty's list and filled her basket with bagels and chopped herring and cream cheese and tea bags, on which there was a special offer. She couldn't see what any of it had to do with the death of her father.

Outside the fish shop there was a queue. It was permanent, the "Jewish" fish shop. The women waited passively, uncomplainingly. They were the same women who had stood patiently in line for the gas chambers. On their backs she had a clear vision of the yellow Star of David.

"Next please!"

Rachel tried to decipher Mirrie's writing.

She heard the slap, slap, slap of the fish as they were slung on the scales.

When she got back, she did as she was told. She buttered the bagels with Auntie Mirrie, then went across the road again to buy a memorial light. By the time she returned, Freda had found one in the pantry. The funeral had been set for one o'clock so that Rabbi Magnus would be back in time for his wedding.

"I'll make some sandwiches for lunch," Addie Jacobs said helpfully. "You'll want lunch before you go."

"Don't let her make them," Beatty said. "She'll use the wrong knife!"

"Lunch!" Dolly shuddered. "I couldn't eat a thing. A cup of a tea and a drop of brandy."

"You'll manage when the time comes," Beatty said. "Is there whisky for the Rabbi?"

Carol came, her face white and small above her black suit; Josh was wearing his bowler hat.

"What about *tefillin?*" Juda asked. "Have you got *tefillin* for the morning?"

Josh shook his head. He had not said the morning prayers or worn his phylacteries since his *Bar Mitzvah.* He had no idea where they were.

"I'll lend you some."

He was expected to pray night and morning for his father.

220

"At least he's got a son to say *Kaddish,*" Freda said. "When Harry goes there's nobody."

The flat filled with people Rachel did not know. Men with pale faces and dark suits, wearing hats they did not remove, women, with their wordless embraces, anxious to be of use. Through it all Kitty sat in a corner while they came to kiss her, hold her hand. She let them, politely, saying yes and no when they spoke to her. At twelve-fifteen she put on her hat.

The men came, uniformed, from the Burial Society to screw down the coffin. When they left, they held out their hands discreetly for tips.

"You'll need something for the grounds," Juda said to Josh. "They'll all have their hands out. They're not supposed to but they do."

The flat was full, overflowing. People were standing in the outside hall and down the stairs. Rachel wondered where they all came from.

The coffin seemed too small a box to contain her father, whom she'd always thought of as a big man. They carried it out, cutting a path through the silence, through the respectful corridor made by the mourners. They carried it down the stairs. Kitty and Carol and Josh and Rachel went down first in the lift and out into the sharp sunshine into the waiting limousine.

Following the hearse, with Carol and Alec, her mother and Josh—and Beatty who had got in without asking—Rachel felt detached as if she were watching the entire parade on film.

It was not quick, Sydney's last journey. They were held up by the lunchtime traffic, the column of funeral cars getting infiltrated by buses and delivery vans and taxis. On the dual roadway they kept in the slow lane, allowing the living to overtake them, reminded, by the somber cavalcade, of their mortality.

221

"I always think you can breathe better once you get past Hendon," Beatty said.

No one answered. They did not feel like being drawn into conversation.

The procession turned off the main highway, easing its way through the countryside to the cemetery. Rabbi Magnus, looking anxiously at his watch, was awaiting its arrival.

The modern prayer hall was comparatively new. The men stood opposite the women as if about to engage in some macabre country dance. The coffin, covered with a cloth, lay on its bier in front of them; Rabbi Magnus and the Cantor from the synagogue stood at the central reading desk. They led the prayers, which the congregation followed from the books that had been handed to them by the sexton. The black cloth covers were impregnated with sadness. "The soul of every living thing is in thy hand," Rachel read. "Blessed be the true Judge, all whose judgments are righteous and true." She did not believe it.

"We are here today," Rabbi Magnus said, "to pay our last respects to Sydney Shelton, a pillar of our community and one who will be sadly missed." He allowed himself a pause. "Sydney Shelton was a just man, a good man, a family man." He looked at Kitty and Carol and Rachel and Josh. "He was a valued member of the synagogue, a constant worshipper, a valued friend. Above all"—he was warming to his theme—"he was a *tzaddik,* a righteous man. He was also a learned man, a regular attender at our *Talmud* discussions until his last days." He clasped his hands in front of him, looked at the floor as if his lines were inscribed upon its tiles and shuffled his feet. "Sydney Shelton," he continued looking up, "Sydney Shelton . . ."

Class One funeral oration, Rachel thought, personalized to fit the remains of Sydney Shelton. She looked round her at the mourners—friends, family, colleagues, acquaintances, neighbours from the flats. It was amazing how the news had got round, how they had assembled so quickly: Norman, like a lugubrious bloodhound; Vanessa in her silk headscarf, next to her mother in a Paris suit; Solly, whom she scarcely recognized in his hat. They hung, for want of anything else to do, on Rabbi Magnus's words, forced by their surroundings into wondering when their turn would come, theirs for the coffin, theirs for the bier on which they would be wheeled to the grave.

". . . and hope that the Almighty will spare"—Rabbi Magnus stole a quick glance at his watch—"the widow and the children and the grandchildren of the late, much beloved Sydney Shelton, for many years to come. Amen."

The "Amen" was echoed by the mourners.

On cue the doors were flung open and the bier wheeled out to wait, at the entrance to the burial grounds, for Josh to take the handles.

It was too nice a day to be buried, Rachel thought. She walked behind Josh on one side of her mother; Carol was on the other. The tombstones flashed white. So many. Row upon row. She hadn't thought the hole would be so deep. One of the gravediggers, young and thickset, looked at her with admiration, holding her gaze. She lowered her eyes and fantasized a sexual encounter with him, a Mellors and Chatterley affair. When she pulled herself together, the men were taking turns to fill the grave with earth. They were throwing it in thudding spadesful onto the coffin, onto her father. She looked at her mother in horror, expecting her to stop them. Kitty stood quietly. Rachel looked round for help. Nobody moved except the line of men, each paying, with the clay, his last resepcts. Old Mr. Gottlieb dug feebly into the ground picking up a thin sprinkling of dirt. There were murmurs of protest at his evident frailty.

"He's no business doing that!" Beatty's voice could be heard.

The last man, soiling his black City shoes, contributed his

clod; and the spades were then handed to the gravediggers, who would finish the job.

On the way back to the cars, the mourners washed their hands in the fountains, praying to the Lord God who "wipeth away tears from all faces."

Kitty's was a pale, dry mask.

Not even the Day of Atonement had seemed so long. They came back from the cemetery, leaving Sydney behind, beneath his coverlet of humped earth. Rabbi Magnus, close family and men of retirement age who had nothing better to do came with them. The mourners sat on the strange, hard chairs in a semicircle, Rachel choosing one as far from Auntie Beatty as possible. The members of the Ladies' Guild, helped unenthusiastically by Leonora, brought them plates on which were a hard-boiled egg, half a buttered bagel and a piece of herring whose bones splayed out like whiskers.

Rachel looked at the food. She would rather die than eat it.

"You have to eat it," Beatty said, licking the butter off her fingers.

Rachel looked at her mother.

"Take a bite," Kitty said.

The hard-boiled eggs reminded her of picnics.

Rabbi Magnus stood in front of them. He started with Auntie Beatty, who was by the window, and worked his way along the row until he reached Rachel, taking each hand and muttering words she could not catch, smelling of the whisky he had downed. His example was followed by the others in the room. They worked their way along the row, wishing each "long life." Rachel wasn't sure what she was supposed to say in return, but wished the women wouldn't bend over her to kiss her, leaving behind their lipstick on her face and the aura of their perfumes and of the herring they had eaten. In dribs and drabs they came and went all afternoon. The Ladies' Guild made tea.

After dinner, cooked by Mirrie, it was time for the evening prayers.

"Do you think there'll be a big crowd?" Freda said.

"Bound to be if this morning's anything to go by."

"I've never seen such a big funeral on a weekday. Sundays you always get a crowd."

The furniture had been pushed back against the walls to make room.

Stretching up so that you could see the pink slip beneath the black dress, Beatty closed the top of the sash window.

"Don't do that," Dolly said. "It'll be unbearable as soon as they all come."

"I'm not sitting there in that draft," Beatty said. "I'll be in bed with a stiff neck."

"Change places then," Dolly said. "I feel faint with no air in the room. Sit where Rachel's sitting."

Beatty got up.

"I like it here," Rachel said, not moving. She preferred to be by the door so that she could make her escape if she wanted to.

"They've got no respect," Beatty said. "Young people today . . ."

"I'll change with you," Mirrie said.

"And sit next to Juda's cigar? With my chest?"

Josh stood up. "Sit here, Auntie Beatty."

Rachel kicked him. It would bring Auntie Beatty next to her.

Kitty moved down one. "Sit here, Beatty." She indicated the chair between her and Carol.

"Talk about disobliging," Beatty said, looking at Rachel and lowering her bulk onto the low seat from which she overflowed onto Carol. "With your father not cold in his grave."

The doorbell rang.

"It's open," Kitty said. "We've left it on the latch." Nine pairs of eyes swivelled towards the door as the first visitor in his overcoat and hat sidled into the room. The evening session had begun.

The arrivals crowded into the room, a faceless parade, overshadowing the mourners for whose dear departed they had come to pray. They spoke among themselves in low tones while they waited for Rabbi Magnus, who would lead the prayers. The women stood in the hallway. Prayers had been announced for eight o'clock. It was eight-fifteen when Rabbi Magnus arrived, apologizing for his lateness. The prayerbooks had been given out. They decided which was the east and turned to it.

"*Lammenatzeach . . .*" Rabbi Magnus intoned. The swaying crowd joined in, in unison, with the Psalm. From outside, in the corridor, you could hear the chatter of the women.

The prayers droned on. Feeling suffocated by the heat in the room, Rachel thought that the service would never end. When it was time, Josh recited the *Kaddish,* his words echoed by the mourners among the crowd. "*Yisgadal ve-yiska-dash . . .*" He stumbled over the unfamiliar syllables. By the end of the week he would be word-perfect.

When the prayers were finished, Rabbi Magnus spoke again, into the quiet. His message, a personal one to Kitty, was simple and sincere. Rachel revised her opinion of him. When the last "Amen" had died away, the books were collected and the long procession started to shuffle along the row of chairs. She shook the hands of people she had never met; strangers wetted her cheek with their tears. She clung to Solly, wanting to talk to him, but he was swept away relentlessly by the crowd. Friends of her mother's told Rachel how they'd pushed her in her pram, as if the memory were interesting, others, that they had been at her parents' wedding. A man who said his name was Cohen wept

226

openly and was unable to speak at all. If all the "Long lives" she was wished were strung together, she would live to be older than Methuselah. She was getting a cramp in her hand.

The visitors said good-bye, but they did not go. Instead they stood talking in groups, renewing acquaintances, forgetting where they were.

". . . we booked up at Arma di Taggia but Rose can't take the heat so we're going back to Knokke . . ."

". . . my daughter-in-law's expecting in August, so we'll wait till October, please God, after the holidays . . ."

". . . he got mugged in Hatton Garden coming away from the vaults . . ."

Here and there, there were pockets of laughter.

Old acquaintances pulled chairs up to sit in front of Kitty, holding her hands.

Austin, who had come posthaste from "up North," and Charles, who had not made the funeral, both of whom had children of their own, sat in front of Beatty and were introduced as "my boys."

Finally, one by one, the visitors went.

"Auf simchas!"

"Wish you long life!"

"Please God on happier occasions!"

"Look after yourself."

"Long life."

"Long life."

"Long life."

It was a nightmare. Six more days. She would not be able to stand it.

Rachel took the hand which was extended in front of her.

"I wish you long life!"

27

Norman cared for his mother and went to the office. Looking at him, his coworkers said the flu must have pulled him down. Like a nagging tooth, the pain was with him every day; he was never without it. Sometimes, his thoughts catching him unaware, he would look up expecting to see Della, in her mauve jumper, at the reception desk. Instead there was Mrs. Treadweil with her blue-rinsed hair. Had he never known the happiness he had had with Della, the pain would not have been so bad.

Sometimes, trying to cheer him up, Dolly said, "What's the use of a woman who can't cook!" or "Come on, Norman, you know she wasn't for you."

But she was. There would never be anyone else. He was too old. He was lucky to have found Della. He looked for her in Golders Green where he guessed she might be working. Sometimes he drove to Kingsbury and stood near the flats, behind a tree, where he could not be seen, waiting for her to come out. A couple of times he had caught a glimpse of her walking down the road. She looked neither happy nor unhappy. He did not speak to her, knowing it was no use.

The woman from Home Help telephoned to say she had twisted her ankle and wouldn't be coming anymore. Norman knew that Dolly had upset her. In the evenings he came home and peeled potatoes and did the cooking and the fetching and carrying that Dolly couldn't manage with the use of only one hand. Since the stroke she seemed to have shrunk to a shadow of her former self. She needed him as much as he needed Della. Della had her parents, would meet another man. His mother had no one. Now that his uncle Sydney was dead, the family scarcely seemed to bother with her. He was all she had. You did not walk away from a situation like that, not if you were a human being.

Tonight his heart was aching badly. Dolly had not had a good day. All evening she had kept him on the run. As he helped her undress, she said, "I don't know what I'd do without you, Norman."

She often said it. It was his reward.

He closed the curtains in what would have been his room and Della's.

"It's time you forgot about her," Dolly said from the bed, watching his face. "You're making yourself ill over it and what good's that going to do to you? Me either for that matter. It's not very jolly having to look at that miserable face every day."

She was right, of course. It wasn't very nice for her. His work was suffering as well. His commissions had fallen so low they were practically negligible. There were dozens of bright youngsters eager to take his place. He would have to pull himself together.

"I wouldn't mind another hottie, if it's no trouble," Dolly said, handing him the hot-water bottle he had put in earlier. "And 'praps a little drop of warm milk. I've got shocking heartburn."

He allowed himself to dream of Della as he warmed the milk and waited for the kettle to boil.

He settled Dolly and turned out her central light.

"Call if you want anything," he said. He always did.

"Good night, Norman."

"Good night."

In his room he opened the drawer and took out the velvet

box in which nestled the ruby ring. He closed the box and, taking the photograph of Della from his dressing table, he locked them both in the attaché case he kept on the top of the wardrobe.

"There's no one to eat, so I don't bother to cook," Kitty said.

Josh had gone round at dinnertime to find her alone in the dining room with a cup of tea.

She didn't bother to cook, and she didn't bother to do anything else either. She had been fine for the week of the prayers, borne up splendidly while people were in and out of the flat from morning until night, especially at night. The numbers did not dwindle, as they came to pay their last respects to Sydney. She had been numbed with the pain. Afterwards she could not remember who had come, who had not. When the week of mourning was over and they had come from the Burial Society to take away the low chairs and the books, leaving her only the black-bordered card with its message of sympathy, she had remained in the midst of the emptiness listening to the silence, waiting for Sydney to call "Kitty," "Kitty"; but there was no sound. She stood in the middle of the disordered room, not bothering to set it to rights, she who had been so house-proud, and let the warm tears run slowly down her face for the first time. They did not stop. She wept in the day and she wept in the night, not sleeping. Lennie gave her pills and said it was normal to grieve, essential. She slept fitfully, haunted by dreams; woke before light, before dawn, wondering what to do with herself, how best to get through the day. The children had been good; the family; the Ladies' Guild. She had sat at Freda and Harry's table in the open-plan living room, looking out with blind eyes through the picture windows over the golf course which so stirred their blood. She had sat blankly in the bosom of Beatty and

Leon's family, who had been invited especially to dinner with her. Neither Beatty's tongue nor her *hubergritz* soup roused her; apathetically, politely, she endured the evening. She sat coldly in Juda's cold dining room. He and Leonora served her fish. Their meat was not kosher. They could have given her stones, she did not care. She did not care either that Vanessa had become engaged to the scion of one of England's premier Jewish families, that on her finger she sported one of the family emeralds. She had sat with Norman and Dolly on the moquette chairs, gazing at the television whose picture got no farther than her blank eyes. Twice a week Mirrie came to keep her company. She was grateful and polite. The only reality was Lisa and Debbie when she went to Carol's. She hugged them close to her and for a moment their warmth pierced the barrier that surrounded her. Rachel came and searched for words to comfort her, to bring her out of her apathy, but when she left, it was as if she had not been. It was the same with Josh.

"Let me bring Sarah to dinner," Josh said. "She'd like to meet you."

"I'm sure she would."

"Make one of your nice dinners, one of your specials."

"Your father would turn in his grave."

"What about next week? Tuesday. Not too early. I have to go to synagogue."

"Your father was worried about the *Kaddish*. Whether you would say it."

"Until the month is up."

"He meant for the year."

Josh looked at her, feeling the guilt of the intention he had not yet carried out.

"It wouldn't hurt."

Eleven months, morning and evening, Sabbath and Festivals, to synagogue. It was already an effort to get up each day at six. The evening prayers interfered with his life.

231

"He was very anxious about it."

He knew he would do it.

"I'll bring Sarah then?"

She recognized the quid pro quo and that Sydney would not have compromised.

Josh looked at his watch. "I must be going."

They always had to be going. They came; they tried; they stayed; but always the moment came when they went back to their lives, leaving her alone in the empty flat in which there were no longer flowers, a filled fruit bowl, small dishes of sweets and nuts. She had stopped noticing whether or not the curtains needed washing.

One morning the bell had rung. A plastic carrier was delivered from "Jonelle." Inside was the dress she had chosen with the pleats, with the navy and red on the cream ground, the one that was washable although it looked like silk. You could wear it to a function, they had said. Or even under a fur. She hung it in the cupboard, knowing that she would never wear it.

She would have to do something with Sydney's clothes, with his suits hung neatly, his shirts, his ties, his shoes. The Friends of the Sick, Mirrie suggested, would take it all away for her. She did not ring them, did not open the wardrobe. His razor and toothbrush were still in the bathroom.

Josh kissed her, noticing the grey roots she had not bothered to cover.

"I'll see you on Tuesday then."

He took her silence for consent.

If it hadn't been for Mirrie, she could not have assembled the dinner. She put on the same dress every day, not being able to think what to wear; a menu was quite beyond her. Chopped liver, Mirrie said, and a chicken, which was easy. Mirrie would make a pie.

She took Kitty to the shops. It was the first time she had been out. She held Mirrie's arm.

Abe Feldman was on the seat, the sun on his face. As he raised his hat, she noticed that his collar was too big and that his skin was an unhealthy ocher colour. He looked as though the operation had not been very successful.

Bella in the butcher's and Fred in the greengrocer's greeted her kindly, with tenderness and sympathy, realizing the wound was still raw. She smiled politely and let Mirrie shop. Before she left, Mirrie made her brush her hair, change her dress and put on some makeup. She did as she was told, applying lipstick and eyeshadow and mascara to the drawn, lined face of the woman in the mirror.

"This is Sarah," Josh said.

She was not bad for a *shiksa*. Long blond hair and sapphire blue eyes. An attractive girl without doubt, but it was Josh Kitty looked at. It was the first time she had seen the love in his face, making it splendid. He had never looked like that, even with Paula.

Josh poured sherry.

"I'm so sorry about your husband," Sarah said. "You must be feeling very sad."

Kitty looked at her. They were the first words which had got through to her in weeks, the very first time her misery had been acknowledged. Nobody, she had discovered, wanted to talk about Sydney, and she did not like to bring up the subject herself. People seemed so embarrassed, mouthing phrases concerning the healing properties of time, telling her how she would come to adapt when she had pulled herself together.

"Josh has told me all about his father. He sounded such a nice man."

"He was my life," Kitty said.

"You must have a lot of happy memories."

She sipped her sherry. The girl was right. She had been dwelling on Sydney's deterioration, on his last days, his last day, which had blotted out the preceding months, the preceding years when they had been young together and the children small.

They sat down to the chopped liver, which had been made by Mirrie.

When they had finished, Kitty only playing with her portion, Sarah said, "What super *pâté*!"

She ate the chicken and Mirrie's pie with enthusiasm, thanking Kitty when they'd finished for what she called a "banquet." Anyone, Kitty said, could stick a chicken in the oven. She was not in the mood to cook.

Afterwards she found herself showing Sarah the family album. Josh as a small boy on the sands at Westgate, herself and Sydney sitting in deck chairs; Rachel and Josh on horseback; Sydney playing cricket with Josh in the sunlit garden in Hendon; Josh in his first long trousers; family picnics with Josh and Rachel and Carol acting the fool.

It was ten-thirty before she knew it. Usually the unfilled evenings went so slowly she had to check her watch to see if it had stopped.

Sarah had kissed her, not like Rachel, who felt it was her duty, or like Josh, on the top of her head, but warmly, as if she had warmth spilling over, as if there were plenty to spare.

As she got undressed, she realized that for the first time a shaft of light had pierced the darkness of her mood.

Carol sat in the corner of the carriage, an olive-skinned woman in a white dress, a gold bangle on her arm, gold chains round her neck. The heels on her white shoes were four inches high and ended in a point no larger in diameter than a shirt button. On the seat opposite, Debbie and Lisa

234

read the comics she had bought them. It was Sunday, and no one else was in the carriage.

She wasn't sure what it was that had decided her to go to see Alec, to go to Godalming. Her decision had something to do with her father's death. He had always been there when there were choices to make, about her life, about the house, about the children. She had never made a move without consulting him, although he had rarely waited to be asked. Alec had called it interfering, not realizing that she waited for it, depended on it. His absence had made her more lonely than the absence of Alec. Twice she had made the journey to the cemetery to stare, weeping impotently, at his grave.

Anyway, she had promised the girls that as soon as the baby was onto two bottle feedings and could be left for a few hours, she would take them to see the horses. It would be a day out. She was beginning to enjoy herself.

Alec met them at the station. He hugged Carol, held the children in the air where they squirmed with delight. In the car she told him about Mathew and how he had started to sit up. On the way they passed the post office, "Antiques and Bric-a-Brac," the garage, an art gallery, a stud farm. She could see no cinema.

The door of the house was lopsided with age, framed with wisteria. Carol did not notice; she was only shocked that there was no *mezuzah* on it. Inside the house was dark and smelled of polish. She saw it with her father's eye, thinking what it needed was fitted carpets, not those old rugs scattered round and looking fit for the dustbin.

They went through the French doors and into the garden. The lawn rolled down to the white fence; beyond it you could see the fields with the horses. Debbie and Lisa, their arms spread wide, their hair flying in the wind, ran like airplanes towards them. She thought of the patio behind the terraced town house where they played sedate hop-scotch, grazing their knees when they fell.

Debbie turned. "Come on, Mummy, we're going to see the horses!" "Horses" echoed back from the hills, on the breeze.

"Come on," Alec said.

She took a step and her white heel sank into the lawn. She grabbed Alec's arm. "I can't!"

She wore his boots, which looked strange with the white dress, the gold bangle, the long red nails. The horses chewed and gazed at her with their soft eyes. Alec stroked their noses and gave the girls sugar to feed them. They slobbered and Carol would not touch them.

The four of them saw the wishing well and the copse that Alec was clearing and the greenhouse where he picked tomatoes for her to take home.

Back in the house, she put on her shoes again, noticing that Alec was contemplating her legs while her eyes adjusted to the light.

In the kitchen, which had a stone floor, a wooden table, an ancient gas stove and a dresser with cups hanging from hooks, a middle-aged woman in a flowered cotton dress stood at the open fridge, in which, Carol noticed with horror, was a packet of Danish bacon.

"This is my wife. Mrs. Hodges housekeeps for me."

There was lard, too.

"It's a pleasure working for the doctor, although he does miss his little family."

Carol hoped she wouldn't give them any of that *chazerai* for lunch.

She saw the bedroom with the windows on three sides, just the way Alec had described it. There were no fitted cupboards, only a wardrobe with a door that would not shut.

The bathroom was bare and smelled of disinfectant.

236

There were hard brown toilet paper and a bathbrush that looked as if it had been there for a century. There were two other large bedrooms, and at the top of the house was the attic, where Mrs. Hodges slept. Her lisle stockings were drying on the back of a chair.

"I told you it was fantastic!" Alec said.

Carol looked at him with disbelief.

They had mushroom soup from a tin and grilled mackerel, which the children would not eat ("Doctor said you'd rather have fish, although I'd sooner have given you a nice roast"), and an apple pie with a stodgy crust, which Carol hoped hadn't been made with the lard, and thick custard.

"Don't eat much, do you?" Mrs. Hodges said, clearing the plates. "Doctor's got a very good appetite."

"How could you?" she asked Alec afterwards. "It was disgusting!"

"Fish isn't her line," Alec said. "She's what they call a plain cook."

"That's not what I'd call her," Carol said. "Lucky I brought some sandwiches for the children. They didn't eat them on the train."

"To tell you the truth, I don't really notice," Alec said. "I spend every spare moment in the garden." Out of the window they could see Debbie and Lisa down with the horses.

"Come upstairs," Alec said. "I've missed you so much."

28

LENNIE SAID she was anemic. It was the cause of the black-outs. They were having a family conclave to decide what should be done.

"You've no business living by yourself, Kitty," Beatty said. "That's what you have a family for."

Kitty had been on the step stool reaching up to the top shelf of the kitchen cupboard when the first one happened. One minute she had been wondering whether to open the peaches or the black cherries for Lisa and Debbie, who had come for lunch, and the next she was on the floor, the frightened children standing over her.

The second time she was quite alone. She had banged her head and cut her leg. She had managed to crawl to the telephone and Josh had come. It was an unsatisfactory state of affairs.

"Rachel will have to stay here," Freda said. "It won't hurt her."

"I'm sorry, Mummy," Rachel said, "I'm going to India. It's been arranged for ages. I told you."

"Your father thought the world of you, Rachel. He's not dead three months and you're gallivanting round the world with your *yok*."

"I'm going with Patrick."

"You told me."

"Patrick Klopman."

Kitty stared at her. "Klopman? Why didn't you say?"

238

"You didn't ask."

"I thought Patrick . . . What does he do?"

"Medicine. We're going after his finals."

Kitty smiled. "Is the weather nice in India this time of the year? Perhaps I'll go and stay with Carol. This flat's too big now anyway. I rattle. She'd probably be glad of a bit of help with the children. Mathew's getting to be quite a little handful."

Rachel stared at her. "Hasn't she told you?"

"Told me what?" Kitty said.

"She's going back to Alec."

"Alec's in Godalming."

"She's going to live there," Rachel said. "Carol and the children."

Carol had given the house to Norman to sell, as Alec had instructed her, but hadn't yet gathered the courage to tell her mother.

She had come back from Godalming on wings. Not because of the rolling lawns and the horses, not because of the clean country air. A miracle had happened. When she'd made love with Alec—it was the first time since her father had died—she had experienced pleasures she had not dreamed existed. When it was over, she wept with joy, with love and gratitude for Alec, for the wondrous sensation that drove all other thoughts from her mind. For the rest of the day she had floated. On the platform, waiting for the train, they had embraced like young lovers for whom every moment apart was torture. She did not remember the journey home.

The children never stopped talking about the horses. They drew them; they borrowed horse stories from the library. Debbie decided she was going to be a stable girl. They begged her to go and live with Daddy in the country.

Three weeks later she woke up one morning and was

sick. Debbie, watching wide-eyed, offered to call a doctor, but Carol knew that she was pregnant and made her decision. It was the first without her father. We'll have the meat sent down on the train, she told him silently, and start a synagogue, as Alec had said. She'd put proper carpet down in the hall and with the money from the town house do up the bathroom and the kitchen, put fitted cupboards in the bedroom. It would be nice for Mathew and the new baby, and there would be somewhere to dry the diapers.

"Stick yourself away in the country?" Kitty said after hearing the news. "You won't like it."

"I won't know until I try."

"When will I see you? I won't see the children."

"You'll see them."

"Every day?"

"You can come down."

"Everything's going to pieces," Kitty said.

"Rachel's going to India," Kitty said.

"Well, she's no right," Beatty said. "I'll tell her if you won't. What about Carol?"

"Carol's going to Alec. Norman's selling the house for her."

"*Meshuga,*" Beatty said. "What's in the country? What about Mirrie? She can live with you."

"I'm going into the hospital," Mirrie said, "to have my veins done. I got the letter yesterday."

"You'll have to get a housekeeper," Juda said. "You can't be on your own."

"You can come to us," Freda said. "The house is big enough."

Beatty looked at her. "What does she want to be stuck out there for?"

"Housekeepers aren't easy," Freda said. "They don't

grow on trees. When you do get them, they want the earth."

"I'll manage," Kitty said.

And she did. Lennie sent her to a physician. Her anemia was not too serious. He gave her pills.

Slowly, piece by piece, she picked up the life that had shattered when Sydney died. She began to take an interest in her appearance, went back to the open arms of the Ladies' Guild, played bridge in the afternoons. Her status had changed. She was one of the widow women. There were many in the flats. They sought each other out, huddled together for comfort. It was all they could do. She washed the curtains, although she knew she should not have been standing on the ladder to take them down, polished each piece of furniture until it shone. She asked Josh and Sarah to dinner. Sometimes she went to Josh's flat and Sarah cooked Cordon Bleu messes—which she pretended she liked—taking care not to use anything which was not kosher. She had got used to seeing Sarah's patchwork quilt on Josh's bed, but she never felt quite comfortable. Josh said *Kaddish* night and morning for his father. It was Sarah who encouraged him.

She went down to visit Carol and the children in Godalming, but was always glad to get back to civilization. She had to admit that Carol had never looked so happy and put it down to her pregnancy. She kept herself busy going to John Lewis's and Selfridges, from where she sent Carol things she needed for the house. She was glad that Sydney had not lived to see his grandchildren spending Saturday mornings at the riding stables instead of in synagogue. Sometimes when Carol phoned, she put her daughter through the hoop.

"How are you, Mummy?"

"I'm all right *today.*"

"What do you mean, today?"

"Nothing. I'm all right today."

"What was the matter yesterday?"

"Nothing. I was all right yesterday."

"When weren't you all right then?"

"Friday. But it was nothing."

"What was wrong?"

"Nothing much. It doesn't matter."

"What was it?"

"I didn't feel too good."

"Why didn't you ring me?"

"It was nothing. I didn't want to worry you."

"Why are you telling me now then, if it was nothing?"

"You asked me how I was . . . it's nothing to worry about. How're the children? Aren't you coming up? They'll be all grown before I see them."

From Rachel there were postcards from Ankara and Lahore, signed Rachel and Patrick. A doctor, Kitty thought, reading the cards, how pleased Sydney would have been.

At the end of August she went to Bournemouth with Dolly and Norman. She had to pay for her widowhood by spending a holiday with Dolly and her ailments. Norman was consideration itself. He walked them along the front, chauffeured them to the shops, sat them by the pool with rugs- round their legs on breezy days.

When they got back, it was almost New Year. Her first without Sydney.

Strengthened mentally and physically by the Bournemouth air, she decided to do something with Sydney's clothes. "Let someone get the benefit," she said. "They're not doing anyone any good hanging there waiting for the moths."

She telephoned the Friends of the Sick.

"They belonged to my late husband," she said.

"We'll collect them for you"—as though they were doing her a favour—"Monday morning."

Sydney had taken care of his suits. Some of them were twenty years old. Often he'd say, "How old do you think this suit is?" And putting a hand to the inside pocket, he would peer at the label—"Eighteen years old!"—as if he were trying to create a record. His shoes, too, pairs and pairs of them. It was a sin to give them away. Josh helped her on his half day. He forced her to put them into the box as she stopped halfway from the wardrobe, reminiscing over a tie that brought back memories, a special pullover. He left the boxes by the front door ready for the Friends of the Sick when they called.

It took them no more than a few minutes to carry the boxes to the lift, to thank her for her support, to remove all that was left of Sydney's physical presence in the flat.

After they had gone, she stood in the hall with tears in her eyes. "Sydney," she said to the walls. "Sydney." She knew that if she was not to break down she must keep occupied. It was the only way. She decided to get down her winter hat to see if it would do for New Year. It would have to. She was not going to buy a new one. There was no one to wear it for. Sydney had always liked her to look nice.

She took the step stool from the clean, silent kitchen into the bedroom and, opening it in front of the wardrobe, climbed up until she could reach the top cupboard. She could see the hat behind the eiderdowns and the winter blankets, the burgundy hat she had put away in a plastic bag to keep out the dust. She remembered thinking that it could probably do with a steaming.

When she opened her eyes, she was in bed and there was the taste of blood in her mouth. Lennie was leaning over her, and she could see Josh and Sarah dimly in the far corner of the room.

"You gave us a fright," Josh said.

Kitty stared at him.

"Lucky I called in at lunchtime to see if they'd remembered to collect the stuff. I found you on the floor. You'd hit your head on the corner of the dressing table."

"I put a couple of stitches in," Lennie said. "It'll be sore for a bit and you're not going to look very pretty! You must remain where you are for forty-eight hours."

"Sarah's going to stay with you," Josh said.

Kitty opened her mouth.

"It's all arranged."

She closed her eyes. She was too tired to argue.

Lennie snapped the hasps of his case. "I'll pop in tonight. You're bound to feel weak. Just lie quietly." He squeezed her hand.

"I'll come down with you," Josh said. "My waiting room will be full." He kissed his mother's head above the sticking plaster. "Take it easy," he said, "and no more stepladders."

She wondered what he was talking about, then remembered the hat.

She had never slept so much. On and off all day, waking to ask the time and not believing when she was told it. Sarah made her a milk pudding for lunch and sat by the bed, encouraging her to eat. She could not understand why she felt so weak. She slept all afternoon and woke up at five, feeling more herself.

"That's better," Sarah said. "I've got the kettle on. I'll make a cup of tea."

The tea was good. She felt stronger every minute. She gave Sarah the cup and pushed back the covers.

"Where are you going?"

"To have a wash." She held her hands in the air and looked at them. "I feel sticky, horrible." She touched her hair. "God knows what I must look like."

"You look fine." Sarah covered her up again. "Stay right where you are. I'll be back in a moment."

She came back with a plastic bowl, Kitty's washcloth and

244

a towel. She was wearing long earrings and a gypsy skirt. Wringing out the cloth in the warm water she had brought, she washed Kitty's face, wiping away the dried blood. She patted it with the towel, then washed her arms, her hands. When she had finished, she took the hairbrush from the dressing table and, avoiding the bruised forehead, brushed her hair with gentleness.

"That's better," she said.

She took the hand mirror and gave it to Kitty.

"What a sight!" Kitty fingered the plaster. "Did Lennie say he put stitches in?"

"Just two," Sarah said. "The cut was rather deep."

"How long do they have to stay in?"

"Ten days You'll have them out before New Year." She held out her hand for the mirror and put it back on the dressing table, together with the hairbrush. She plumped the pillows on which Kitty lay back, tired once again, drained of all energy, and straightened the sheet and the eiderdown. She collected the bowl and the washcloth and the towel.

"I'm going to see about something to eat for tonight."

"There's some fish in the fridge," Kitty said. "A lemon sole."

"Leave it to me," Sarah said. "Don't worry about a thing. Would you like me to close the curtains? Then you can go to sleep until Josh comes."

"I can sleep," Kitty said. The evening was already drawing in.

Sarah stood by the door, a tall, slight figure with flowing hair over her shoulders.

"I'll see you later then. I'll leave the door open in case you want anything."

"You're a Good Soul," Kitty said. "A *gutte neshumah*."

It was the Nobel Prize, the O.B.E., the Academy Award.

245

29

Y‌OU COULD TELL THE CHANGING OF THE SEASONS by the
hats. The single girls went hatless, long drifts of hair falling
over their faces and their new clothes. From her front-row
seat, Kitty Shelton, in her burgundy tweed suit with the
padded shoulders that were no longer fashionable and her
burgundy felt hat, from which hung self-coloured rouleaux,
looked down through her bifocals onto the black and white
mass of the male congregation below.

Her outward appearance was the same as last year, but
the similarity ended there. It was a hollow image of her
former self who sat in the same row as poor Rose Ingram,
poor Ettie Green, poor Myra Graham. Beneath the burgundy suit there was a grieving soul, a numbed spirit and
an aching heart. It was as much as she could do to look
down onto the men at all. When she did, her sad eyes
searched the rows, in particular the one directly facing the
warden's box, her silent voice calling Sydney.

Of the white shawled shoulders, the covered heads, none
belonged to her. There was no one to smile to, no one to
signal to, no one to tell her the page. Like Myra Graham,
whom last year she had pitied, she was on her own. A year
ago she had thought, complacently, that this New Year
would see her happily ensconced in her seat, her husband,
a year older, below her, Carol next to her, Debbie and Lisa
in the Children's Service, her third grandchild on her lap.

246

She had reckoned without the Almighty and without Alec.

As far as Sydney was concerned, time had mitigated but not relieved the pain. She knew that no matter how long she lived she would not get used to life without him. She would go through the motions; she must. She was not a stupid woman and was aware that from day to day one had to live in the world, but her heart would no longer be in it. There was not a moment during her waking hours or in her dreams that she did not miss her partner, her soulmate, her companion for so many years. Kind as people were, and they were kind, their consideration was no compensation. The young were cynical about marriage, but for a good one no satisfactory substitute had yet been found.

Rachel was going to be married to Patrick Klopman. There had been a postcard from Krishnapur to say they had decided. Kitty's eyes filled with tears as she thought how very happy Sydney would have been, how proud; his little Rachel, whom all the time he had misjudged. Her heart was in the right place after all. All that business over *Yom Kippur*. She was as stubborn as Sydney himself, his mirror image; in Kitty's opinion that had been half the trouble. She hoped Rachel and Patrick wouldn't live too far away; but, knowing Rachel, she had her doubts that it would be round the corner.

She missed Carol; missed the children; missed the small landmarks in the life of Mathew. Oh, how she missed them! There was no popping round to Carol in the morning or for tea, no Carol to shop with, no Carol on Friday nights. The weekends on her own were the worst. No childish voices, no hugs for Grandma, no requests for the sweeties selected with so much love.

She was amazed about Carol. She hadn't thought—and she'd told her so—that she'd last two minutes in the country, not Carol, who had enjoyed pushing the pram along

247

the busy streets. But she had. And how she had. Kitty did not know if it was the new pregnancy—ridiculous having another one so soon—or the country air, but Carol was a changed girl. Where she had been tense, taut, a mass of nerves, often irritable with Alec, with the children, she was calm, serene, relaxed. She even looked different. She had put on weight, and not merely from her pregnancy; her eyes shone and her skin had a glow that owed nothing to cosmetics. She had done wonders with the cottage. It was carpeted throughout, had a gleaming new kitchen and bathroom, and she had filled it with the furniture she had brought from the house, throwing out, together with Mrs. Hodges, all the old junk. Although he preferred the old furniture, Alec had let her; it was worth it to have his family with him.

He and Carol seemed to be getting on better, too. There was less friction, more fun, but then in the country Alec did not have to work so hard. Grudgingly, Kitty had to admit, the move was turning out all right; but the knowledge did nothing to diminish her loneliness. She did go down, for the weekend. She didn't like the wind when it was windy or the sun when it was sunny, and anyway she missed the noise of the traffic; it was too quiet. She spoke to Carol every day. Well, almost every day. Carol rang her. When she did not, Kitty would wait a few days, then pick up the phone to chastise her daughter with a "Hallo, stranger" or "I thought you'd forgotten my number." She had to admire Alec for one thing. He had kept his promise. They had formed their own little religious community. By dint of perseverance, they had dug out a few Jewish families who lived in the vicinity and on one Saturday in four and on the High Holy Days, of which this was the first, the services were held in Alec's house. She had begged Carol to come up for the holidays with the children to stay with her. Alec had been adamant. "Start as we mean to go on," he'd said to Carol. She did not relay the message, only that they would not be coming. Carol lit her candles on Friday nights, saw to it that the children did not forget their Hebrew and had the meat sent down on the train. What would happen when Mathew got older Kitty did not know, but for the moment, she said silently to Sydney, he did not have to worry, Lisa and Debbie would not grow up to be little *shiksas*. Little *shiksas*. She was a one to talk. She asked Sydney, as well as the Almighty, to forgive her; for next to her in synagogue, the only company she had—and she turned her head to smile at her—was Josh's *shiksa*, was Sarah, looking as unlike the Jewish girls dressed to the nines as chalk and cheese. Had Sarah not been there, she would have had no one. Kitty Shelton of the large family, the close family, the lucky and blessed family, would have been alone this New Year, her first as a widow.

It was strange about Sarah. Ever since she had fallen and banged her head and Lennie had put stitches in and Sarah had nursed her, she had felt for her like a daughter, as if she were her daughter. Her feelings were so strong that sometimes she wondered if Sarah really was a *shiksa*, although Josh had assured her on that point. She could not imagine herself having such a powerful rapport with any person outside her own faith. Aware of her betrayal of Sydney and of his ideals, she had to admit that she loved the girl and sometimes felt closer to her than to Carol or to Rachel.

Kitty knew what they were saying about her, what they must be saying. Ruthie Wiseman and Rika Snowman and Barbara Brill, in their tweeds and their gabardines, must be pointing their fingers at Sarah in her gypsy skirt, at Sarah and at Kitty. Kitty held her head high. What did they know? Compared with some of their spoiled, self-centered daughters, Sarah was a jewel. No, not a jewel. A fresh rose among a box of glittering stones. Sydney, she knew, would never have accepted her. He adhered to the letter of his principles. She bore the guilt on her own shoulders. Sarah was all she had. You will see, Sydney, my darling, she told him, you will see.

She fingered the cut on her forehead where the stitches had been taken out and which she had tried to disguise with makeup. Since she had been taking the pills, thank God, she had not fallen. And if she fell, she fell. She no longer worried about such things. The happenings of the past year had made her philosophical.

Of course she had time on her hands, no Sydney, no Carol and the children. After the holidays she was going to help at the Jewish Day Center, with the old people. The benefits would be mutual. Eventually she might move to a smaller flat, away from her memories, where the essence of Sydney was not in everything she saw, everything she touched. She had to take her new life slowly, picking up the threads one by one until eventually they might make some sort of pattern to replace the old one. How "stiff-necked" she had been last New Year to imagine that her life would continue, unchanged. "Lord, what is man that thou regardest him, or the son of man, that thou takest account of him? Man is like to vanity; his days are as a shadow that passeth away. In the morning he bloometh and sprouteth afresh; in the evening he is cut down and withereth." How many times had she repeated those words on Passover and on Pentecost, on Tabernacles and on *Yom Kippur*.

There was no *Yiskor* today, no Memorial for the Departed. Josh had said his *Kaddish* and gone to work. With his father no longer alive, he did not feel it incumbent upon himself to attend the synagogue services. In his place he had sent Sarah.

Sarah had her finger on the page. A page. It was not the right one. Kitty took the book—she was using Sydney's and had lent Sarah hers—and, listening for what had been going on while she had been daydreaming, found the page and pointed out the place. The congregation rose to its feet. Kitty got up and Sarah followed her; they stood together like mother and daughter.

The Cantor, in his quiet tenor, sang into the silence: "The great trumpet is sounded; the still small voice is heard; the angels are dismayed; fear and trembling seize hold of them as they proclaim Behold the Day of Judgment!"

"*Yom Hadin,*" Kitty sang. She turned the page again for Sarah.

"On the first day of the year it is inscribed, and on the Day of Atonement the decree is sealed, how many shall pass away and how many shall be born; who shall live and who shall die . . ."

What was the use, Kitty thought with tears in her eyes, of struggling. What was going to happen would happen. It was all *beshert.*